LANDSFOR

FROZENFIRE

Raj Bansal

Absolute Author
Publishing House

Publisher: Absolute Author Publishing House
Cover: Rebeca @rebecacovers
Interior Formatter: Dr. Melissa Caudle
Maps Creator: Raj Bansal
Maps Illustrator: Tim Godfrey using *ProFantasy* software (licensed by Ralf Schemann) and used with permission

Library of Congress Catalogue-in-Publication Data
  Bansal, Raj

  p. cm.

Paperback ISBN: 978-1-64953-746-1
eBook ISBN: 978-1-64953-747-8

Printed in the United States of America

CONTENTS

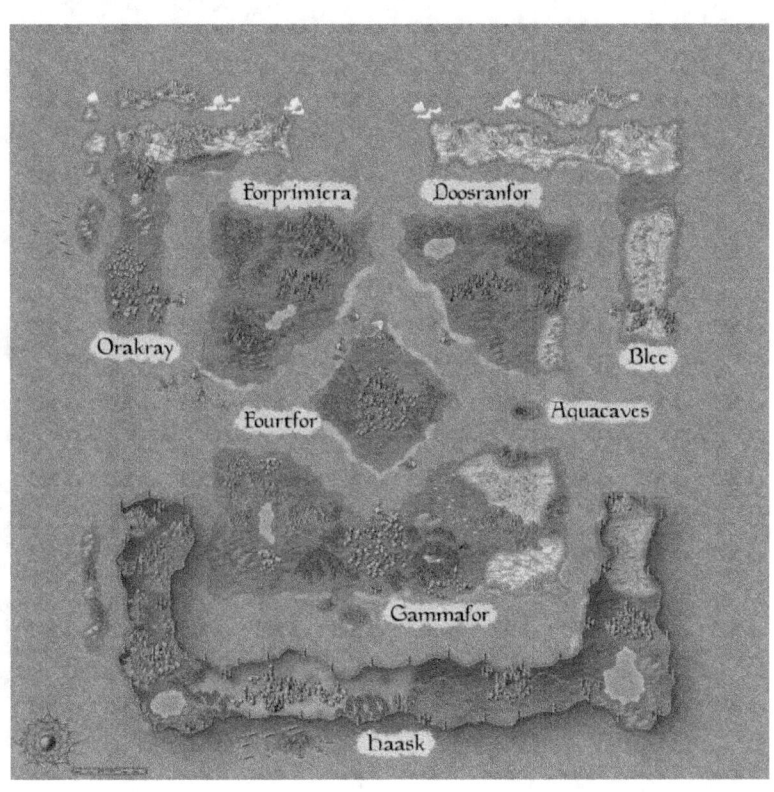

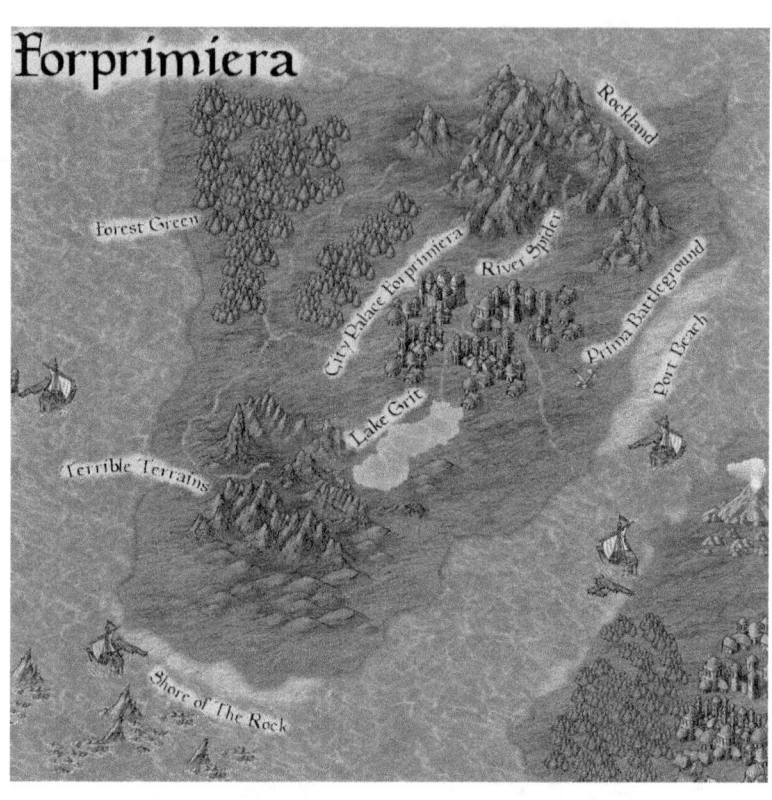

Forprimiera

Rockland

Forest Green

City Palace Forprimiera

River Spider

Prima Battleground

Port Beach

Lake Grit

Terrible Terrains

Shore of The Rock

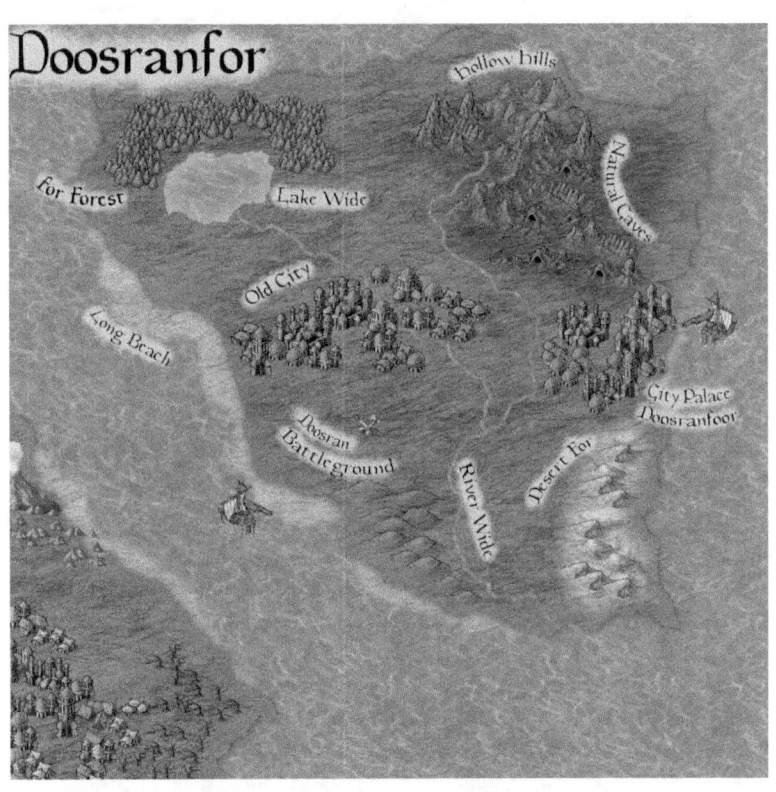

Gammafor

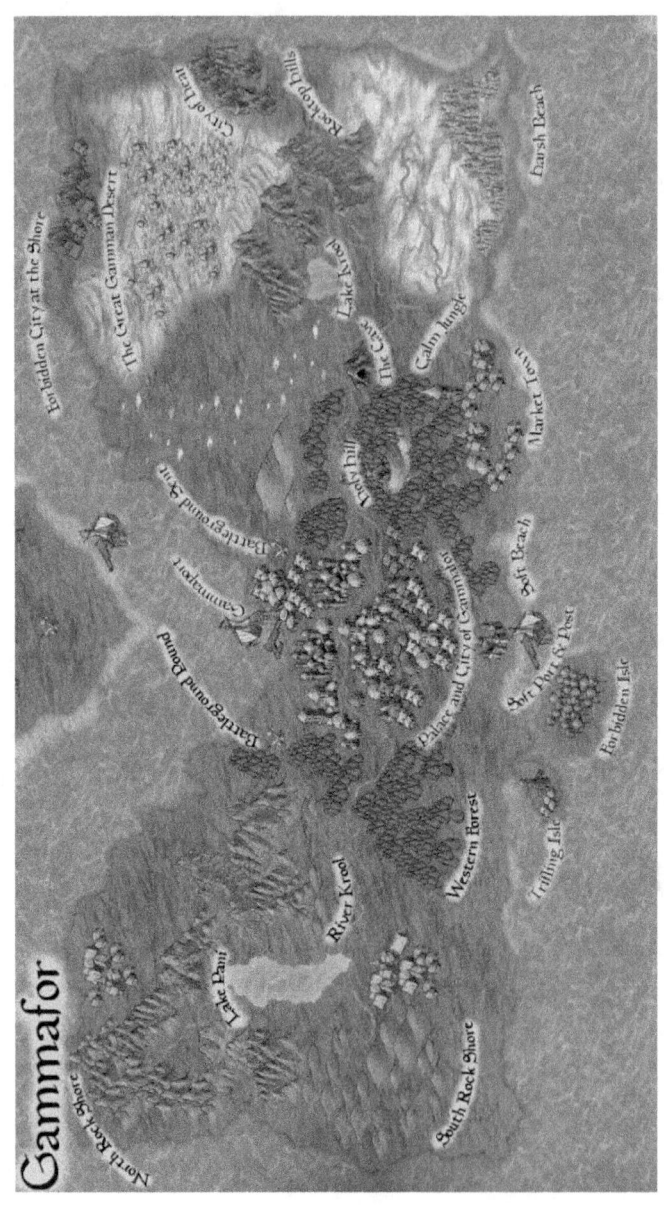

North Rock Shore

Lake Pani

River Kreol

South Rock Shore

Western Forest

Trifling Isle

Palace and City of Gammafor

Soft Beach

Forbidden Isle

Safe Port & Post

Battleground Doned

Cemetery!

Battleground Ant

Holly hill

Market Town

Calm Jungle

The Canyon

Lake Nova

Rock top hills

Harsh Beach

City of Bari

Forbidden City at the Shore

The Great Gamman Desert

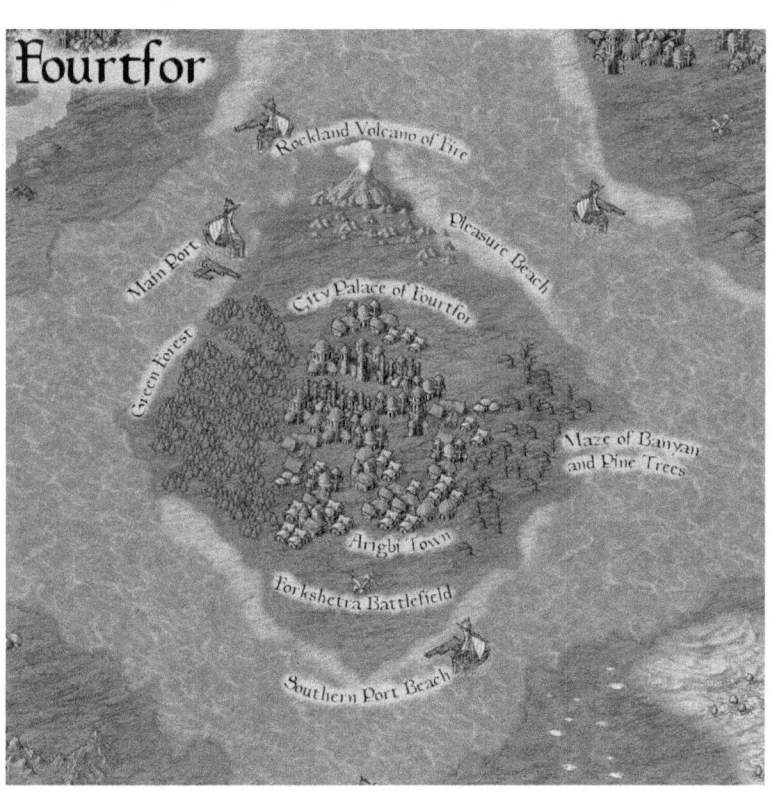

Fourtfor

Rockland Volcano of Fire

Main Port

Pleasure Beach

City Palace of Fourtfor

Green Forest

Maze of Banyan and Pine Trees

Arigbi Town

Forkshetra Battlefield

Southern Port Beach

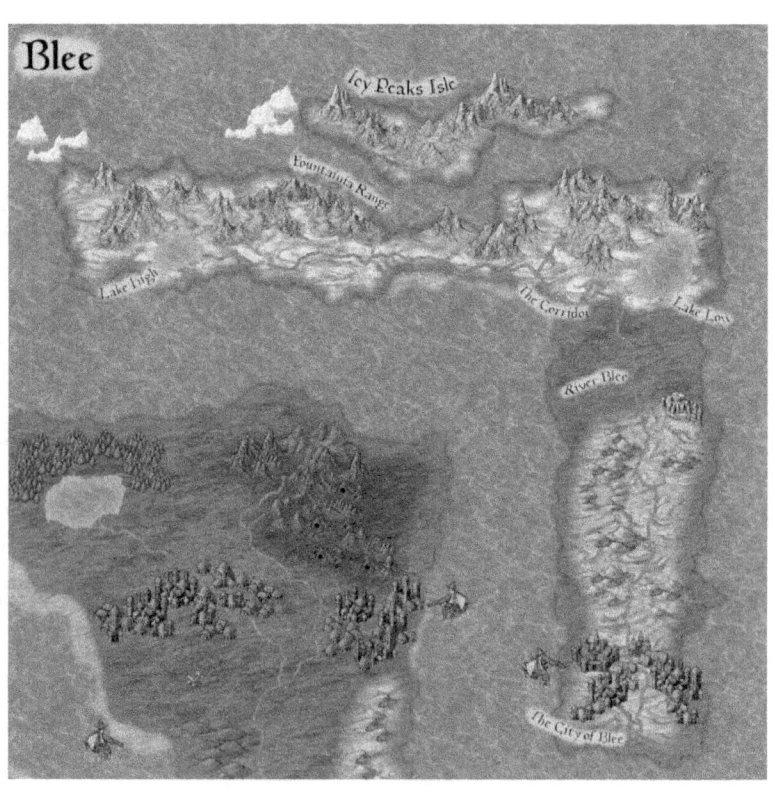

Blee

Icy Peaks Isle

Fountain Range

Lake Tugh

The Corridor

Lake Less

River Blee

The City of Blee

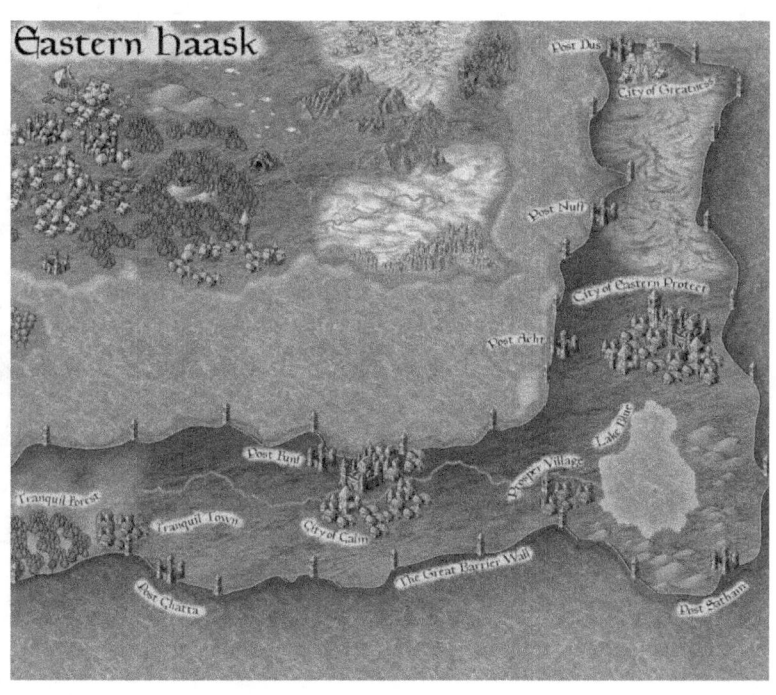

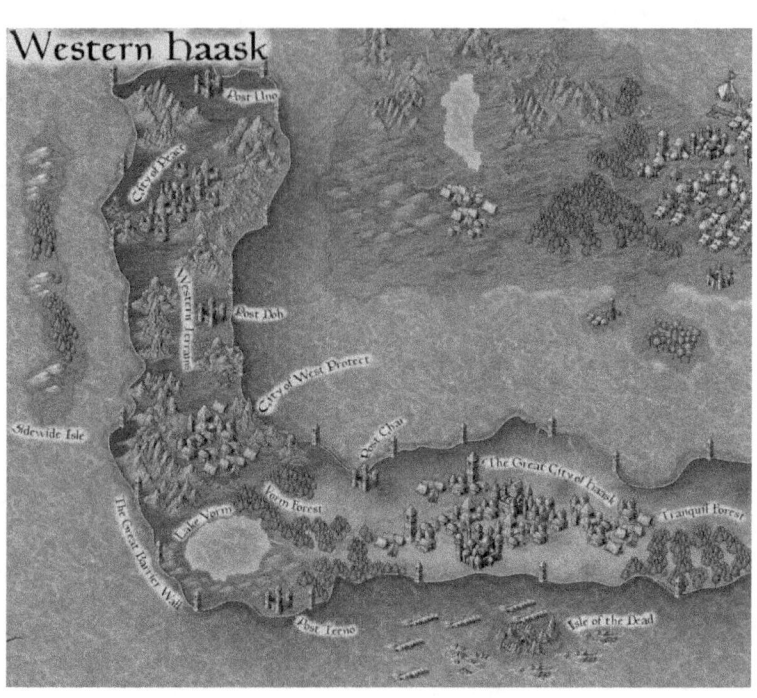

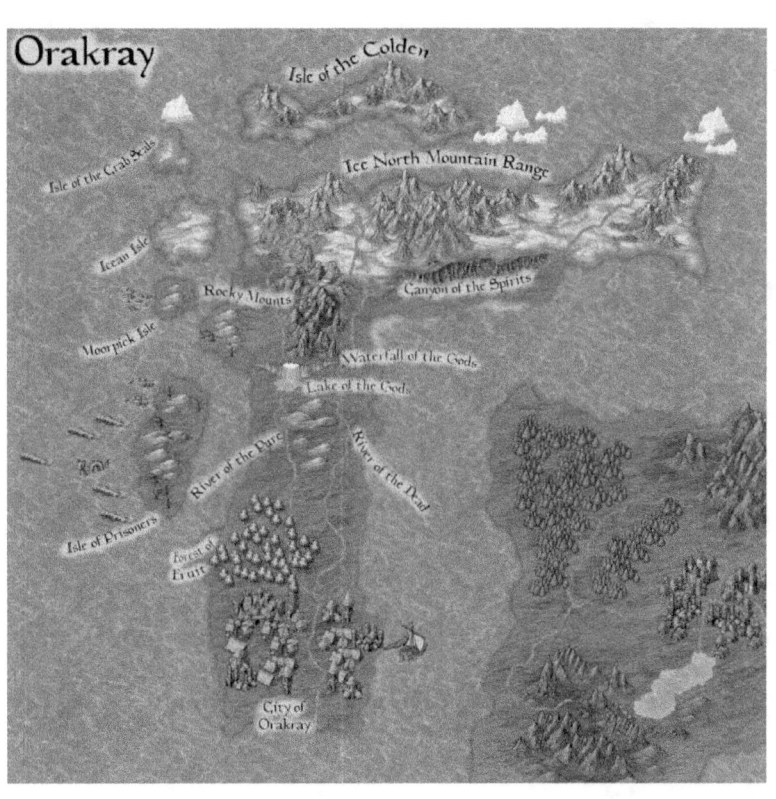

PROLOGUE

THE KEEPERS

L ong ago in a distant realm, an unrighteous Lord rose from the south and advanced north towards the Kingdom of Landsfor, crushing any other lands and Kings that stood in his path. Those were terrible times for the Kingdom of Landsfor. A great evil had befallen the realm and its four islands.

The King of Landsfor, King Solothaar Rain, sought aid from the God of the Gods, Topus, in the temple upon the holy hill. God Topus heard his prayer and answered him by showing him the way to defeat the evil Lord from the south.

The answer was the Emispear, the unsurmountable power of the Frozenfire—a mighty battle spear made up of four parts: three blue, red and green gleaming rods and a yellow blade for a spearhead said to contain the power of the sun. When all four parts were joined, the weapon shone a luminous white.

The God of Gods Topus bestowed upon King Solothaar this divine weapon so he could defeat the evil Lord and protect humankind. The weapon was only to be used against the forces of evil and for the preservation of righteousness. It was a formidable weapon any King would have been determined to keep. But once the weapon had been used and the evil forces defeated, the weapon was to be dismantled once again and its four pieces returned to their keepers.

King Solothaar, being a righteous and responsible King, accepted all terms and adhered to them strictly. He used the weapon to defeat the evil Lord, along with the help of the four keepers. Then, after the war against evil was won, King Solothaar returned to the holy hill as promised and returned the weapon to the God, expressing gratitude for his aid. Though God Topus did not manifest, the four guardians were there to collect their respective parts for safe keeping.

The first keeper was the great fire breathing golden hawk, with feathers of sharp blades. The bird was the keeper of the spearhead. Solothaar placed the weapon upon a rock and a sharp yellow beam shot from the hawk's eyes and separated the head from the staff, and the spearhead resumed its place as one of the feathers of the bird.

The second guardian was a great red bear. He took the red element, one of the three elements comprising the staff, the one known to contain the powers of fire, and held it near his large, white belly until the staff disappeared inside him.

The third keeper was a large blue bear. Similar to the red bear, he took the blue part of the staff, the one bearing the powers of sky, wind and water, and held it near his large, white belly until it, too, disappeared.

Finally, the blue bear picked up the final green piece of the staff and threw it into a moving, green shrub with red berries. The green rod, representing the Earth vanished inside the leaves of the bush.

With that, King Solothaar paid his respects to the keepers before they all went their separate ways. The Emispear was never to be invoked again, unless a similar calamity one day befell the Kingdom.

CHAPTER 1

SLEEPLESS NIGHTS

For King Dymondo Rain of Gammafor and Fourtfor, the wound of losing his mother was still fresh. Though her eventual demise was expected, her sudden death came as a shock to the entire family.

Dymondo tossed and turned on his bed, his lips shivering and his pillow wet from the cold sweat that had formed on his forehead. It was the same nightmare—a memory that had haunted him all his life—an inner guilt that devoured him from inside. The more he tried to forget it, the more it returned to terrorise him in his slumber.

His Queen, Mysteria, awoke to his mumbling and forceful movements caused by his nightmare. She had experienced this many times now and was quickly becoming used to her husband's troubled sleep. She took him in her arms and slowly and gently rocked him, trying to calm him down whilst being careful not to wake him to prevent further shock. It was no use.

Dymondo shot up, momentarily released from his nightmare, but in shock. He was breathing fast, his heart racing like a charioteer in a grand contest. His eyes were wide and his hair drenched with sweat.

"My King," said Mysteria, putting her hands gently upon his

3

shoulders.

Dymondo jumped at the touch, but she held tight.

"It's alright…It's over…"

Dymondo nodded and wiped his sweat-filled forehead. He got out of bed and headed for the water flagon. He did not bother with any goblet or glass, but drank straight from the container.

Mysteria came out from underneath the bed sheets and covered herself with her gown. She went towards a wall lamp and lit it to allow some light in the room.

"Blow it out, my dear, for I am going back to sleep."

"No. We are talking about this."

"About what, Mysteria?"

"About your nightmare."

"I am not having any nightmares," lied Dymondo.

"You hide what you see from me. Why?"

"It is nothing at all, dear. Just a nightmare. Nothing to be concerned about."

She walked up to him and turned him to face her. She had her other hand upon her gown to hold it in place.

"Mysteria, please. I wish to go back to bed." Dymondo wiped the sweat dripping onto his neck from the back of his head.

"You cannot hide such things from me, my King. You'll have to tell me."

"I shall, but not now."

"Why not now? This isn't the first time I've seen you run for the water jug in the middle of the night."

"I know. Perhaps I miss Mother."

"Oh dear, come here." She extended her arms out to him. He walked up and embraced her.

Her gown flung open and she held him tight and close to her skin.

"That was a terrible loss for us all. I didn't even get the opportunity to meet her as her daughter-in-law. But you must be strong, my dear."

"Others may have accepted her unexpected departing to the

4

afterlife, but I am still in mourning, Mysteria."

"I understand…But everyone gave her a great send-off, didn't they?" Mysteria added, trying to apply balm with her words.

"Yes." Dymondo withdrew from the hug. "No doubt. Brother Shilathaar raised the Call straight away after her demise. He preserved her body in a large container filled with oils and other medicines and when we met up for the Call, he had already placed her in Fourtfor castle, where she wanted to be."

"Yes, that was kind of him…surprisingly."

"She was his mother, too," defended Dymondo.

"Of course, My King but… she seemed, as you say, fine and healthy before she left for Forprimiera."

"Yes, Mysteria, but her death was due to natural causes. She was found sound asleep in her chamber."

Mysteria nodded.

"Now she is reunited with Father in the afterlife. May her soul rest in peace. We all gave her the best send-off we could with the great royal funeral in Fourtfor, but I still miss her, Mysteria."

Mysteria held him again.

"I know how much you loved her and how you could confide in her. But that doesn't mean there is no one else you can speak with. You can always speak with me. Tell me…what did you see in your dream?"

"I see…"

"Go on."

"I see my childhood. Three princes of Landsfor playing atop the mountains just outside the jungle. I see myself. I am ten. I see my brothers. They too are children like me. I see another child playing among us. He is the son of the Prime Minister, the one at that time. Syterius, I think his name was. A very talented child, a genius. He'd beat us all in any game or competition, despite being younger than all of us—a rare talent. I see us all playing a game in which he defeats me and Brother Grygerious. One turn is all that remains of the game, and he and Brother Shilathaar are all that's left. He beats Shilathaar. The game gets played again, over and over, and every time, he wins. This makes Shilathaar very angry. Both Grygerious and I know that Shilathaar is going up to strike him, and I can stop him, but I respect Brother Shilathaar… and fear him."

"Then?"

"Then I see Grygerious looking on with a wicked smile, as if this is all entertainment."

"Then…?"

Dymondo stopped and gazed at her not wanting to continue.

"Please, Dymondo…"

"Then…I see Shilathaar grabbing Syterius by his neck and he starts to push him towards the cliff of the mountain…"

"Then?"

"He did not stop. I ran after him and so did Grygerious, but Grygerious was enjoying himself, clapping his hands, spurring Shilathaar on to hit Syterius. I was shouting… "No! Stop, Brother! No!"

"Then…"

"He did not stop… Shilathaar pushed him to the point where there was no ground. The poor boy fell over the edge and dropped far below, into the tall trees of the forest…to his death."

"Oh my gosh! Is this incident true…?" Mysteria put her hands over her mouth,

"Yes…it happened, but only the three of us know the truth. Everybody else thinks Syterius slipped by accident."

***

Around the same time, Lance Sterferep, King Dymondo's most trusted aid, was sneaking into the home of Zircornia Matchiwada as her secret guest. Zircornia Matchiwada was a very beautiful young woman belonging to a privileged household as her father was an influential nobleman at King Dymondo's court. The Matchiwadas lived in a beautiful house with all the luxuries of the royal palace, situated in a prime location in the Kingdom. With her parents sound asleep, Sterferep snuck into Zircornia's chamber and spent the night in her bed.

Zircornia resembled a Goddess and had long, blonde, silky hair with light blue eyes. She would often dress in long, blue and white dresses and rarely chose another colour to wear. A decent, twenty-five-year-old woman she was with much respect for herself and her mother.

She adored Sterferep and he loved her, but this was the first time Sterferep had stayed over at her home, so the brave Lance was feeling slightly apprehensive.

After having made love, they lay together quietly in each other's arms unclad. The skies outside starting to turn from black to red. Sterferep noticed this and got up.

"Oh, stay a little longer," she said quietly.

"I must leave, it is nearly daybreak. I will be wanted back at the palace."

"A few moments longer…?"

He moved to her and kissed her on her lips.

"As much as I'd love to, I must go before anyone gets up. Your father will definitely not be happy to see me here," he said and started to get dressed. She too got out and put on her silky gown.

After he had donned his trousers and boots, she embraced him and could not help but notice the engraving on his shoulder again. It was as if the mark was part of his skin—a mark for life given at birth.

"So, what is this little creature doing here? I have wanted to ask you before, but I never did," she said stroking it gently.

Sterferep put his hand over his right shoulder and sat on the bed with his back to her.

She went over to him and embraced him from behind.

"Tell me. What is it?"

"I've had it since birth. You must not mention this to the King, Zircornia." Sterferep was serious.

"Of course not, but you must tell *me* Sterferep. What is it?"

"It is the Cecrops—a depiction of a man with a serpent's tail."

"I can see that, but why is it there?"

"I don't know, but my parents say it must have been with me

7

since birth."

"Must have? Surely they must know…"

"…No! I was adopted. My parents found me by the riverbank of Krool, and though they were poor, they took me in and raised me as their own. I don't know who I truly am, Zircornia. Hence the reason everyone refers to me as Sterferep Unknown. But my father always asked me to hide this mark and not let anyone know of it. It was like he knew something but never shared it with me. He died when I was eighteen and my mother two years back. As for the mark, I have kept it hidden my whole life. I had forgotten about it, actually…until now. No one else knows about it apart from you. Can I trust you?"

"Of course you can, my love. I am yours and you are mine, along with all your secrets. But…"

"But what, my lady?"

"Three years ago…King Shilathaar came to Gammafor court and brought his wife…Queen Silvenia. I did not look closely then, but…" she paused to think. "I believe…I have seen the same mark on her right shoulder."

"How…?"

"We were all dancing and Queen Silvenia of Forprimiera is known for her loose clothing, as you know. As usual, she was dancing freely. I cannot fathom why she dresses like that."

"Yes, her bosom is often on display," smiled Sterferep.

Zircornia opened her mouth and hit him gently on his bicep in jealousy.

"Where were your eyes?" she asked.

"Ha-ha! You know her, my dear! How could I not see?"

"True, and that day she was wearing a lovely thin silk dress— too thin; her entire figure could be seen. I saw her right shoulder and….it had the same mark. Maybe there is a connection between you and her?"

Sterferep went quiet and Zircornia rubbed his shoulders in consolation.

"I'm sorry to have caused you more concern."

"Its fine, Zircornia. I have been running away from this all my life. Perhaps it is now time to solve this mystery once and for all."

Zircornia smiled and kissed him.

"Just remember, I am always with you. But how will you find out?"

"Gratitude, Zircornia," smiled Sterferep, kissing her. "I'll seek the help of my friend, the King. I just need the right moment."

Zircornia nodded. "We can always trust him."

"But I cannot disturb him about it right now. He is occupied with important matters of state. But I will look for a chance to speak with him."

"You must."

"First, I must get back; otherwise, your parents will not be pleased to find me here."

Zircornia's face dropped and Sterferep finished getting dressed and left through the window from where he had come. Zircornia watched him jump into the bushes, making sure he landed safely and waved him goodbye. He waved back and then silently ran off towards the palace.

CHAPTER 2

THE GOLDEN HAWK

The rest of the night had been a sleepless one for Dymondo, so he was extremely quiet when Lance Sterferep and Lance Kor came to his chamber in the morning. Dan and Dwarpal were with them. Generally, Lance Tamaris would also be with them. But that was a topic Dymondo did not wish to address just yet, hence no one spoke of it. Everyone had been told that Tamaris was away tending to personal matters.

Dymondo walked fast, nearly stomping to court, his cloak floating in the air behind him.

Everyone bowed their heads and kneeled on the ground. Dymondo looked around at everyone prostrated before him.

"Rise!" Everyone stood up and took their seats and positions. Lance Sterferep and Lance Kor posted themselves beside the King, whilst the other two stood among the courtiers.

"Education Minister Olivious Herrerous! Chief Minister Puyol Bryt! Proceed!"

Olivious feared his King's anger and pondered how to break his troubling news. Nervously, he cleared his throat and proceeded.

"It appears that a winged creature has perched itself on the gate of the Kingdom. It does not let anyone enter or leave."

"Why have we not done anything about it?"

Chief Courtier Majesma Lahall stood to speak. "My King, it is no ordinary bird. It is as if some demon has cast its evil eye upon Gammafor…"

"Majesma! I am not interested in hearing praises of enemies that pose a threat to the state. Forsake the fine words and dramatic descriptions for the moment. Simply state the problem and tell me of a suitable solution! Firstly, how has this creature been successful in preventing people from passing through the gate?"

"Forgive me, my King, but the creature injures them," said Majesma.

"People are being hurt because of this bird? I want to know right now what has been done to stop this heinous act. I cannot have the citizens of this Kingdom getting hurt!" Dymondo was furious.

"Force has been used, my King, but all attempts have been futile. The bird breathes fire and, when it chooses, a frozen mist. Any weapon launched its way gets incinerated or turned to solid ice. The burnt objects turn to ash and the iced objects crash to the ground and explode into innumerable shards. We have lost many spears, axes, arrows and swords this way. And any person who tries to attack the bird from close range has been left injured. The bird's feathers are as sharp as blades."

Dymondo looked worried after hearing the description. Sterferep looked over at Kor.

"Any deaths?" asked Kor.

"No, Lance Kor. The bird has not killed anyone. It warns people before it launches its knife-like feathers. If the person persists, only then will it cut their flesh, but so far there have been no mortal injuries. The wounds are deep, but they will heal."

"Go on," said Dymondo.

"We have commenced…talking to it."

"Talking to it? It speaks? It's a bird!" yelled Dymondo in frustration, bringing silence once again to the court. He was still agitated. The King thought the era of mystical creatures who

11

spoke their tongue was long gone, until he met Cattus in the jungle. But that was God Topus himself. He could hardly believe what he was hearing.

"Does it have a name?" Dymondo asked, expecting no answer in return.

"Quilliblade."

The King looked around his court in shock but soon gathered himself and paused to think rationally about the situation. He stopped being so aggressive and began to speak calmly.

"So we have a situation on our hands to deal with?" he clarified.

"Yes, my King," said Majesma, who became slightly more at ease after noticing the change in Dymondo's demeanour.

"So, what does this Quilliblade want?"

"An audience with the King."

"Does it give a reason as to why it seeks one?"

"No, my King."

"When does it desire to visit the palace court?"

"It does not desire to visit the palace court, sire."

"Then how will it meet me?"

"The bird demands the King come to the palace gate and meet it there. Only then will it express the purpose of its visit."

"'Demands?' Choose your words with caution, Chief Courtier," warned the King.

"They are the words of the bird, my King, not mine. I dare not utter such a phrase."

"Disrespectful bird!"

"Have you tried shooting it down with an arrow from a long distance?" asked the defence minister Urayu Dero, turning towards the commander-in-chief of the army, Hitius Opecious. Hitius stared back at Urayu in disgust, then turned to the King, ignoring Urayu completely.

"My King," Hitius began, "we have tried many techniques on this creature, but it has all been fruitless." He lowered his head.

Urayu spoke up again. "But have you—"

"Shooting from far is treachery!" Hitius barked without looking at him. "There is no honour in it! I will not do it! Unless...the King desires it, then it shall be done," he clarified.

"I must say I agree with you, Hitius," answered Dymondo. "Very well! I shall go meet the bird."

Dymondo rose from his throne and everyone followed suit and started walking out in haste.

"My King," the Prime Minister Kriptus Magnus said, getting up from his seat, "you must be careful. Just think a little more before heading straight into this."

"I agree, my King," said Lorca Loray. "You mustn't hurry into this."

"Take men with you, surely!" advised Kriptus.

"I am capable of doing this by myself!" Dymondo was getting annoyed. Kriptus's shoulders dropped in defeat.

"Fine! Sterferep, Kor, Dan and Dwarpal! Come with me!" commanded the King and left the court.

All the courtiers began to murmur among themselves. Olivious ran up to Puyol and Kriptus.

"How many times will he run into danger like this?" he whispered.

"I understand your concern, dear Olivious," answered Kriptus quietly. "But—"

"Give him time." Puyol interjected. Kriptus nodded in agreement.

"How much does he need?" retorted Olivious.

"There is a day when every boy becomes a man and, for the King, that day will come soon enough," smiled Puyol.

Dymondo marched towards the gate of the kingdom as his guards and Lances followed him. As he got closer, he rushed on ahead to the gates, leaving his guards and Lances behind.

"My King!" shouted Sterferep.

"Yes Sterferep?"

"Let us stay ahead of you. There may be danger."

Dymondo conceded and slowed his pace.

When Dymondo and his men reached the gate, they found many broken arrowheads scattered on the ground, along with snapped spear shafts, crunched spearheads, stringless bows and various bloodstains on the ground. There were even a few patches of the ground on fire. It looked like a battlefield.

Two guards remained by the gate with people standing outside the gate waiting for the bird to allow them in. All those that wished to exit the Kingdom had returned to their homes. Dymondo slowed down as he got nearer to the bird, which other than its fire-yellow colour, seemed rather ordinary perched on its pillar.

"Here I am before you," said Dymondo.

The hawk opened its eyes and turned its head towards Dymondo. Its eyes were indeed frightening. They were yellow and difficult to stare into. Dymondo was shocked at their horrific nature, and his own eyes widened with fear.

"The King himself!" the bird said in the strangest voice Dymondo had ever heard. The voice was frightening, sounding neither male nor female, but a mix of the two. The bird's tone was fearless and commanding.

"Yes, this is he. What can the King and his Kingdom do for you, Quilliblade?"

The hawk's eyes widened, and a knowing smile appeared from under its beak. More fear struck in the hearts of the onlookers. It seemed as though the bird was going to attack and kill all the men standing before him, perhaps even their King.

"You?" laughed the bird. The laughter was even more frightening than the eyes. "You are not capable of doing anything for me!"

Dymondo gathered all his courage. He honestly could no longer tolerate any more insults, be they from man or beast.

"There now, great Hawk, no need to be indelicate. Do not speak to me in that way."

The bird's eyes turned red in anger and it flew onto the ground and grew large and larger still, until the King was the size of the bird's claws and had to crane his neck to meet the bird's eyes. The bird continued to laugh, only this time its voice was ten times louder and more frightening.

"The King will do something for me? Ha-ha! Consider

yourself blessed that I have not killed every man in this kingdom and that I have not killed you. I will not answer to *you*! *You* will speak to *me* with humility! Is that understood?"

Dymondo collected himself and chose humility.

"Yes, O King of the Birds, I understand, but please be kind and tell me, what brings you to my Kingdom? And why do you dislike my citizens and prevent them from entering and exiting the gate?"

"I have no care for who enters or leaves this gate. I just wanted to speak with you. There was no other way to get you to stand at my feet," said the bird.

"Here I am. I am standing at your feet. What more do you wish for?" asked Dymondo.

"I said you can give me nothing!" roared the bird, growing larger in size, expanding its bright, golden wings until its feathers seemed like countless sharp swords. The bird opened its mouth and flames began to blaze inside.

These could have easily been his last words, but Dymondo remained calm. "I request O great Bird, please do not misunderstand me for I am here to have a pleasant conversation. Please return to your previous form so that we can talk," he said.

The fire stopped blazing from the bird's beak and the wings retracted and the bird returned to its original size and perched itself on the pillar once more, still looking down at Dymondo.

"Gratitude, O great Hawk, I am merely trying to understand the purpose of our meeting. If there is anything I can do, then I shall gladly do so, and if there is something you have come to tell me, then please do so. I humbly await your reply."

The bird seemed less angry, and its eyes were not as wide as they were before.

"I am here to warn you, King!"

"I am pleased to accept your warning, O King of Birds!"

"No! Not here!"

"Where then?" Dymondo was growing impatient again.

The bird shook its wings, but did not change size. "The warning and the task I am about to give are both confidential! No one must hear!"

"Then, O great Bird, would you like to come into my Kingdom and honour me with your presence in my palace?"

"I have heard good praises of you, O King Dymondo! But no!"

"Command me, then, O great Quilliblade."

Quilliblade grew again but not as big as before and flew from the pillar onto the ground, standing at the same height as Dymondo.

"Ride on my back, Dymondo, and I shall take you high into the skies, where no one can hear us!"

"King, this can be a trap! Beware!" spoke Sterferep.

"Ah, the loyal friend and Lance! I was waiting for you to step in!" laughed Quilliblade.

"The safety of my King is my utmost priority!" replied Sterferep.

"This coming from a man who does not know who he really is! That mark on your shoulder! What is it?"

Suddenly everyone looked at Sterferep. Fortunately, his mark was still concealed under his armour and tassels.

"Mark?" asked Kor.

Sterferep was stunned into silence.

"Never mind, Kor!" said Quilliblade. "He himself can work out what he needs to in due time. Zircornia has already told him where to look! Now get on Dymondo, I do not have all day!"

Dymondo hesitated at first, but then got on. Quilliblade increased in size slightly and shot high into the air like a cannonball. Dymondo and Quilliblade were soon among the clouds and Dymondo could see his entire Kingdom below him. The King held onto Quilliblade's neck as they flew.

"Can you breathe, King? Tell me if you cannot. I will fly lower."

"I can, great Bird. Please go ahead," said Dymondo as he held on tight to Quilliblade's neck. The bird slowed down and began to speak.

"Your wretched brothers conspire against you, Dymondo!"

"What?"

"Yes! They will make an attempt to take your life, to remove

16

you and seize your kingdom!"

"How can you say that? My brothers would do no such thing!"

"They will!" snapped the bird. "I am not here to argue my statements! They are correct!"

"But how can they, Quilliblade?"

"Trust me, they will try! You must prepare yourself!"

Dymondo was silent, thinking of his brother Shilathaar and the kind of aggression he was capable of.

"What? No questions?!" the bird mocked. "Don't you want to know how?!"

"Yes, of course," Dymondo finally responded.

"You must travel to the Aquacaves!"

"Where?"

"The Aquacaves! There is a map…in Forprimiera"

"Forprimiera? A map of what?"

"The Aquacaves! The map is in one of the chambers of the palace!"

"Then my brother, Shilathaar, must surely have it!"

"No! He is a fool. The map has been lost for some time. In the chamber it remains!"

"What is in the Aquacaves?"

"There, the God of Water will help you if you show him reverence. In the Aquacaves you will finds many jewels and riches, but what you seek is a divine weapon which you must attain! The Emispear! The power of the Frozenfire! Only the man who understands its true power can wield the weapon. But be warned—"

"What?"

"The creatures! There will be creatures in the depths! You must face them before obtaining this divine weapon! But you need that weapon! Without it, you cannot defeat Shilathaar and Grygerious!"

"But they are my brothers."

"Yes, brothers who will try to kill you, but they cannot do so without this weapon. They do not know that. What they do know is that you are not really brothers, but what they do *not* know is that they are divine, just like you are. Dymondo, they must never know this! So go Dymondo, go! May the special powers of the Water God Aquinious be with you! Remember if you lose your way inside the Aquacaves; if you feel trapped, then pray to God Aquinious and you will find a way!"

"Can you be more precise on the map's location, O great Bird?"

"Are you a child, Dymondo?"

"I most certainly am not!"

"Do not answer back to me!"

"Apologies."

"Better...so tell me Dymondo, where do children go to learn?"

"School?"

"And where do they go to do research?"

"A library?"

"Indeed! And where is the largest library in the realm?"

"Forprimiera...?"

"Hmm...there is a great room in the palace there, near the guest chambers, where all the old scrolls and slates are stored and kept. These scrolls need proper care and safekeeping, but there are too many, and Shilathaar is no scholar. He has just thrown them in that chamber—the one with the large circular door. I cannot even call it a library anymore. Disgusting! The map is in there."

"But that would be like searching for a pearl in the ocean!"

"Ha-ha! Life is tough, my *boy*! Come, let me return you to your gate."

The bird flew down onto the ground and landed slightly away from the gate. Whilst the bird and the King were airborne, all the people standing outside the gate had seized the opportunity and entered the Kingdom, running quickly to their homes. Dymondo looked for his guards and found them standing a distance from the gate. As Dymondo jumped off, the bird decreased its size. It plucked one of the sharp, yellow, blade-like feathers and threw it at Dymondo's feet so that it stuck into the earth.

"This is the first part of your divine weapon. There are three others! You shall find the second and third part of the weapon in the Aquacaves! The second part is a red shining rod, and the third, a blue shining rod."

"So it's a spear?"

"Yes, but no ordinary one. My feather is the spearhead! Keep it safe!" ordered the bird.

"And the fourth part?"

"The creature that gives you the red and blue rods will tell you where to find the final piece. Remember, you must do what I have said! If you do not, then prepare yourself for the consequences!"

"Gratitude for your help, great Bird, but why don't you just take me to the Aquacaves or show me yourself."

"The map needs to be recovered. It is the one and only map that shows where the Aquacaves are. That should not fall into the wrong hands. Retrieve it and keep it safe." With that, the bird turned and readied itself to take flight.

"Wait...who are you, O great Bird? Please show me your true form. You must be a divine and celestial being!" spoke Dymondo.

The bird smiled in a friendly way for the first time since arriving in Gammafor and its voice became calm and heavenly. "Dymondo, you truly are knowledgeable and clever. It is true, I am no ordinary being. But I cannot tell you who I am or disclose my true form to you...yet."

"Then allow me to bow and kneel before you and fold my hands to seek your blessing," said Dymondo, folding his hands before the bird and kneeling down to the ground and bowing his head. The bird smiled and gently placed its sharp feathered wing on Dymondo's head.

Long may you live, and long may you reign, King Dymondo! Seek the map, and may you be victorious!" roared the bird and flew away into the skies until it could be seen no longer.

Dymondo plucked the sharp spearhead out of the ground. It initially seemed lightweight, but it was not. It was solid gold and firm and shone a blinding yellow like the sun. He held it against the blue sky to admire its magnificence. Suddenly the blade dimmed, lost its firmness and took the form of a normal golden feather. Dymondo walked back to the gate of his kingdom, safely clutching the feather in his hand.

CHAPTER 3

PLANS

Dymondo entered the gate, and Sterferep, Kor, Dan and Dwarpal all ran up to him.

"The King has returned!" shouted Dan.

"My King, are you alright?" asked Sterferep.

"Yes, Lance, I am." There were questions in Dymondo's eyes when looking at Sterferep after what the bird had said about his mark.

"Let us get you inside," said Kor.

They all headed towards the palace, and Dymondo went straight to the court and adjourned it immediately. He required time to digest what he had heard. He was dumbfounded and hurt by what the bird had told him about his brothers. But it made sense. With Queen Ohio gone, Shilathaar and Grygerious no longer had anyone to answer to.

With his head low and drooped shoulders, Dymondo retired to his chamber. Mysteria was away, so he went over to a chest and placed the feather inside. When Mysteria entered the chamber, carrying a beautiful new dress, he greeted her and did not say another word for a while, being so lost in thought.

"My lady," he finally said.

"Yes, my King."

"Are you aware of what took place today?"

"The bird?"

"You heard!"

"I heard some guards murmuring when I went to fetch my new dress."

"Yes, indeed. A golden bird was perched on the gate of the Kingdom?"

"Right, my King."

"It took me up in the skies to convey an important message. I believe the bird was divine—sent by the Gods."

"The Gods?"

"Yes, or perhaps a deity himself, but the bird would not say."

"A talking bird?"

"Yes, my lady, just like the talking panther in the jungle."

"But that was God Topus himself."

"Yes."

"What did it say?"

"It commanded me to go on a mission to recover a divine weapon. But first I must find a map lost within the palace of Forprimiera before my brother Shilathaar finds it."

"That is a dangerous mission, my King, and a grave secret. You should not mention it to just anyone."

"I trust you, Mysteria," said Dymondo, lying on the bed.

Mysteria swooned at the comment.

"I don't even need to ask you to keep it to yourself because I know you will. You're my Queen."

"If this bird was a divine being, then this message must surely be from the Gods."

"The bird gave me a feather from its own wing."

"Those wings were sharp as blades, I heard!"

"Yes! I will show you!"

Dymondo rose from the bed and headed towards the chest in the corner of the chamber and drew out the yellow feather, which now looked rather ordinary.

"This becomes a blade—a golden blade. It is the head of a divine spear! Could you keep it safe in the secret chamber for me?"

"Of course, my King."

"And mention this feather to no one!"

"Have I ever, my King?"

"No, hence why I trust you," smiled Dymondo.

Mysteria took the feather from Dymondo. "I will go now," she said, digging in the chest under some clothes until she pulled out the key to the chamber. "You must prepare to sail to Forprimiera."

"Now?"

"You must not let that map or the divine weapon fall into the wrong hands. Some secrets must remain secrets, but if those secrets are in danger of exposure, it is better they fall into the hands of a righteous man. You must announce your departure in court tomorrow and send word to King Shilathaar."

"You're right, Mysteria. I shall do exactly that."

"In the meantime, I must visit my mother. She will be worried as I have not seen her for a while."

"Did you not send word?"

"I did, through another maid, but she still worries."

"You must go see her then," said Dymondo.

Mysteria smiled. "My King is kind."

"I have one request."

"Yes, my King?"

"That you are here in our chamber tomorrow while I inform the others."

"I will do as you ask."

"I have another request."

"Say it, my King."

"I request you bathe with me in the royal bathing chamber before you depart. I could do with a hot bath after the unexpected flight."

She turned towards him and smiled more. "How could I say no to such a request?"

Dymondo laughed. "Splendid."

"You could do with a good scrub," she winked and disappeared down the stone steps to secure the golden feather.

***

Later that evening, as she was departing the chamber to visit her mother, Lance Sterferep offered to accompany Mysteria to her mother's chamber.

"My Queen, I am worried for the King," Sterferep said in a low voice as they walked.

"Why Sterferep? What happened?"

"He needs to start thinking more before throwing himself into situations."

"He hasn't been sleeping well. A nightmare haunts him—a distant childhood memory I dare not speak of."

Both went silent.

"I shall try my best to speak to him," Mysteria finally said, "but indirectly. And you should do the same. Don't hurt his ego with a direct launch. The King has the habit of asking for opinions from time to time and when he does…coach him."

"I shall do that. Gratitude Queen Mysteria. I know I can always count on you for good advice."

"Gratitude," smiled Mysteria as she headed for her mother's chamber.

***

The next morning in court after the important proceedings came to an end, Dymondo made his announcement.

"I shall be leaving for Forprimiera in two weeks' time to visit my dear brother, Shilathaar, and sister-in-law, Silvenia…Chief Minister Puyol!"

Chief Minister Puyol Bryt stood up. "Yes, my King?"

"Please send a message to my dearest elder brother, Shilathaar, regarding my impending visit."

"Of course, my King, I shall do so immediately," said Puyol and turned to his two assistants and nodded at them. The assistants left the court immediately to get on with the task.

"Excellent! Now! While I am gone, Chief Minister Puyol, Education Minister Olivious, Chief Courtier Majesma and Defence Minister Urayu shall take care of all the court proceedings under the guidance of Prime Minister Kriptus Magnus. Commander-in-chief Hitius Opecious, you are to remain vigilant in my absence and ensure that the borders and the waters remain well-protected. Seek advice from Defence Minister Urayu if necessary; however, in the direst circumstances, may God Aquinious never bring such a day, you send word for me." All those mentioned nodded in acknowledgement.

"Lance Sterferep, Lance Kor, Dan and Dwarpal, you shall accompany me to Forprimiera."

Dan nodded with an excited grin on his face. Kor too smirked and gave a quick nod. Sterferep, though, looked concerned. He was accustomed to hearing Tamaris's name mentioned on the list of men to accompany the King. Dymondo noticed Sterferep's face, but chose to ignore it. Zircornia quickly looked over at Sterferep and he too looked back. She smiled at him and he managed to return the smile. With the announcements made, Dymondo headed towards his chamber with Sterferep, Kor, Dan and Dwarpal following him. Dymondo invited them in, and Mysteria stood in the corner.

"My trusted men, we are on a mission to Forprimiera. I am not travelling for fun." All four looked at one another. "There are only five people I fully trust and those five people are now standing in this room," Dymondo said.

The four men bowed in gratitude, then looked at Mysteria. Mysteria smiled and nodded.

"We have to remain vigilant and alert when in Forprimiera and trust only ourselves."

"What is the mission, my King?"

"We are to retrieve a map, Dwarpal. It is lost among scrolls in a chamber in Forprimiera—a large chamber with a circular door. It is a library, but it is in shambles. We must find it and then the map. It will not be an easy task. Time is not a luxury, and getting caught is not an option. We have fourteen days until we set sail, and we will be training up till our departure. This should appear as a vacation, but it is a mission. Treat it as such."

"What is this map? How will we know what it looks like?" asked Kor.

"That I will disclose later. Right now, just prepare yourselves. Formulate a strategy on how we can penetrate the security and move past Shilathaar's guards to obtain what we require."

"Indeed, my King," said Kor.

"You must not utter a word of this to anyone! I strictly forbid it. Sterferep, not even Zircornia must know." Sterferep nodded in acknowledgement.

"Kor, Dan and Dwarpal, be wary of drink and taverns for the next fourteen days. Too much liquor can loosen a man's tongue! I shan't forbid you from consuming any liquor or from taking women to bed, but do not lose yourselves or let your emotions wander."

They all bowed.

"Gratitude my King, for showing this faith in us," thanked Dwarpal.

"Yes, after what happened, with scholar Lorca—" Dan began.

"We won't talk about that. That is in the past." Dymondo interrupted. "Lorca is fine and you have learnt from your mistakes. We now look to the future. Sterferep believes you both have potential. Soon you shall be Lances. Just focus on learning as much as you can from Kor and Sterferep," explained Dymondo. "Sterferep."

"My King."

"At court you seemed displeased at some of my instructions."

"I was hoping you'd take along Tamaris Putyn as well."

"Yes where is he? We haven't seen him." asked Dan.

"He is away due to personal reasons," spoke Kor.

"Yes, his fortunes do not yet favour him for such an important mission, though he is great young man—a great Lance." Dymondo tried not to say much in front of Dan, Dwarpal and most importantly Mysteria.

"So go now and prepare physically and mentally for your departure," the King continued. "Spend time with your loved ones, but do not mention a word of this to any of them."

"My King?" queried Dwarpal. "In Forprimiera…if we get caught…then—"

"Then we all remain together and prepare to strike down

anyone in our paths. Our ship will remain at the shore at the ready in case we need to make our escape. But we do not leave any man behind. Kor will look after me; I will look after Sterferep; Sterferep will look after, you, Dwarpal; and you will look after Dan and Dan after Kor."

"If that happens, we will be at war with Forprimiera!" said Kor.

"Yes, and we cannot afford that right now, hence the secretive nature of the task. We must be as discreet as possible and avoid bloodshed. Is that clear?"

"Yes, sire!"

"Now disperse and do not let any other soul know of our true reason for the visit. It is a holiday, gentlemen. Act as such."

The men nodded and left the chamber. Dymondo took a deep breath and looked over at Mysteria. Mysteria smiled at him.

Dymondo sat on the side of the bed and began to remove his boots.

"My King…"

"Yes, Mysteria?"

"I was thinking…"

"About what?"

"You say the golden feather is part of a divine weapon? The tip of the spear as you state it?"

"Yes."

"And you are setting out to retrieve the other parts of the weapon?"

"Yes, but the map must be retrieved first."

"I gathered that part, my King."

"Then what is it?"

"What if you find the map and the other parts of the pear?

What good would it be for the spearhead to be sitting here in Gammafor?"

Dymondo nodded.

"I understand what you're trying to say, but it's too risky to take it with me to Forprimiera?"

"It is a risk, but the beauty of the feather is that it

looks ordinary, so no person will suspect it," smiled Mysteria.

Dymondo thought for a while. It would be a risk to take the feather, but Dymondo knew if he found the other parts of the spear, he would be impatient to construct the weapon. He decided the risk was worth it.

"I shall do as you suggest and keep the feather with me."

Mysteria smiled. "When it is time for you to depart, I will make sure you have it for your journey."

CHAPTER 4

THE ARRANGEMENT

Princess Nilharia, the King's sister, had severed her ties with Dan and Dan too had forgotten about the moments of intimacy he had spent with the Princess. Words remained unsaid and feelings unconveyed until the day Nilharia decided to call Dan into her chamber. When he arrived, Velvia, Nilharia's lady in waiting, was in the chamber with her.

Velvia gave Dan a foul glare as he entered.

"You summoned me, Princess? How can I be of assistance?"

"Dear Dan, I don't know how to express this, but I just wanted to clear the air," explained Nilharia.

"You do not need to, my Princess. All is well from my side."

"O Dan, you are a gem, aren't you?"

Velvia rolled her eyes and Dan caught the look.

"Dear Princess and Lady Velvia, I offer my heartfelt apologies to you both for what has happened, but I assure you, I shall no longer be of any concern to you."

"It is not your fault, Dan," spoke Velvia sternly.

"Nevertheless, I do regret what happened. Please accept my apologies. But you are right, I did not know, and believe me no one else apart from me knows and shall know," clarified Dan.

Velvia nodded, though she remained standing with her arms crossed.

"Yes, it was my fault. I apologise Dan," said Nilharia.

"Oh no, dear Princess, please do not apologise," he said and bowed and knelt. "No apologies are required."

"It is not *all* your fault Nilharia," spoke Velvia as she held her hand. They both smiled at one another.

"Rise, Dan," said Nilharia. "Gratitude for keeping our secret."

"Of course, my Princess. Your secret is safe with me. If anytime you need my help or aid with anything then you can always trust me," smiled Dan and bowed again.

"Well, there is one thing…" started Nilharia.

"Command me."

"Well…it depends on Velvia. My dear, what do you reckon? Would you be happy with this arrangement…?"

"What arrangement?" asked Velvia hardheartedly?

"It's just a suggestion."

"Nilharia! Speak!" Velvia was getting annoyed.

"Alright!" Nilharia snapped back. "Well…as we all here know, you and I are in love."

"Yes," replied Velvia.

"But we also know that I don't just like women. I like men as well."

Velvia huffed in discontent. "Yes."

"So from time to time, do you think Dan could—?"

"No!" shouted Velvia.

"Please! Velvia at least try for me!" begged Nilharia.

"I don't like…men," stated Velvia.

"Well I do! Won't you even try it for me?"

Velvia thought as creases formed on her forehead.

"Alright, I shall try once, but if I don't like it, then it won't happen again!"

"I assure you…you'll like it. Dan, are you in agreement?"

"Your wish is my command."

"Why would you say no?" smiled Velvia. Dan smirked and lowered his eyes.

"Fine. It is settled. You will remain at my door. When I call you inside, then you will know what it is for," winked Nilharia.

Everyone went silent, then Nilharia's eyes lit up.

"Why not now?!"

"No, not now! I need time to digest—"

"Quiet! The both of you. Lady Velvia, you are my lady in waiting. Dan, you are my guard. I command you to kiss Velvia…gently."

"No! Nilharia! I—"

"Ssh. Just let him do it…you'll like it," smirked Nilharia.

Dan placed his spear against the wall and walked over to Velvia and held her face in his hand. He gently brought his lips close to hers and began to kiss her. She was apprehensive at first, but it wasn't long before she reciprocated and passionately kissed him back. The kiss finished and Velvia wiped her lips.

"Well…how was it?"

"I don't know—"

"Excellent!" clapped Nilharia. She walked up to Dan and kissed him. She then kissed Velvia and the three shed their clothes and fell on top of the sheets.

Lance Sterferep walked past Princess Nilharia's chamber and found Dan away from his position. Sterferep did not know he was inside. All he saw was no one standing guard outside the Princess' chamber. Furiously, he looked around for Dan in the neighbouring corridors and eventually decided go back and stand guard himself until Dan returned to his position. Just as he started to walk back up the corridor leading to the Princess' door, Sterferep witnessed Dan emerging from her chamber. Sterferep immediately hid behind a pillar to watch. He saw Dan adjust his kilt and wipe sweat from his forehead. Sterferep knew.

After a few moments, when Dan had resumed his guard position, Sterferep emerged from behind the pillar and walked up to him.

Dan and Sterferep looked at one another and smiled.

"Lance Sterferep!" bowed Dan.

"Dan, how do you fare?" asked Sterferep.

"Very well, Lance," assured Dan.

"I walked past earlier, but you weren't here…where were

you?" Sterferep asked, his smile intact.

Dan's face turned red from embarrassment.

"I was here all along, I may have stepped away for a comfort break, Lance," lied Dan.

Now Sterferep was angry. He expected the truth from Dan, not concealing lies. Sterferep got close and spoke to him in a low but stern voice.

"It has to stop!"

Dan felt physically sick. His legs went numb and sweat broke once more across his forehead.

"What has to stop?" Dan asked in a lowered voice, trying to act innocent.

"Shut up...You take me for a fool. I see everything, Dan!" Sterferep growled under his breath.

A few guards and Lances appeared in the distance. Sterferep stood next to Dan and put on a false smile.

"Just smile like I am, so no one suspects us," he said through gritted teeth. Sterferep was furious. "I know what you have been up to. It has to stop!"

"I...I don't know what you are saying, dear Sterferep," maintained Dan.

The guards and Lances walked past greeting Dan and Sterferep who had not let their false smiles fade until the guards and Lances had reached a distance. Once they had, Sterferep wheeled on Dan.

"You have to stop fucking the Princess!""I swear it was her. She commanded me to do it. She invited me into her—"

"I know! She can be frivolous. I saw how she danced with you at court. I should have said something then, but I saw you two kept your distance from one another, so I thought I'd just let sleeping dogs lie. It seemed the issue had resolved itself."
"It had, but just now—"

"Quiet, lower your voice!" Sterferep again spoke under his breath. "We stand outside her chamber. Dan ... it has to stop!"

"Does anyone else know?" asked Dan.

"No!"

Dan breathed a sigh of relief. "Please don't tell—"

"I won't! But if the King finds out, then I will not be able to save you from his anger. I vouched for you, Dan!"

"Apologies."

"Your apologies are worthless!"

"What if she commands me? Then what shall I—"

"Just stop!" snapped Sterferep and stormed off.

Dan was petrified. He felt punctured and feared what the King would do if he ever found out. He couldn't let that happen, but his desire for Nilharia was overwhelming. To balm his wounded heart and to conceal his fear, he resolved that for the next few days after his duty, he would set off towards the distractions of women and wine.

Raj Bansal

CHAPTER 5

SILVENIA

At the court of Forprimiera, the court doorkeeper made his announcement.

"All at court, the crown prince of Orakray, Kratos Laaris and Prince Yatus Laaris!"

Two, strong, tanned, muscular figures strutted into the throne room. Both were dressed in golden armour and red, silk tunics with sharp blades hanging from their waists belts. Shilathaar was pleased to see the princes. They both smiled at the King and he smiled back.

"We pay our respects to the great King of Forprimiera, Shilathaar!" proclaimed Kratos in a strong posh voice.

"Welcome! Greetings Prince Kratos. Greetings Prince Yatus! You are welcome to court. Please take a seat near me!"

The two bowed and approached the King's throne.

Kratos had long, wavy, medium-brown hair. He was a year or two younger than Queen Silvenia. He had a large forehead and it was difficult to determine whether his hair was receding or not, though he often ran his fingers through his hair to check. He had a long chin and a sharp nose, and his brown eyes had a glimmer of deceit in them. He frequently wore a toga in the blood-red colours of the Laaris clan of Orakray (the flag and crest of Orakray were both blood red with a depiction of a fearsome black bear), along with golden-tasselled armour and golden trinkets. He also kept his muscular body well-moisturised with oils and scents. Many women took a liking to him.

Yatus was two years younger than his brother, though just as cunning. He had the same evil grin and the same brown eyes.

34

Unlike his brother, though, Yatus had thick hair. He would at times allow his dirty-blonde hair to grow long and at other times would have it cut short. He too was muscular but without the oils, and he generally got more attention from women than his brother did, making him the more playful and mischievous of the two.

The pair took seats close to the King.

"What a surprise! How does King Orayus Laaris fare? Why did you not send word?"

"If we had sent word that we were coming, how would we have surprised you? King Orayus is well, my King," replied Yatus. He too had a strong, posh voice.

"Ha-ha! And the Queen?"

"Again well," said Kratos.

"Marvellous! It is always a delight to see you both. What brings you to Forprimiera, gentlemen?"

"All is well, my King. We merely decided to give the King a pleasant surprise. The warmer summer days are approaching fast. Therefore, we thought we could enjoy them with you, the gracious King, and our brother-in-law, Shilathaar, and the Queen, and our beloved sister, Silvenia," said Kratos.

"But of course," agreed Shilathaar.

"I propose in the coming days we go hunting and strike down the most fearsome creature in the forest and eat its meat over the fire," proposed Yatus. "After that, we can drink sweet wine until we can no longer stand or even sit up!"

"Ha-ha! You continually manage to strike the nail on its head, Yatus! Yes Indeed! We shall! You both must be tired from the journey. Feel free to rest in our royal guest chambers. The Queen and I shall dine with you both this evening and make plans and arrangements for the hunt and any other tasks in preparation for summer. Be prepared for lots of wine, singing and dancing!" laughed Shilathaar.

The two stood up in delight and bowed. "The King is gracious. Long live the King!" shouted Yatus.

The courtiers repeated the chant.

"We take your leave, my King, for we shall meet later this

evening," said Kratos.

"Indeed, do proceed my good sirs."

"One other request, O great ruler!" requested Kratos. "Do we have your permission to visit Queen Silvenia in her chamber prior to the evening feast? As you can understand, we yearn to meet our beloved sister."

"Granted! Do as you wish, gentlemen, for we are family. You need not ask," announced Shilathaar.

Shilathaar enjoyed the respect Kratos and Yatus gave him, and Kratos and Yatus knew it. The King's brothers-in-law were not senseless, but shrewd. It was a requirement to be obsequious towards Shilathaar, so one could extract the desired results from his mouth.

"Hah! That wasn't too difficult, Brother!" said Yatus, giving his brother a wily smile once they had made it a good distance away from court.

"It never is! Our much-loved brother-in-law is easily persuaded!"

"We know what he requires. Ha-ha!" mocked Yatus.

"Nevertheless, Shilathaar is not a bad man."

"Most definitely not! I rather enjoy his company. He is good with our family, and above all, his cock pleases our sister continually!" laughed Yatus. "Come, let us visit her before we rest in the royal guest chamber!" Both laughed and strutted down the corridor towards Silvenia's chamber.

When the two got to the Queen's door, they were granted permission to enter.

"Kratos! Yatus! Welcome to Forprimiera, my brothers!" greeted Silvenia, walking up to her brothers. She first went up to Yatus and stood on her toes to give him a kiss. He hugged her tight, then lifted and swung her around in joy as she kissed him and they both laughed loudly.

"How do you fare?" Yatus asked.

"Well, Yatus, and you?"

"Cannot be better," he smiled back. She then walked up to Kratos. Again, she had to tiptoe to plant her kiss on his lips. He too hugged her tight and lifted her off the ground and both continued laughing with joy.

"Kratos! How are you?"

"Very well, my Queen!" he joked as he put her down.

"Oh, leave it will you! Queen?" she pushed him away and smiled back. "Leave us!" she commanded her maids. She then grabbed the strong arms of her brothers and took them towards her bed where they all sat down to talk.

"So how have my two lovely brothers been? And how are Mother and Father?"

They both chuckled. "Yes, all is well my lovely, dear sister. Mother sends you her love and Father… he sends blessings and an entire list of things you must and must not do," said Kratos.

"Ha-ha! As if I've ever listened to what that old man had to say," jested Silvenia.

They all laughed loudly at that. Just like her brothers, Silvenia was very cunning and selfish and had no care for anyone but her siblings and her husband. All three siblings frequently spoke ill of their father behind his back.

"Yes, the old fart can keep his words to himself. I just let them go in one ear and out the other!" laughed Yatus.

Silvenia lay sideways on the bed and her breasts nearly escaped from her dress. The two brothers removed their sandals and sat comfortably on either end of the bed.

"Oh, it's been such a long since he's allowed you both to visit Forprimiera," she said. "You must visit more often and not listen to what he has to say," she added, whilst picking at the bed cover.

"Of course, dear Sister. That we will from now on. Even now he did not permit us, but we insisted and he let us go," explained Kratos.

"I often fail to understand the reasoning behind his words," complained Silvenia. "In fact, I cannot take his words seriously ever since news of his love child in Gammafor."

"Oh, I despise Father's love-child. My blood boils at the thought of him!" said Yatus.

"Mine too. Poor Mother. She was faithful to him her entire life and he repaid her with an illegitimate step son! What a phallus!" cursed Kratos.

"Ha-ha!" laughed Silvenia as they mocked and ridiculed their father.

"He is only King because he is still strong," said Kratos. "Shilathaar adores him for his courage."

"Yes, strong he is, no doubt," confirmed Yatus.

"Not interested at all," said Silvenia and sat up on her knees, her bosoms bouncing back into her dress. "I shall arrange a large feast for us three and only we shall dine together in my chamber and stay up all night and prattle!" she announced.

"What of your husband?"

"What was court like today?" she asked.

"Same old: 'I am not the King of the four lands!' Ha-ha!"

"He said that, did he?"

"Yes, I heard him!"

"Well, in that case, we need not wait for him for he will not be visiting my chamber this night. He will insert his shaft into one of his mistresses and curse his youngest brother whilst doing so," clarified Silvenia.

"Ha-ha, but does he not utter those words every day?" mocked Yatus.

"Yes! Ha-ha!" said Silvenia laughing so mischievously and slapping her hand against Yatus's. They all laughed so loud that they could not stop. The brothers fell onto the ground and Silvenia fell back down onto her bed and her breasts fell out of her dress. She laughed even harder at that and at her brothers sprawled on the floor. With one hand she reached out to Kratos and with the other hand she tried to place her large bosom back into her dress. Kratos too was still laughing, and as he grabbed her hand to get up, he saw his sister adjust herself.

"Your dresses! Only the Gods can help you! Just like when you were unmarried, you could never keep them in!" laughed Kratos.

They continued to laugh even more after this comment. She laughed back, "I remember we all used to run in the fields, ride horses, and climb mountains and they would always get in the way!" she continued to laugh.

"I ended up seeing them every day!" said Yatus as he too stood up from the ground still laughing.

"I remember Mother once strapped your breasts down with a cloth!" laughed Kratos.

"Oh Gods! I could not even breathe properly. I couldn't run, ride or climb!" laughed Silvenia.

"I remember you went running back to Mother and we followed you and you asked her to remove it."

"Yes, and she refused and told me I must cover myself in front of my younger brothers." They all laughed at that.

"Her face dropped when you just threw off the cloth in front us!" laughed Yatus, and they all laughed more.

"I was only nineteen back then?"

"It was hilarious!"

"Wait, wait, wait…gentlemen. It happened like this," she said as she temporarily stopped laughing and stood on the bed "…behold!" she said and laughed as she lowered her top to reveal her breasts and then covered them in the same movement. This time they could not stop laughing for a very long time.

"Oh, great fun!" Kratos said catching his breath after the laughter had ceased. "So, why will the King not be present at the feast this evening?"

"Did he say he would be present?" asked Silvenia.

"Aye, he did."

"Then the feast will not take place in my chamber, dear Brother. We must do as the King says!" sighed Silvenia.

"After which he…will bang his mistress!" joked Yatus. They all laughed again.

"Who is he shafting these days? Last time it was that slave girl from the village… what was her name…?"

"I do not wish to know!" said Silvenia seriously.

"Suppose… why would you?" smiled Yatus. Silvenia did not smile back. Yatus too terminated his grin. Seeing this, Kratos got disturbed as they both could not bear the frown on her face.

"Sister… honestly… are you happy with this oaf?" Kratos asked holding her hand.

39

"I am, Kratos. He is brash and crude, but he treats me with respect."

"And care?"

"No, not care."

There was silence.

"He is a man, Kratos. He breathes war…anger…fire…and weapons! He does not have a place for delicate, soft items in his life."

"But you my sister are soft as a petal. Does he not hold you with caring hands?"

"Hah! No Kratos, No!"

"Absurd! Does he hit you?" Kratos was angry.

"No, Brother! I will strike his crotch with my knee before he even contemplates that!" laughed Silvenia. "Actually, I *enjoy* his rough hands upon me. I like the way he is. I could not have survived with a man who forever spoke of love and flowers, rivers and moonlight. I like a man to be a *man*! He is what he should be! My father is a man! My brothers are men! And my husband is a man! I love it!"

"And what of all the mistresses he takes into his bed?"

"I know of them all, even this village bitch. Cloutia was her name. But shall I disclose one of our secrets…? A secret both him and I share"

"What is that?"

"You must *not* mention this to anyone!"

"You have our word, Sister."

"If he takes mistresses, then I too am occasionally permitted to take part in similar pleasures with soldiers and slaves and gladiators!" squealed Silvenia.

"Are you serious? Shilathaar is aware of this?"

"He suggested it."

"Ha-ha! What a peculiar arrangement!" laughed Yatus.

Kratos sat in shock and Silvenia grinned. Yatus continued to laugh which eventually triggered Silvenia and Kratos into loud laughter as well.

"I see your mark fades, Sister!" said Kratos.

"Is that so?" replied Silvenia as she looked at her upper right shoulder. "I cannot tell."

It bore the image of the Cecrops; half man/half serpent.

"Never let it fade. The serpent man is our protection!"

"Yes, yes, I know, Brother."

"You must not scrub hard over it!" shouted Yatus.

"Relax, you two! It will never completely vanish!"

"The Cecrops prolongs our life."

"Yatus, I know how important it is," said Silvenia in a stern voice. "I know that we cannot be killed by just any person. Only the person that bears this same mark can rob us from our lives."

"Ssh! You must not speak that out loud!"

"C'mon. How many people are out there with a Cecrops on their right shoulder? Us? I have not seen anyone else."

"Even so, we must take caution. Keep it covered at all times if you can. Does Shilathaar know?"

"No! He just thinks it is a family mark. That's what I told him!" sneered Silvenia.

"No harm in that then."

"But…"

"But what, Yatus?" asked Kratos. Both he and Silvenia turned to their brother.

"Father has a love child… he too will bear that mark…will he not? He too…is a Laaris…"

Kratos and Silvenia had no reply, and a stunned silence engulfed the chamber.

CHAPTER 6

SYMERA

As Grygerious lounged in his chamber in Doosranfor, Karnigol entered and bowed.

"My King…I present to you…Symera," announced Karnigol.

A young lady walked into the King's chamber. Cresenia lifted her head with pride as she looked down upon the young woman with the perfect figure.

Symera stood before the King dressed in black leather trousers and black boots. She wore black leather gloves and a tightly fastened, black, full-sleeved, hooded leather jacket. Her nose and mouth were covered with black face concealment, but her light brown eyes were visible. They displayed a strange combination of confidence and calm. She stood straight and looked directly into Grygerious's eyes.

Cresenia walked around her examining every inch of her body, but Symera kept on looking at Grygerious.

"A fine figure she has, Karnigol," said Cresenia. "But that is all I can see right now."

Grygerious tilted his head to the side and looked carefully at the visitor. He put his one hand on his chin and ran his fingers through his silky blonde hair. Cresenia's eyes lit up when he did that. She loved his hair.

"Is there anyone outside, Karnigol?" asked Grygerious.

"No, my King. I made sure. In this chamber there is no one but us four."

Grygerious moved around the motionless young woman, not taking his eyes off her. "I suppose I'm taking a risk."

"I have a blade, my King! Any ill movement from her and she will die! You are safe."

"You know how to wield a sword?" laughed Grygerious.

Karnigol felt offended, but kept his composure. "I do, my King!"

"Hah! Good for you...and for me I guess!" he laughed more and Cresenia smiled.

"Remove your mask, young lady," commanded Grygerious.

The woman did as she was told.

"Pretty face! Beautiful eyes! I like it so far, Karnigol," commented Grygerious. "It seems as though I may have seen you somewhere—"

"Hah! Cresenia waved her hand at the beautiful young woman.

"Cresenia...there, there!"

"Trying to woo her, are we? You've seen her somewhere? Hah!"

"She is not as beautiful as you, Cresenia!" Grygerious opted for flattery, but was still looking at Symera.

"I know," said Cresenia and turned to pour some wine.

"Get me one as well!" said Grygerious as he walked close up to Symera, still keeping a safe distance.

"Your hair! Show me!"

The young woman took off her hood. She had thick, silky brown hair.

"Straight hair!" Grygerious said as he took the goblet of wine Cresenia had extended to him.

"Yes," agreed Karnigol.

"You believe she can do the task?" Grygerious asked Karnigol.

"Hah! I can do a better task than her!" said Cresenia in

43

arrogance, drinking her wine.

For the first time, Symera looked over at Cresenia. Cresenia was too busy drinking from her goblet to notice Symera's glare. Grygerious turned towards Cresenia for the first time since Symera had entered the room.

"Yes, but Cresenia, you are not poisonous! She, on the other hand…" Grygerious looked back over at Symera and smiled.

Karnigol saw the King's smile shift into something more thoughtful.

"What doubt comes into your mind, my King?"

"I am thinking…would I fuck her? Yes…but is she irresistible? I don't know."

Grygerious turned his back towards the woman and Karnigol looked towards Cresenia.

"Get me another! She won't do, Karnigol! Take her away!" pronounced Grygerious as he drained his drink.

"But my King—"

"I said no!" shouted Grygerious. "Away with her!"

"How do you know I am not irresistible?" the presented woman spoke for the first time.

Grygerious turned around in a huff and threw his goblet on the ground.

Cresenia closed her eyes and Karnigol jumped at the sound. Symera did not flinch but kept looking ahead.

"You dare question me? Then listen! You are not insurmountably beautiful. How can you ensnare a man in your trap? I do not find you irresistible!"

"What is beauty?"

"I know when I see a beautiful woman!"

"What do you look at? Her eyes, her face, her hair or her figure? I ask you, my lady," said Symera turning towards Cresenia. "What do you look at in a man? His hair, his eyes, his smile or his frame?"

Grygerious and Cresenia both went quiet.

"A pretty face is the not the only point of attraction. There have been many cases where a man does not have remarkable facial features, but his body is thigh moistening. There have been many times where I have seen great facial features in a man but his frame and body were not equal to his face. Though…some men have both."

"I can agree to that," smiled Grygerious.

"There! So the same can be said for woman. Do you agree to that?"

"Yes!"

"Then how can you say I am not irresistible when you have not seen my body."

Grygerious's eyes lit up, and a wicked grin appeared on his face.

"That won't be necessary!" Cresenia intervened. "Karnigol, take her away! Rude woman! My King, you should have her punished for answering back to you!" The jealous Cresenia spoke.

"No, no, wait! I am now intrigued!" said Grygerious.

"But my King—"

"Cresenia! Why are you getting insecure? Even if I want to, I cannot fuck this woman, or even kiss her. She's poisonous!" clarified Grygerious which shut Cresenia up.

Grygerious turned towards Symera and his filthy smile returned.

"Remove your clothes," he commanded her.

Symera gave him a subtle smirk and removed her boots, followed by her trousers until she was semi-nude. Karnigol looked away in shame. Grygerious stared at her legs.

"I suppose nice legs…" he said as he walked around to her back. "Very nice arse, I must say! And yes, desirable sex, but I prefer shaved…though yours is well groomed."

Cresenia rolled her eyes at Grygerious.

"Tell me, why remove your trousers first?" asked Grygerious.

"Have you heard the saying…saving the best for last?"

"Indeed!" Grygerious's evil eyes went ever so wide.

"Then…behold!" She removed her gloves. Her nails were sharp but groomed. Grygerious knew very well to stay far away from them. She then slowly and gently unfastened her jacket and it let hang on her unfastened.

Grygerious's heart skipped a beat. Through the gap he could see the inner curves of her breasts.

Symera pouted coyly, then with an extravagant smile, removed her jacket to display her breasts.

Cresenia's goblet dropped as did Grygerious's face upon seeing them. He had never seen such a beautiful pair of breasts in his life! They were amazing. Large, perfectly round and with desirably pert nipples.

"Oh my!"

Symera smiled.

"Fuck, they are magnificent!" Cresenia spurted out and then swiftly placed her hand over her mouth.

"Oh!...Oh!" Grygerious had no words.

"What were you saying about being irresistible?" asked Symera as she stood stark naked before him with her hands upon her hips.

"Forgive me! You are stunning! I cannot take my eyes off you!"

Symera strutted toward him and Grygerious caught hold of his crotch as she did.

She came close to him and whispered. "You must avoid nail contact, lip contact and genital contact…but you can touch any other part," She winked at him and then looked down at her bosom.

Grygerious placed his hands on her bosom and squeezed her breasts hard as he could. He groaned as he did and immediately got close to climax. He let go and sat down on a chair to catch his breath.

"I need a moment," said Grygerious.

Symera smirked at Cresenia.

"Why on Landsfor are you a poison damsel?" Grygerious shook his head.

"You said Landsfor!" Karnigol and Cresenia spoke in unison.

"For those breasts, I wouldn't mind if Brother Shilathaar parted my head from my body for saying that word. I have no care in the realm for anything at this moment," replied Grygerious wiping the sweat from his forehead.

"Put your clothes back on, Symera, for you are irresistible. I cannot control myself. Please at least cover your breasts!"

Symera smiled and put her clothes back on which gave Grygerious time to gather himself.

"Marvellously done, Karnigol! You have found the right damsel!"

"My King." Karnigol was still looking away.

"You can look now! She has put her clothes back on," said Grygerious.

"Gratitude, my King."

"I will give you a golden ring for just finding her, Karnigol. Set her to task and see it through to the end and you shall receive four more. Five remarkable rings, specially made. One for each finger of your chosen hand."

Karnigol's eyes lit up.

"My King is gracious."

"Wait a moment. Why is it that you seem familiar to me?"

"Oh leave it, will you?" interrupted Cresenia.

"No, I am serious. Who are you?"

Symera looked around and lowered her eyes.

"My father was the Prime Minister of Landsfor."

Grygerious looked off in the distance and tried to remember.

"Sygma," Symera told him.

"Prime Minister, Sygma?…but of course! He retired when I was a child! Yes, I vaguely remember."

"He died!"

Grygerious went quiet.

"He did not retire. He died," she repeated.

"Right… my condolences…I must have seen you at court."

"Yes, you did. My face hasn't changed much."

"Did you get kidnapped after your father died?"

"What do you mean?"

"You are a poison damsel. Surely you have not chosen this path."

"You are wrong. I did. In fact, my father chose it for me!"

"Your father? Why?"

"To avenge my brother."

Grygerious again searched his memory.

"You should remember him very well!"

Karnigol looked closely at her. Symera's eyes were beginning to display anger.

"Syterius," said Symera.

"Ah yes! Oh the Gods! You are Syterius's sister! Syterius and we three brothers were friends! We used play together all the time!"

"My father told me."

"Poor Syterius. My heart weeps for him! He was taken from us too soon."

Symera lifted her head and contained her anguish. There was an awkward silence in the room. Grygerious was now being cautious and trying not to say much more. He was looking for the opportunity to give her the instructions.

"My father said he was killed," Symera said.

"Killed? He slipped. He fell from the edge of the mountain. It was an accident."

"My father thought he was pushed by someone. He said on his death bed that I should avenge my brother and showed me this path."

Grygerious was now afraid but his conniving mind was fast at work.

"Symera! What are you implying?" shouted Karnigol unsheathing his sword.

Undeterred, Symera continued to speak.

"Was he not pushed?"

"You are right!" replied Grygerious.

Symera's face dropped.

"He was pushed. Syterius was killed," said Grygerious lowering his head as he began to shed crocodile tears.

"Speak! Tell me who pushed him."

"Fate!"

"What?"

"Fate! Destiny!"

"What at your saying?"

"Destiny also brought you to me. For the person I am sending you to poison happens to the killer of your brother!"

"Who is that person? Tell me!"

"My brother...Dymondo Rain."

Symera put her hand on her chest and her anger turned into shock.

"No! You say an untruth. My Dy would never do such a thing!"

Grygerious wiped his tears and looked at her. She evaded eye contact.

"*Your*...Dy?"

"Dymondo Rain is known to be righteous. He can do no such thing! Tell me the truth!"

"Watch it, Symera!" Karnigol extended the sword and pointed at her throat.

"No, Karnigol. She is in distress."

Karnigol lowered his weapon.

"I can understand your plight, but—"

"It was one of you three Princes that took his life! I ask whom?"

"I am not strong, Symera. Nor do I have the will and courage to fight anyone. Why do you think I need poison damsels to remove my enemies?"

Symera pondered that for a while.

"How come your brother is your enemy?"

"They both are! I wish to rule the four islands. I want to bring peace and joy to the realm. No destruction and no violence! See how peaceful Doosranfor is? You live here, do you not?"

Symera nodded.

"I cannot fight them, so I will remove them."

Symera said nothing.

"Fine. You do believe that I am the least likely of the three brothers to have killed Syterius, do you not?"

Symera again nodded.

"So it must be either Dymondo or Shilathaar...right?"

She again nodded.

"Fine. Then kill them both. One after the other. Go to Gammafor and kill Dymondo and then head over to Forprimiera and kill Shilathaar. Then your brother's death shall be avenged."

Symera thought before she said another word.

"I need to know who it is!"

"Why...? Why would you not believe it is Dymondo? Why is he *your* Dy?"

Symera lowered her eyes.

"Tell me, Symera. What is it that you hide?"

"Dymondo was ten when Syterius died. Dymondo and I are of the same age. Our mother only lived for another year after Syterius's death. My father kept on investigating secretly. He would go to the mountain by Syterius fell from every day after court, looking for evidence and clues. I do not know how, but he managed to ascertain that Syterius was pushed."

"And?"

"Time went by. For years, Father kept me away from court, but on Shilathaar's birthday celebration, he called me in to help out with preparations for the banquet. It was there I met Dymondo for the first time. We must have been nineteen."

"Go on."

"We became good friends. We began to meet more often and go riding to the ocean to see the sunset. By that time my father's health had begun to deteriorate. He loathed our friendship."

"What is it with Dymondo and riding up to sunsets?! He and my wife used to do that too!"

"It is romantic," Cresenia offered.

"Am I not romantic? I don't go riding to the shores with women to behold the sun sink into the ocean!"

Symera said nothing.

Grygerious shook his head and said, "Continue!"

"One day, it was late, so on the way back we camped at the banks of the river Krool. It was a cold night and we held each other to keep each other warm."

"You had sex?" said Grygerious, killing the sweet intimacy

Symera was about to describe.

Symera looked at him and paused. "We fucked!"

Grygerious folded his arms and raised his eyebrows.

"Next morning, we bathed in the river naked. Oh my! We were so happy!"

"Damn fuck, got to suck those breasts!" said Grygerious under his breath.

Symera heard him but just smiled and nodded.

This infuriated Grygerious.

"Then what?"

"I got home. My father, who was bedridden, was worried for me. I knew he did not have long to live. He knew that too. Then he told me about my brother and what he suspected—that one of the Princes pushed him over the cliff. My hand and feet turned cold. He told me I must avenge his death. He spoke of the ways in which I could get close to royalty. Coitus being one. He spoke of poison damsels but said I was too old to start now."

"You could have just found out who it was out of us three and then killed us after having sex? Why the poison damsel route?"

"As much I liked to believe that Dymondo could not be the one, I was not sure. So the last thing I was going to do was to bed the man that killed my brother. That night my father died, and in the dark of night I disappeared to this island. The poison damsel path was dangerous, but I had no choice. If I didn't want to bed the man, I would have to lure him and just scratch him, or kiss him. And that can be done anywhere."

"Yes, it gave you options. That was a daring and dangerous decision."

"I survived."

"But are you as poisonous as the others?"

"I'd give you a demonstration, but are you man enough to risk your life for your word?" smiled Symera.

"Karnigol...fetch two guards."

"But my King!" Karnigol was shocked.

"Do it!"

Karnigol lowered his head and went to summon the guards.

51

Cresenia looked on in shock.

"I want you to kiss one and scratch the other!" ordered Grygerious as Karnigol walked out.

"Keep it short and quick."

Symera nodded.

Karnigol walked in with two slim handsome guards dressed in fine, white linen togas, and they all bowed to their King.

Symera walked up to one and forcefully kissed him, and whilst engaged in the lip lock, she scratched the face of the other. Both went crashing to the ground to their deaths and their bodies turned blue. Symera looked back at Grygerious and wiped her lips upon her sleeve and smiled.

"Hmm! Marvellous! Head to Gammafor and finish off Dymondo."

"Tell me who it was first!"

"Lady Symera, if you do not wish to believe me, then the choice is yours. The truth won't change. It was Dymondo. I am telling you. As I said, kill them both, and you will be avenged."

Symera still could not believe what she was hearing. Her heart was not prepared to believe it.

"Why would Dymondo do that?"

"Competitiveness! Dymondo liked to win. Syterius always won in any game he played. Dymondo got fed up with losing and grabbed hold of Syterius's throat and pushed him off the cliff!"

"Silence!" shouted Symera and covered her ears.

"No, you listen, Symera. Syterius fell to his death because of Dymondo!"

Symera shook her head vigorously like a women possessed. Her eyes turned blue as her blood boiled. Grygerious jumped in horror at the sight of them.

Anger makes their eyes go blue. "Calm down, Symera. Save your anger for Dymondo!"

Symera closed her eyes and reopened them. They were still blue. She stood staring at the ground breathing heavily.

"Go now, Symera. Go right way and take your revenge. Dymondo must be wondering where you went. Use your old friendship to get close, then....strike!"

Symera nodded. Her eyes were still blue but now wet with tears. She wiped them.

"Go now! May victory be yours!"

Symera turned and she and Karnigol began to head out.

"Before you go...may I ask you a question?"

She turned around to face him again. He placed his hands upon his hips.

"You said some men have both. Great facial features and a body!"

"Yes, I did."

"Although we would never fuck, if you could...would you?"

Symera stood looking at him for a while and walked up to him.

"I don't know. I haven't seen your body."

Grygerious had no reply.

"I take your leave, my King. The task shall be done."

Grygerious's ego was hurt.

"Wait!" He took off his white toga until he stood before her stark naked. Karnigol again looked away.

Cresenia rolled her eyes in anger. Symera looked amused.

"Answer me!"

"Fine," she said as she walked up to him and around him, examining his frame.

"Truthfully yes, you are handsome. Toned body and a handsome face."

Grygerious smiled and began to redress.

"But I would not fuck you!"

"What? Why?" Grygerious was angry.

"Because your heart is the ugliest thing I've ever seen."

"Symera!" shouted Grygerious as he moved towards her grabbing onto his half-tied toga. Symera extended out her hand displaying her deadly nails and keeping her blue, poisonous eyes fixed upon him. He halted immediately. Cresenia's face turned blue with fear. An inch closer and he would have made contact. Symera shook her head slowly, prompting him to step back and lower his filthy eyes. She then tud to Karnigol, who had unsheathed his sword, and gave him a look that prompted Karnigol to put the sword back in its scabbard…slowly.

With that, Symera left Grygerious's chamber intent on seeking her first target, the youngest Rain prince whom now had become the King of Gammafor and Fourtfor.

CHAPTER 7

THE TYRANT'S GUESTS

I n Forprimiera, the next few days passed like this with Kratos and Yatus attending court each day and spending the evenings cavorting with Silvenia and feasting with Shilathaar. On the fourth afternoon, when the Primieran court was in full session, Shilathaar turned to his chief courtier.

"Anymore, Orpictus?"

"Yes, my King. Your younger brother, King Dymondo of Gammafor and Fourtfor has sent word that he wishes to visit. His messenger just delivered the announcement. He will arrive in ten days' time."

Shilathaar's face dropped at the mention of Fourtfor. *Why did Orpictus insist on reminding him that his youngest brother controlled two of the four islands?* Nevertheless, he tried to keep a straight face.

"Very well… promptly send word in return that he is most welcome. I would be delighted to receive him and have him visit Forprimiera. Does he mention any particular purpose for the visit?"

"No, my King. Just that he wishes to see his brother."

Shilathaar scratched his beard, pondering why Dymondo would suddenly come to visit.

"Very well, that will be all for today! Disperse! Kratos, Yatus and Orpictus; you remain!"

All the courtiers stood and bowed and quietly left the court, all except the three the King had mentioned.

"Everyone has gone my King. What is it that bothers you?"

"Nothing bothers Shilathaar, Orpictus! However, I am mildly perplexed as to why Dymondo is visiting."

"I understand your surprise, my King. Generally, King Dymondo visits only on special occasions. I may be wrong, but I believe he is coming here for a purpose."

"I too! But he has veiled that purpose under his sweet words by saying he's coming to visit his brother," said Kratos.

"I believe so too," said Orpictus.

"Hmm…let him come. But I want everyone to keep a close eye on him. I want to know what he does and where he goes. Everything!"

"Indeed, my King. I will tell the guards. It shall be done."

"Remember, though! Should he become aware that he is being watched, do not touch him or harm him in anyway."

"Absolutely."

Ten days passed and Dymondo's ship touched the shores of Forprimiera. Standing at the shore was Shilathaar himself along with his Queen, Silvenia, and his many guards, soldiers and musicians, all there to welcome Dymondo with great pomp and grandeur.

Shilathaar could not help but notice the towering Sterferep standing next to his brother. The Lance was as tall as him. The frames of the other three standing behind Dymondo were similarly impressive.

"Brother!" shouted Dymondo and ran up to embrace Shilathaar.

Shilathaar received his embrace. Dymondo then turned to Silvenia and bowed and approached her for a gentle hug. She on the other hand grabbed his face and kissed him on his lips and laughed. "How are you young Dymondo?" she asked.

"I am well, my Queen," replied Dymondo wiping his lips.

"Come! It is so good of you to visit, Brother!" roared Shilathaar in his loud voice, putting his large arm around Dymondo and beginning to walk.

"Brother this is—" Dymondo began.

"Ah yes, your Lances! Yes, they too can come!"

Shilathaar had brought chariots to ride back to his Kingdom. Shilathaar got on his great chariot; a large black conveyance with a red dragon depicted on its front. The flag on the chariot was purple with the same red dragon sewn into its fabric. The red dragon had replaced the golden lion when Forprimiera became an independent Kingdom. Dymondo chose to ignore the modification.

Shilathaar extended his hand for his wife to join him on board his chariot.

"My King is kind," she said, "but I would like to ride back to the palace with young Dymondo, in my chariot." Smiling, she grabbed Dymondo's arm and pulled him to her conveyance.

Shilathaar laughed and smiled. "Very well!"

"Come Dymondo, we shall ride together!" she said sounding excited and pointed towards a grey chariot which was slightly smaller and did not look large enough for two.

Dymondo smiled back sceptically.

"My men?"

"Yes, yes! They too will ride on a chariot!" announced Shilathaar. "They are welcome to take any one! Charioteer! Head to the palace!" And he was off.

The four men got on the chariot just behind Silvenia's grey chariot and waited. Dymondo got on first and extended his hand to Silvenia. She grabbed it tight and jumped on. The chariot was very tight, forcing them to stand very close to each other. Silvenia couldn't have been happier. She loved every moment of pressing her frame tightly against his. Dymondo, however, was very uncomfortable.

On Silvenia's orders, her chariot rode off. The chariot with Dymondo's men had no charioteer, so Sterferep grabbed the reins with his strong arms and ensured their chariot remained close behind their King's. Wind blew through Silvenia's dark hair and across Dymondo's face as they rode on. Shilathaar's chariot was far ahead and Sterferep's was marginally behind, but enough away that the conversation between Silvenia and

57

Dymondo could not be heard by anyone.

Silvenia pressed herself against Dymondo and begin speaking to him in a sultry voice. "Dear Dymondo, how are you?"

"I am fine, dear Sister-in-Law."

"Good to know. Dymondo, how is your new Queen?"

"My Queen is well."

"I hear you do not take mistresses."

Dymondo remained quiet. As she talked, he noticed the Cecrops on her shoulder and instantly thought of Sterferep and looked back at him but kept quiet.

"Everything alright down there?" She said grabbing his crotch, but letting go straight away. Dymondo hid his annoyance and irritation and tried to remain calm.

"My lady, your jests are just…"

"…Just remarkable aren't they!" she laughed.

Dymondo said nothing.

"Jests aside…Dymondo, you must fuck!" she said as she ran her fingers through her hair. "Shilathaar and I have arranged a beautiful young virgin for you. She will entertain you throughout your entire stay with us."

Dymondo smiled again regrettably. "The Queen and King are kind, but I don't—"

"Don't take mistresses! I know! But I am saying you should! Your brother does! And Grygerious, your other brother, is the King of fucks! He fucks more than he talks," she laughed, then brought her mouth near to his ear. "Had you ever fucked before you got your Queen?"

"Of course, I had!" Dymondo instantly answered.

Silvenia laughed out loud and could not stop. "I like that, young Dymondo!" She continued to laugh much to Dymondo's disgust.

The chariots rode through the city and Dymondo suddenly forgot the Queen's jibes as his eyes took in the scene around them. He had been to Forprimiera before and had even met some of the Kingdom's subjects during the time of King Balathaar's challenge, but now Dymondo witnessed an unhappiness and a fear on the faces of the Forprimiera's subjects that he had never seen before. The people's shoulders were low and their heads drooped as they bowed to their King as he rode past in his large black chariot. They had no choice but to pay deference to their King. There were guards everywhere. Countless guards. The atmosphere was chilling, and the sun hiding behind clouds made it even more foreboding. There was hardly a murmur among the people. Dymondo could not discern one smiling face.

Shilathaar's chariot reached the Kingdom gate first and he waited there for the other chariots to arrive. Mercifully, Dymondo's ride with Silvenia was finally over as Shilathaar asked him aboard his own chariot.

"Come, Brother, now it's time for you ride with your brother."

"We are having a fantastic conversation, my dear!" objected Silvenia.

"Ha-Ha!" boomed Shilathaar. "I am sure you are! I am sure Dymondo will come to your chamber to pay you his respects. You can resume your conversations then," he said as he winked at her and she smiled back.

"Most definitely. With your permission, dear Sister-in-Law…" Dymondo said, moving to leave her chariot.

"Of course," she replied and planted another wet kiss on his lips. He loathed it when she did this to him. Dymondo swiftly got off and hopped upon his brother's chariot. Silvenia's grey chariot rode through the gate and straight to the palace.

"Come, Dymondo. Let me show you my artillery!"

With Dymondo's comrades remaining steadily behind, Shilathaar moved his chariot through the gate and turned toward the preparation ground. Dymondo saw hundreds and thousands of soldiers. Blacksmiths forging innumerable swords, spears and arrows. Catapults, cannons, ballistas and trebuchets everywhere and innumerable horses and elephants. Between it all, soldiers practiced the art of warfare. Indeed, Shilathaar was preparing for war.

"That is incredible, Brother!" Dymondo exclaimed, feigning

enthusiasm. "What a magnificent sight!"

"Isn't it?!" shouted Shilathaar in excitement. "A King must always be prepared for battle. As you know, I am a great tactician, but my soldiers train every day! Practice and training can never be enough! We make a hundred thousand arrows and one thousand swords per day! We have the greatest arsenal ever assembled!" boasted Shilathaar.

"Brother, this is truly remarkable! I am very pleased to see this."

"Good! Recently I visited the Kingdom of Blee."

"Did you see their banners?"

"Blee's crest is a large black eagle upon faint, green fabric. Blee has wonderful artillery and a great army, too! But not as good as mine! Ha-ha!"

"What of Orakray and Doosranfor? Does Brother Grygerious have great artillery?"

"No, but he does not require it. I will snap the neck of the man that lays evil eyes upon him, just as I would for you, my brother. Orakray are my in-laws. Of course, their artillery is magnificent!"

Dymondo smiled hesitantly. He knew he would have to strengthen if he was ever going to be a match on the battlefield against the armies of Orakray, Blee and Forprimiera."

At last, they reached court and Dymondo was greeted by everyone. Kratos and Yatus had not left since their last visit, so Dymondo got the opportunity to meet them as well. The court session was full of joy, wine, music and dancing in Dymondo's honour. All of this was an infrequent trait of the Primieran court, so everyone savoured the moment.

Kor and Dan took part but not to great lengths due to the mission. Sterferep and Dwarpal refrained from wine completely. Sterferep looked toward Dymondo, wondering when he would have a chance to speak to him. The fact that Dymondo was still distant from him after Quilliblade revealed his secret mark was killing him. They had not had a proper conversation about it since. His eyes were distracted for the moment, though, by the antics of Queen Silvenia and her brothers, dancing wildly before the court.

As he watched them, he looked closer at the mark on Queen Silvenia's shoulder. It was the very same mark as his. And as they danced more vigorously, he saw the same mark on her brothers' shoulders. Sterferep was baffled and dumbstruck. He had to remain focused on the mission, but he had his own answers to find.

Dymondo too watched the wild scene before him, but more absently as questions boiled in his mind. *Why is Shilathaar preparing his artillery? Why did he show it to me? Why did he go to Blee? Was the bird telling the truth? Is my brother really preparing for a war against me?*

CHAPTER 8

THE DEFIANT BROTHER-IN-LAW

The court session finished and Shilathaar was well-inebriated. He stumbled over to Dymondo.

"Dymondo! My brother! I am now heading to my chamber. Your sister-in-law has already retired. You must rest now, too. Your soldiers have been given a chamber right next to yours."

"Gratitude, my King."

"Oh, and Silvenia has asked if you could visit her chamber before heading to your own. Remember, you said you would pay your respects?" Shilathaar laughed.

"Yes, and I shall, Brother." More awkwardness awaited Dymondo.

Orpictus showed Dymondo and his men to their chambers, but on the way, they made a stop at Silvenia's chamber.

"My Queen!" shouted Orpictus. "King Dymondo Rain of Gammafor and Fourtfor wishes to meet you. He awaits to pay his respects."

"Ah yes! Dymondo of course," Silvenia called from inside. "It will take me few more moments. Please ask him to wait."

Orpictus turned to Dymondo "The Queen—"

"I heard," replied Dymondo, knowing the delay was deliberate.

Eventually, Silvenia asked Orpictus to send him in. With his men waiting outside, Dymondo walked in slowly. He found the Queen standing in front of her mirror, combing her long, silky hair and very drunk from all the wine she had consumed at court.

"Greetings, my Queen," said Dymondo, standing some distance away with his hands behind his back.

"Ah yes, Dymondo!" she cried out and put down her comb. She turned and strutted over to him without stumbling in the least. She wore a tight, transparent dress and as she strutted, her ample breasts bouncing nearly out of the fabric. Dymondo did his best to avoid looking until she got nearer.

When the Queen reached him, she gave him a light hug and big kiss on his cheek. Dymondo thanked the Gods she didn't kiss him on his lips. No doubt she had a magnificent figure, but her manner of dress always took away all decency and elegance.

"How do you fare, youngest one?" she asked in her sultry voice.

"I am well, my Queen. How do you fare?"

"Oh, Dymondo, do call me Silvenia. I am only the Queen in court. Be at ease as you have come to visit your brother's wife."

"That's kind of you. How do you fare then, Sister-in-Law?"

"You know how difficult life can be for a Queen, but oh gosh, do pardon me… I forgot your Queen is new to this…and royalty!" she smirked.

That wiped the smiled off Dymondo's face. "That I know, but when time is right she will grow accustomed, and because I've found the right woman, she'll make a great Queen!"

"Tongues are wagging, Dymondo, do forgive me, but Primierans believe that something is suspicious…" she smiled.

"Meaning?"

"Well you do not take mistresses… Is all well, youngest one? Is your Queen happy by you?" she mocked.

Dymondo sighed deeply and narrowed his eyes. The Queen gave an evil smile back.

"Well…Dymondo?"

"You must not believe what people say my Queen—"

"Silvenia!"

"Yes...As I was saying, Primierans are hasty to judge situations and do not give it much thought!"

"Don't let your brother hear that. Ha-ha. That is not true, and even if it is, I believe the subjects of Doosranfor and your land are the same, because they too speak of such words... under their breath," she said whispering the last of her words in his ear.

"My people are not subjects. They are citizens. I assure you, all is well!" Dymondo was growing very perturbed but trying to keep calm.

"Well that is good, my dear, but your brother and I would have loved to have seen you get married to a lovely, beautiful princess. That way you could enjoy life a little. Princesses that become Queens know their Kings will take mistresses," she added with a smile, but meaning none of it.

Dymondo ignored the remark.

"Your wedding took place too soon after Mother's departure," Silvenia added. "I found it difficult to enjoy myself."

"Of course."

"How is life in your Kingdom? Made any allies yet? Shilathaar has made many friends!"

"I too have many friends, dearest Sister-in-Law," replied Dymondo.

"Silvenia, dear Dymondo!" she smiled, "I don't count Lances, guards and courtiers of your Kingdom to be friends. I mean, have you made any proper strong friends?"

Dymondo looked at her in amazement as to how she knew of his friendship with the Lances, guards and courtiers? *Primieran spies must linger in Gammafor and Fourtfor,* he thought.

"Oh, come on, youngest one, we know everything, my dear. Nothing is hidden from us," she said politely but her dagger eyes told another story.

"Seems to me you know much about what goes on in my land."

"Of course, darling. Shilathaar is your elder brother, and an elder brother must look after his younger brothers, right? The middle one is useless, I say. He can fuck for sure, but you…you are the clever little baby," she viciously laughed.

"That is gracious of the King. Now that Father and Mother rest in peace, he is like a father to me. So, it is good to know he is looking after us."

"No youngest one! That makes me your mother!" she laughed out loud and came close to him again—so near that it caused Dymondo discomfort.

"Now do I really look old enough to be your mother?" she said, running her soft fingers slowly from his temple down to his cheek. Her lips were close to his face. He could smell the wine on her breath and her perfume. Her eyes pierced his with sharp, villainous, yet ravishing, looks.

"No, of course not, dear Sister-in-Law, you are not old at all," said Dymondo, keeping a straight face.

She smiled and held his face in her hands: "You will not address me as Silvenia…will you, youngest one?" She brought her lips even closer to his. He stayed firm and did not flinch. She smiled as she kissed him on his forehead and walked back. Dymondo took another deep breath as she turned her back on him.

"So, my dearest youngest *brother-in-law*, I hope asking you to visit me in my chamber hasn't caused any inconvenience to you before you retired to bed!" she smiled.

"Oh, that hurts, dear Sister-in-Law. Of course it did not. We did not get a chance to meet properly earlier and exchange kind words. I could not have retired without greeting the Queen appropriately or without having met with my beautiful loving and caring Sister-in-Law. Please call me Dymondo," Dymondo said using her own medicine against her. He was now being diplomatic. Sweet poison.

She raised her eyebrows in astonishment and an upward curve developed on her face. "My, my, I do not ever remember you saying such kind words to me! I will only call you Dymondo, if you call me Silvenia. Go on, no one is listening."

"Forgive my audacity, but my lady forgets…I have *forever* been kind to you."

"Well, what can I say…you left me nothing to say back to you," she smiled. "What do you have planned for tomorrow, hunting?"

"Perhaps. For now I do not wish to stress about tomorrow. I desire sleep."

"Oh well, be on your way then, dear baby, and have a good night's rest," she said with a forged smile. "I enjoyed our conversation—the one we could not finish riding upon my chariot."

"I enjoyed it too. Good night, my Queen."

She smiled back at him.

"The Queen believes in wishing good night lovingly. Come over here and give your sister-in-law an embrace and let her kiss you good night," she said, holding out her arms.

Dymondo hesitantly walked over. He did not like being in her presence, let alone going near her. Nevertheless, he walked up to her and she put her arms around his muscular shoulders and embraced him tightly, pressing herself completely against him. He lightly reciprocated the gesture and put his arm around her back. She withdrew from the embrace gently and, with one arm still around his shoulder, she lightly licked her soft fingers and styled his hair with them.

"There…that looks good now," she said softly. She again brought her lips very close, so close that the tips of their upper lips were touching. Dymondo was embarrassed but again he did not flinch or move. She strategically did not go any nearer but spoke softly and slowly. "Goodnight… have sweet dreams…" she whispered, her lips softly brushing against his before moving back.

"Oh!" she exclaimed. "Wine has made your lips rather dry." She put her thumb in her mouth to moisten it and rubbed it over his dry lips. "Oh gosh! They are very dry!" She licked her lips and gently kissed him on his lips slowly wetting them. "There!" she laughed. "From now on, I will *always* kiss you on your lips when I greet you or say goodbye. Otherwise, you will let your lovely lips grow too dry," she laughed and moved away.

Dymondo again took a deep breath and was pleased that she

was no longer close to him. This time he could not hide his reaction at which Silvenia laughed loudly. He stood there with wet lips truly disgusted and humiliated by her eccentric behaviour.

"Why that look, Brother-in-Law?"

"My Queen, you already kiss me on my lips every time you greet me."

"Noticed, have you?" she asked winking at him.

"May I ask——?"

"I kiss everyone on their lips! Think nothing of it, dear Brother-in-Law. You should have seen Gilgenia's face when I greeted Grygerious with a kiss when he came to visit last time. He doesn't pull faces like you. A hug and a kiss. Nothing else. He didn't make any fuss. Why do you make such a big issue of it?" she asked and laughed again.

Dymondo lowered his head.

"Oh! You must be shy! Oh! Poor Dymondo Rain! Don't be shy, dear Brother-in-Law. Are you sure you have fucked before?" she laughed again.

"Yes!"

"Then why are you so shy? I'll tell the King to give you your present tomorrow morning," she winked and smiled at him.

"Goodnight, my Queen," said Dymondo and left the chamber feeling disgusted and disgraced, slamming the door behind him as he went.

"Goodnight! Ha-ha!" she shouted and laughed. He could hear her laughter all the way down the corridor as he walked with his head down, following Orpictus as the chief courtier showed them to their chambers. Outside their chambers, stood two Primieran guards. Dymondo thanked Orpictus and turned to his men.

"Sterferep, Kor, Dan and Dwarpal, follow me in."

The four followed him inside. "Is everything alright, my King?"

"Forget titles, Ster. I am not in the mood," said Dymondo and slumped into an armchair.

"Kor, secure the door," advised Sterferep. Kor shut the

chamber door firmly.

"What happened?" asked Dwarpal.

"Queen Silvenia…"

"What of her? What did she do?" asked Kor.

"What did she *not* do?...Bitch… She has no regard for anyone or her dignity!" growled Dymondo.

"I would ignore her," said Sterferep. "Everyone knows what she is like. I suggest focusing on the task at hand."

"Correct! Come hither," said Dymondo as he rose and walked over to the desk. They all stood around the rectangular desk to confer.

"As I told you back on Gammafor, we are here to search for a very important document," began Dymondo in a very soft voice.

"Document?" whispered Dan.

"A Map!" Dymondo whispered back. "It is most likely kept in the scroll chamber I told you about, the one with the round door. I hear many unsorted and miscellaneous scrolls and slates are kept within this chamber. You need to locate the chamber and let me know where it is."

"How can we do that? There are too many guards on patrol," whispered Kor.

"Two hours after midnight, when I hear the necks of the guards drop into sleep, you four will search. No armour, no weapons and no sandals. You must be as silent as shadows," replied Dymondo.

"Naked?" grunted Sterferep under his breath.

"No!" replied Dymondo. "Wear your tunics and togas but cover them in black cloaks. But no trinkets that may make a sound. Clear?"

Kor smirked at Sterferep who glowered back. The Lances turned to Dymondo and nodded in understanding.

"You need to do this tonight. We are merely here for three or four nights. Finding the chamber is the uncomplicated task. Finding the map will be more difficult, so we must find the chamber tonight."

"What shall you do then?" asked Dwarpal.

"Once you find the library, I will enter and take the scroll on the second or third night. Now go and rest until it's time and report to me in the morning."

Dymondo's men nodded and retired to their chambers while their King rested in his. All lay awake in their beds until two hours after midnight had passed. Sterferep then snuck his head outside to inspect the guards. Dymondo was right. The guards had slumped into slumber. Sterferep carefully opened the chamber door, and the four men stepped out into the corridor, all dressed in black cloaks. They tip-toed past the sleeping guards and began their silent search.

CHAPTER 9

THE MAP

A fter Dymondo had gone to bed, Shilathaar visited Silvenia's chamber. "My dear Queen!" roared Shilathaar. Silvenia was having her hair scented by her maidservants and looked over to see her giant bully of a husband. Her eyes lit up and narrowed into a lustful gaze. She got up in her silky translucent night gown, and Shilathaar could see she wore no undergarments.

"My King! How wonderful for you to come and visit me. Would you have me ask the maidservants to fetch wine?"

"Yes!" he roared again as he examined his wife's beauty. Silvenia clapped her hands and three maidservants ran to get wine.

"You! Stay!" commanded Shilathaar, pointing at one of the maids.

The maid stopped and turned to him, speaking in the most frightened voice. "My King."

"Over here and help me with my clothes."

The maidservant quickly ran over to him, and whilst the other two ran to get wine, she started to unclip and remove his heavy armour.

"Tough today!" he said to his wife.

"Always is! When is it not?" taunted Silvenia.

"Queen, Queen! There now! No need!" said Shilathaar.

Silvenia giggled and jumped and lay on the soft royal bed. Shilathaar removed his armour and the maidservant started to remove his linen white shirt. Silvenia placed his hand between her thighs as his white shirt was removed, eyeing his gallant frame and perfect broad chest. It was as though the God of War Terradeus himself stood towering over her.

"Did Dymondo do as he was commanded?"

"Hah! Yes, the little wimp came...to pay his respects!" laughed Silvenia.

Shilathaar mocked his brother with laughter. "He has a sweet tongue."

"You must not believe any of it. Remember you need to seize your Kingdom back. Do not get swayed by emotion." Silvenia was serious.

"You are right. I am the King!"

"Yes, you are the King. You will crush him like an insect!"

"What of Grygerious?"

"Now he is the real wimp. He poses no threat whatsoever. If he stands against you, one strike of *my* hand, and Grygerious will never get up again."

"An iron fist!"

"Stronger than iron, like my dear husband."

"True...Tell me, my love. Why do you flirt with him so much? Do you like him?"

"Dymondo? Urgh! Never! I just do it to annoy him. I want him to feel embarrassed all the time. I enjoy watching him cringe."

"He hates it."

"That's why I do it. I know you like it when he is uncomfortable. I do it to see you smile."

"Ha-ha, yes, dear wife. Keep on making him feel sore," said Shilathaar as he kissed her.

Silvenia savoured the kiss. "It has been too long, my love. Do not leave it so late again," she said.

"Ha-ha! How long have you been without cock?"

"A long while!" purred Silvenia.

"Mock me do you now, love? May I ask which of my gladiators' cock have you not had?" laughed Shilathaar. Silvenia started laughing and rolled around on the bed and stretched.

"Aye! I had Pritanicus visit a few days back!"

A cunning grin appeared on Shilathaar's face as though he was aroused when Silvenia said that. After the maidservant removed his fur underwear, he began rubbing his bare privates. He slowly walked over to the bed and lay beside his wife. She gently stroked his abdomen and clasped his chest muscles.

"Pritanicus! Ha-ha! That fool! If only he was as good in the arena! Did his cock grow to a decent size?"

"Fairly decent! But it is yours I crave day and night."

"And I crave you!"

"Ha-ha!" said Silvenia and rose from the bed. "You! Here!" she ordered, pointing at the maidservant that had just helped Shilathaar with his robes. The young woman ran across to the other side of the bed and began undoing the Queen's night gown.

"Why do you laugh?"

"You *crave* me, love? You cannot get enough of all those mistresses you take. How many do you have in your bed at one time?" sneered Silvenia.

"My Queen, they are as important to me as your gladiators are to you."

"I bet you want this one here to get you started," winked Silvenia. The maidservant had removed Silvenia's dress by this time and Silvenia lay down before him on the bed stark naked.

"Ha-ha! I do not need any assistance, my love, but yes, you know me too well. I enjoy being started off!" laughed Shilathaar.

Silvenia gestured to the young maidservant and pushed her towards her husband. The maid hesitated for a while but then placed her mouth around his privates.

"Ah yes! That always feels great! Stop and remove your dress, slave!"

She stopped and did as she was told. Once she too was naked, he squeezed her soft breasts and ran his fingers through her hair as she got on with the task. Silvenia in the meantime lay beside him and began to passionately kiss him. Eventually, the maidservant helped Shilathaar to climax.

"That is more like it!" he shouted and then turned towards his wife. The maidservant moved back and began to get dressed.

"See that the wine is ready by the time we have finished!" commanded Shilathaar and the poor young woman ran to obey.

"Now my love let us embark!" he said, clutching Silvenia tightly in his strong arms. She loved the ruthlessness of her man.

"Ssh! No more speaking!" she whispered. Silvenia grabbed his privates hard. Shilathaar held her breasts in his hands tightly and both jumped on each other. The loving making was the complete opposite of gentle. She moaned in excitement at his violent grunts and scratched his back with her shiny nails as he penetrated her. After the steamy encounter, the couple drained an entire flagon of wine and fell into slumber.

***

Dymondo waited anxiously in his chamber, hastily pacing from one side to the other. Ill thoughts came to him as he waited for his men to return with good news. He was certain they would not fail; however, part of him couldn't help anticipating Primieran guards entering his chamber with his brother to seize him for conspiracy. As time went by, and he became more nervous, he sat on the side of his bed and looked out the window, fighting the temptation to open the door and peek outside, which would only bring the mission to great jeopardy.

Suddenly, he heard the chamber door move slowly inwards. He walked over to the table and clasped the handle of his sword, watching the door continue to open in silence. At last a head peered in and Dymondo sighed in relief.

"You!" he whispered loudly. "I thought it was someone else!"

Sterferep quietly entered, followed by Kor, Dan and Dwarpal.

"So...?"

"Ssh!" gestured Sterferep, slowly closing the door after them and taking a deep breath when the creaky door was finally shut. Sterferep, Kor, Dan and Dwarpal silently approached their King and all spoke low.

"Did you find it?"

"We did!"

"Excellent! Where is it?"

"You were right," spoke Dwarpal. "It was a large, wooden, circular door—the scroll chamber, or library, as you said."

"Where is it?"

"Fortunately, it is not too far from our chambers. When you exit from this chamber, walk straight down and it's the fifth corridor on the right. It's very dark."

"Rats down there!" snapped Dan.

"Ssh! Keep it down!" said Sterferep harshly under his breath and continued to explain to Dymondo while the rest remained quiet.

"Yes...Rats are there. Take a lamp from the wall nearest to the fifth corridor and you shall be able to see as you walk. You will have to walk for a while. It is very easy to miss the circular door, but it's on the left as you get towards the end of the corridor. At the end of the corridor is a wall with a small hole that allows in some light. Tonight the ground shone blue from the moon's beam. When you go, you'll have to be very careful."

"Are there guards down there?"

"Yes, so again... be vigilant. But like tonight, they should be asleep. Stupid! Sleeping on duty."

"Would the lamp not awaken the guards?"

"It didn't tonight... I believe the guards drink wine at night."

"And on the way back? Were you seen?"

Sterferep paused.

"Answer me!"

"One of the guards awoke, but I grabbed his mouth hard. He did not breathe after that!"

"What?! You killed a guard?! Where is he now?"

"He is still sitting on the stool, dead, but we shut his eyes and, because his mouth was open, Dwarpal grabbed a rat from the corridor, twisted its head and placed it inside the guard's mouth."

"Oh, dear Gods!"

"We couldn't think of anything else! If we had thrown him out of the hole at the end of the corridor, then it would have looked like someone had killed him. Now it looks as though a rat crawled up his mouth during his sleep."

"Rats are not poisonous, they do not kill men!"

"I am aware."

"And they will not believe that the rat choked the guard."

"I…I… do not know what to say."

"Me neither."

"We also entered the chamber."

"You did?"

"Yes."

"But I did not ask you to do that."

"Nevertheless, it is good that we did because Dwarpal was able to gauge how the scrolls are kept."

"Fine. How are they kept then?"

"They are sorted by colour."

"Go on."

"The red scrolls are education laws. Yellow for defence. Green for agriculture. Hazel brown scrolls relate to weaponry and the army. The blue ones are peace treaties and arrangements with other nations. Black scrolls are for sanitation and the white scrolls are old maps."

"That's what we want!"

"Yes."

"Aye! Great work Dwarpal. How did you manage to see in the dark and discern this colour coding?"

"I shall tell you when we return to Gammafor, my King," said Dwarpal softly. "Right now, I suggest we remain quiet and return to our chamber…and…" he hesitated.

"Go on," Dymondo urged. Dwarpal looked at Sterferep and Sterferep nodded for him to continue.

"…that tomorrow we conduct no action for when they discover the death of their guard, they shall be on extra alert. You must do this task now on the third night."

"Yes, you are right," agreed Dymondo

"One more thing, my King. There is senile old man in the

scroll chamber," mentioned Sterferep.

"What? A man inside the chamber? Did you—?"

"No!" snapped Sterferep. "He was asleep right at the back of the chamber in pitch darkness. We only noticed him because he mumbled in his sleep."

"More of a snort really," corrected Kor.

Sterferep glared at him. "Gratitude, Kor, now if I may?"

Kor gestured for him to continue with a smile.

"We walked over with the lamp and he was fast asleep. A rat even crawled across his belly, and he didn't move a muscle. He shouldn't be a problem for you."

"Very well. Great work. Now you all head to the chamber next door and do not be seen. I shall have you here tomorrow at the break of dawn."

"My King," they all said and bowed.

"One other thing, my King," said Dwarpal. "Scroll chambers are drafty rooms. Over time, things get blown by gusts of wind on to the ground and even underneath tables and chairs, so search high and low for the white scrolls."

Dymondo nodded at Dwarpal and the Lances and guards left the chamber.

***

The next day was bright. Despite a restless night, Sterferep, Kor and Dan, and Dwarpal managed to find some sleep and woke up in good time. They got dressed and headed towards Dymondo's chamber. As they approached his door, they noticed a cluster of guards gathered around the entry to the fifth corridor from Dymondo's room.

Sterferep beckoned the others to follow him, and when they reached the corridor, sure enough, there were more guards at the end gathered around the corpse from the night before. The commander-in-chief of Forprimiera, Retchia Snapp, was with them.

"Does anyone know how this is happened?" he asked everyone. "The King is on his way, so whoever knows, speak now!" he snarled.

Sterferep, Kor, Dan and Dwarpal went up to the crowd and

looked over their shoulders at the commotion.

"Do you know anything?" Retchia asked them.

"Of what, Commander?" asked Sterferep.

"This, you imbecile!" Retchia did not notice his Lance uniform as Sterferep stood behind a few guards.

"Excuse me, sire, your rank is most definitely higher than mine, no doubt. But Lances are not accustomed to being spoken to in this manner," replied Sterferep.

"Lance?"

"Sire, these are the guards that have come over from Gammafor along with King Dymondo Rain!" whispered another guard into Retchia's ear.

Sterferep, Kor, Dan and Dwarpal walked passed the guards and stood in front of Retchia. He then noticed Sterferep and Kor's uniforms.

"We are not guards, but Lances, solider!" corrected Kor.

"Oh! Of Course, Lances! Ha-ha! Yes, yes, I know of Lances," jeered Retchia as he examined them. Sterferep was not impressed. "And what of these two?" asked Retchia gesturing to Dan and Dwarpal.

"Not yet, but they will be soon." informed Sterferep.

"Ha-ha." Retchia laughed again

"Can we be of any assistance?" asked Sterferep.

"Assistance?!" laughed Retchia.

"Yes, can we be of some help?"

"No, no! One of our guards died last night in his sleep with a rat in his mouth, look!"

Sterferep looked over with interest. "Urgh!"

"Looks as though this bastard fell asleep and the vermin crawled into his mouth and stopped his breathing," said Retchia.

"No, Commander," corrected Sterferep

"No?"

"Rats do not kill men. Men kill men. It looks as though the poor guard was killed and someone placed a rat in his mouth to cover their act!"

Retchia looked at Sterferep and all the guards murmured among themselves. Though shocked at Sterferep's disclosure,

Kor, Dan and Dwarpal remained quiet and stood still with innocent faces. Sterferep maintained his typical stern demeanour.

"How do you know this?"

"I do not *know*, Commander. I merely state what I believe has happened based on the evidence before me!" said Sterferep in his strong voice.

Retchia did not know what to say.

"We in Gammafor never consider such incidents as an act of nature. We investigate thoroughly. I believe someone could be behind this, even if it is true that the rat killed this man."

Retchia could not be proven wrong amidst all the guards of Forprimiera and was determined to remain by his initial conclusion. "And what if the rat *did* kill this man?"

"Then thanks to the Gods, we do not have an intruder in the Kingdom, but we must eliminate any doubt through investigation."

"Excellent!" The booming voice came from behind. It was the King of Forprimiera, Shilathaar himself, followed by Orpictus. All the guards jumped with fear and moved aside and made way for the King. They all bowed before him as he walked up to Sterferep and Retchia. Retchia too bowed.

"Kor, Dan, Dwarpal, salute!" said Sterferep and he, Kor, Dan and Dwarpal all bowed and knelt to Shilathaar. Shilathaar was much pleased. Kneeling was not a custom in Forprimiera. Shilathaar was pleased to see his brother's men kneeling before him.

"Rise, good Lance." shouted Shilathaar. Sterferep stood up. He was as tall as Shilathaar.

"What is your name?"

"Lance Sterferep."

Shilathaar placed his hand on his shoulder. "Strong Lance! I have heard what you said!" he laughed. "So, you believe it is not a rat that killed this man?"

"It is possible, O great King, but as I was telling Commander-in-Chief Retchia, there is no harm in investigation."

"Excellent! I agree."

Retchia was fuming and now adamant to prove Sterferep wrong. "I believe this is very clear, my King. The rat killed this man!"

"Retchia! This Lance has a point. Tell me, Sterferep, what would you do in these circumstances?"

"Well…O great King, I would search the corridors, passages, chambers and the entire palace for anything strange. I would lead the hunt myself. That is what I would do," smiled Sterferep as he stood tall.

Shilathaar turned to him and smiled. "Yes! I like this! "

"I would search for one entire day, O great King!"

"Then that is what we shall do! Lance Sterferep, would you kindly guide my guards on how to conduct this search?" Shilathaar was not used to asking, but he knew he could not command Sterferep.

"O great King, please do not ask, but command me!" Sterferep had never been so humble to anyone ever before. Kor, Dan and Dwarpal kept mum despite their surprise at Sterferep's diplomacy. He was learning, they thought.

"Marvellous!"

"O great King. If you grant permission, I would like to lead and conduct the search with the help of my men, Commander-in-Chief Retchia and all the guards of Forprimiera. We can start now and conclude the search at this time tomorrow morning."

Sterferep glanced at Kor and Kor understood Sterferep's plan—to cunningly lead the guards on a wild goose chase in order to wear them out by keeping them busy all day.

"You have my permission! Find me that man!" ordered Shilathaar.

"O great King, if there is an intruder, then, delightfully, I shall bring him to you, but if not, then we must believe Commander-in-Chief Retchia's conclusion. He may be right… it could just have been the rat."

"It *was* the rat!" shouted Retchia grinding his teeth.

"Commander! I very much hope you're right, but the search is important!" shouted the King.

"I believe it is a waste of time, my King!"

"Enough!"

"Apologies, my King," bowed Retchia.

"Better! Now do as Sterferep says and get on with it. Remove the corpse and hand it over to his relatives. Promptly!"

"One request, O great King," said Sterferep.

"What is it?" asked Shilathaar.

"Do we have your permission to pay our respects to King Dymondo before we embark? Just so I can inform him as to where we shall be the entire day. He will be delighted to know that we are helping the great Kingdom of Forprimiera. He truly loves you, my King."

Shilathaar paused and for a second his heart skipped a beat at the Lance's honeyed words, but he soon returned to his usual character as he remembered his wife's words from the night before.

"No need, good Lance. I am going to meet him now! I shall tell him that you will return this time tomorrow!"

"Tremendous! Now with your permission," Sterferep bowed and knelt.

"Go and may you be successful!" roared Shilathaar.

Sterferep turned back down the corridor. Kor, Dan and Dwarpal bowed and knelt to Shilathaar and set forth after him. The other guards too followed, all except Retchia, who remained behind, dumbfounded at this sudden usurpation of his authority.

When the others had their backs to them, Shilathaar grabbed Retchia by his collar and brought his angry face closer to his. "Learn...To...Be...More...Like...Him! Why were the guards sleeping on duty? If this happens again, I shall have your head!" Shilathaar shoved him away. "Now catch up with them!"

Retchia nodded. He tried to emulate Sterferep and attempted to kneel after his bow to Shilathaar, but he failed miserably. His knee grazed the ground and his shield banged against the side wall. He looked absurd.

"Leave it, will you?! Just go!" shouted Shilathaar.

Retchia nodded and ran after the group.

Shilathaar turned towards Dymondo's chamber, followed by Orpictus.

"This incident! Do you think it was Dymondo?" asked Shilathaar.

"The wretched guards were asleep! No one knows!"

"I said to you Orpictus, keep an eye on him! Keep those stupid guards awake!"

"I will see that Commander-in-Chief Retchia deals with this."

"That's better!" Shilathaar kept walking. He came to a halt at his brother's chamber door. "You remember what else I need from you?" he asked Orpictus.

"Yes, my King."

"Very well. Then I will call for you when its time."

Orpictus bowed and turned down the corridor and Shilathaar knocked on the door.

"Enter," spoke Dymondo.

The large King walked in. "Brother!" he said, walking up to Dymondo and grabbing him hard against his armour.

"Good morning to you, dear Brother," said Dymondo.

"Enjoyed breakfast, Dymondo?"

"Indeed…it was filling."

"Great! And slept well?"

"Again yes, Brother."

"Tremendous! Now you can enjoy your time here in Forprimiera. As you know, this land has many pleasures to offer!"

"Brilliant, but I'd just like to rest and relax these few days," Dymondo responded.

"Why? Enjoy yourself! Go hunting!"

"I dare not refuse your command my dear brother, but for some reason, I feel at home here. Sleeping under your protection relaxes, like when I slept in my chamber as a child when Father was King. I know Father has left us, but you have loved me so much in the same way that I have never felt his absence. When I embrace you, it feels as though I've embraced him. Brother let me sleep and relax and feel like a child again for many moons have passed since I have felt this at ease."

For a moment, again, Shilathaar's heart turned dewy from his brother's words, and his eyes became compassionate, but Silvenia had poisoned him well against Dymondo. Shilathaar gathered himself while keeping a smile on his face. This time he embraced his younger brother softly.

"Great! Rest, Little Brother, and remember, as long as I am alive, no one can touch my family," Shilathaar said softly before assuming his grand voice again. "However, you must accept a small gift!" He clapped his hands and Orpictus walked in with a fair, young woman with her head down carrying a large flagon of the finest sweet wine. She wore only silver jewellery that just covered her private parts.

"This is Gracia! The finest wine in the land!" He smiled at Dymondo.

Dymondo smiled back and nodded.

"Her name is also Gracia!" he laughed and tapped his brother on his shoulder before he started to walk out.

"Oh, and one other thing! I have asked your Lances to help my commander-in-chief today! One of our guards was found dead this morning. My stupid commander-in-chief thinks the rats did it, but your Lance thinks we may have an intruder."

Dymondo forged his astonishment. "Really? Is that so?"

"Yes, so your Lances are working with my men. I hope you don't mind me commanding your men around like this?"

"Brother, you have the complete right to command me and any of my Lances! You are not only King, but my brother…and father."

Shilathaar nodded. "Did you go meet your sister-in-law last night?"

"Yes, Brother, I have paid my respects."

Shilathaar smiled. "She loves everyone! Isn't she kind?" he asked.

Dymondo smiled tentatively and nodded. "If you wish, Brother, I can lead the investigation into this scandal. Who dares intrude into my brother's Kingdom?!" said Dymondo, grabbing his sword.

"Ha-ha! No need, Little Brother, you rest. Your tall Lance is leading the investigation. You need not worry," said Shilathaar and left.

Dymondo took a deep breath. *Brilliant,* he thought. Sterferep had positioned himself well.

The girl walked up to the table and placed the flagon upon it.

"Would you like me to pour you a glass, O King?" she asked in her soft voice. She was in her early twenties. Dymondo noticed a shiver in her voice and goose bumps on her soft thighs and arms from the brittle cold air that had started to flow in through the window. Her nipples, visible through the long silver necklace, were erect as well. Dymondo walked over to the posh wardrobe and took a warm blanket from inside. He walked over to the young woman and gently covered her with the woollen sheet. She grabbed the blanket tight around her and looked at him in gratitude. Dymondo smiled and caressed her cheek gently.

"So your name is Gracia?"

"Yes, my King." She lowered her eyes again. "Shall I pour you some wine?"

"How many cups do you have?"

"I have four cups, my King."

"Pour me some wine and pour yourself some as well and come sit beside me."

The girl paused and looked startled. She had not been treated as an equal before. Still, she did as she was told. She gave him the wine and sat beside him holding her own cup, but remained staring at the ground. Dymondo drank his cup in one go.

"Drink, Gracia. It's good wine!"

She drank half a cup. It was true. The wine was nice. She was not accustomed to such good taste. Some of it ran from the side of her mouth down to her neck. "Apologies," she said, wiping her face and neck with her hands. Dymondo got up and gave her his silken handkerchief. She took it with gratitude.

"More wine for you, my King?"

"No, thank you."

She nodded and took the wine cup from Dymondo and finished her own. She then got up and put the cups upon the table next to the flagon and turned towards Dymondo. With him watching, she walked up to the other side of the bed, removed the blanket, and placed it on the bed. She then removed her long silver necklace and waist ornament, covering her down below. She was very beautiful. She had pale skin and a thin frame, but she was very attractive with small, perky breasts and very smooth skin. She looked at Dymondo and lay on the bed for him. Dymondo walked around, picked up the warm blanket and again placed it over her.

"My lady, you will catch a chill," smiled Dymondo and walked away to the table. "Now keep the blanket on. The winds are nastier here in the north. I am certainly feeling the draught."

She was surprised and rose to sit up with her breasts now visible again. Dymondo gestured to her to pull up the blanket to her shoulders so she was fully covered. She did so.

"My King, may I ask you something?"

"Of course,"

"Do you not find me attractive?" she asked, lowering the blanket again to show him her breasts.

"Oh, my word, of course I do, Gracia. You are marvellous," Dymondo said, then again gestured to her to pull it back up.

"Then why do you refuse me?" she said again covering herself.

"Because I am in love with someone else."

"But you are King"

"So? A King too is a man, Gracia. My heart beats for another, and I'd like to remain faithful."

"But if you will not have me, then King Shilathaar will sentence me to death."

Dymondo paused to look at her and smiled again.

"Do not worry, for I shall not tell him. I shall tell him that you took very good care of me."

"He will know!"

"How?"

"He will….I…I…have not laid with a man yet and he will—

"

"Stop! Fine…then I'll ask him to gift you to me. You shall come with me to my Kingdom and serve me there…but only if that sounds good to you?"

She could not believe the generosity shown by a man of Dymondo's stature.

"Oh, that would be wonderful! You would do that for me?"

"Indeed, I shall. Now, if you can fetch me some scrolls, ink and a stylus from the wardrobe, I would like to write. You can stay here and get some rest." She again did as she was told.

"Would you like more wine?" she asked.

"Hmm…it is nice, isn't it?"

"After all it is…Gracia," she joked.

Dymondo laughed. "Why don't you pour both of us a cup?"

She did as asked and Dymondo drank it all in one gulp. She did too.

"May I know the name of the lucky woman you are in love with?" she asked, already slurring her words.

"Mysteria."

"Does Mysteria love you?" she asked, now swaying on her feet. Dymondo smiled at her drunkenness.

"Very much."

"I forget my place, sire. Apologies," she said and lay on the bed, wrapping herself in the warm blanket. "The wine has taken my senses, and I must sleep." She sounded truly intoxicated.

Dymondo looked over at her lying on the bed. Her eyes were closed.

***

That evening, when Gracia's slumber broke, Dymondo sat with her and made sure she drank more wine with him. Dwarpal had advised him to conduct the map retrieval on the third night, but with Sterferep was leading the searches, he knew his Lance would steer the guards away from the scroll chamber. Dymondo wanted to be away from Forprimiera as soon as possible, so this was his night to act.

At two hours past midnight, Dymondo rose from his bed and still barefoot, he donned a thick, dark cloak with a hood. He looked back at the bed at Gracia. After consuming so much wine, she would not be waking anytime soon.

Dymondo tiptoed to his chamber door, and luckily, the door opened without a creak. Outside he found the two guards were once again asleep, with one leaning against the wall and the other sitting on a wooden chair with his heading drooping forward. The Gods were helping him. *If these were the guards of Gammafor. I'd have their heads dunked in excrement,* he thought.

He slipped past them carefully and quietly, and swiftly made his way down the long, dark corridor. He took one of the three remaining lamps from the wall along the way and turned down the fifth corridor. Just as his Lances had told him, the visibility was low. Unlike the corridors of the palace in Gammafor, the Forprimiera palace corridors were dark and sinister, and frighteningly silent. Dymondo could hear himself breathe as he wandered deeper into the darkness.

At the end of the corridor, a single shaft of pale moonlight shone on a large, circular door. The door looked blue in the low light. Dymondo held up the lamp up to it and found the handle. The door made a light sound as it opened, but there were no guards around to hear it. They were too busy with Sterferep's search.

Dymondo stepped inside the chamber and gently closed the door. He shone the lamp around, gathered all the white scrolls in sight and went through them carefully.

"Who goes there?" an old voice came. Dymondo jumped in surprise.

"It is I…" replied Dymondo cleverly.

"What brings you here young man?" the voice said, belonging to a figure now coming into view under Dymondo's lamp. It was the old librarian. He could hardly walk, but unlike Shilathaar's hearty young guards, he was not asleep but wide awake.

"I came to the library to select a few scrolls to read and study."

"Library?!" The old man was annoyed. "This look like a library to you, boy?" he shouted under his breath. "This is a

86

dump, my dear boy. You will never find anything here!"

"I'm sure if you will help me—"

"I will not! Who sent you? The King? That arrogant man; he has no respect for books and scrolls. It pains me…" the old man sobbed.

"There now," Dymondo said, placing his hand on the old man's shoulder. "I came of my own accord. Will you help me?"

"Promise you aren't sent by Shilathaar?"

"I promise you."

"Then I shall. Normally the King's guards and ministers throw in scrolls and slates with no regard for order. After all these years, to have someone come here to take something away to read…?" The old man placed his weary hand on Dymondo's head and patted it gently. "…What are you looking for, young man?"

"I am looking for a map."

"Ah…a map. White scrolls then, young man. Mostly kept over on that shelf," said the old librarian, pointing to a shelf of dusty white scrolls. Dymondo started looking through them. Providentially, there were not many to rummage through. Unfortunately, there was no map that read "Aquacaves." Then he remembered what Dwarpal said about looking underneath the tables and chairs. He headed straight to the large desk in the middle of the room and looked underneath.

"Why look under there?"

"With the guards being so careless, I assume some must have fallen under the furniture."

"What map are you looking for?"

Dymondo stared at him for a while, but the old man's gaze remained innocent.

"The Aquacaves."

The old man got up from his seat and walked up to Dymondo.

"I haven't heard that name in eons. Let me help you…" he said as he bent down to look himself. "Bring over your lamp, boy." Dymondo had started to grow fed up of everyone in Forprimiera calling him "boy." Nevertheless, he brought over the lamp.

"Ah-Ha! You hide there, do you? Come hither..." the old man stretched to reach for something and pulled a muscle in his shoulder. "Haaye!" he exclaimed in pain.

Dymondo held him up and placed him upon the chair. "Are you alright?"

"Yes, yes, I am fine. Just old age, son. "Tell me... you seem very young to know about the Aquacaves. How do you know about them?"

"It is under there?" asked Dymondo ignoring his question.

"I think so. Underneath the desk."

Dymondo left him to rub his shoulder and went to look.

"Peculiar times those were..." the old man continued as Dymondo struggled under the table. "Bears that could talk. Birds with wings as sharp as knives... and giant snakes..."

Dymondo was focused on his search, but he was subconsciously listening, especially when the old man spoke about birds and snakes. Under the desk, he saw a dusty white scroll that looked as though it had fallen under there quite some time ago. After a few failed attempts, he managed to get a hold of it and pull it out, along with a considerable amount of dust.

Holding the lamp up with one hand, he unrolled the parchment with the other. It was a map of Landsfor, but there was something peculiar about it. Apart from depicting the typical land features of the realm and the surrounding outer Kingdoms, there around the eastern gulf between Fourtfor, Gammafor and Doosranfor, was an illustration of a circle in the ocean, and next to it, the label he had been hoping to find.

"The Aquacaves" read Dymondo quietly to himself.

"Yes! The map to the Aquacaves," said the old man.

"May I borrow this?"

"Of course," the old man nodded.

Dymondo was now in a rush to leave the chamber,

"And when will you return it?"

"Very soon, I must take your leave now, Librarian. Gratitude for your help."

The old man smiled upon being referred to as "Librarian."

"You are welcome...I think back in those day there were talking plants as well—"

"Gratitude for the information, but I must leave. It is rather late."

"Yes, yes, do go on...son."

Before the old man could finish his sentence, Dymondo rolled up the scroll and secured the map deep in one of the inside pockets of his cloak. He promptly left the chamber, shutting the door behind him, strode down the corridor, placed the lamp back in its position, quickly made his way to his door, slipped past the sleeping guards and into his chamber. After quietly securing the door, he expelled a long breath and looked at the bed. Gracia had not moved a muscle.

CHAPTER 10

THE MARK

Dymondo got up the next morning before Gracia's slumber broke and started gathering all his belongings. Gracia got up and immediately began helping.

"Let me do this, please," she said, taking over whilst still dressed in the warm blanket. Dymondo let her work while he dressed, checking the jacket once more for the map. It was still there. Dymondo walked up to the chamber door and asked one of the guards outside to send two other maidservants along with a spare set of women's clothes. The other guard he asked to send for his men and send word to the King that he was leaving. The guards did as they were asked, and the maidservants and his men arrived all together and entered the chamber. Gracia secured the blanket around her and Dymondo nodded to the two maids bearing the fresh set of clothes.

"Help her dress," commanded Dymondo. "Then, you are free to go. Gentlemen! Turn toward the wall, please!"

Dymondo and his men, turned to face the wall, and Gracia smiled at the King's discretion. The two maidservants came and dressed her up in a fine purple outfit and left once they had done so. Gracia then prompted the men to turn back around, then helped Dymondo finish packing.

Once packed, the King and his men left the chamber and headed straight to the Kingdom gate, followed by a fearful Gracia. There stood Queen Silvenia and King Shilathaar along with Kratos, Yatus, Retchia, Orpictus and the King's guards waiting to see them off.

"Very well, Brother, I hope you have enjoyed your stay! You should have stayed longer."

Dymondo embraced his elder brother and thanked him. Silvenia then stuck out her arms at Dymondo and threw herself around him. Sterferep saw the Cecrops on her shoulder as the Queen slapped a large kiss directly on Dymondo's lips and began to laugh. Dymondo hesitantly looked over at his brother to find him laughing as well.

"Travel well, young Dymondo. Do not mind the jest!" laughed Silvenia.

Dymondo timorously smiled at the two. "I take your leave now, Brother and dear Sister-in-Law. Before I go, though, if I asked for something, would you give it to me?" he added.

Shilathaar stopped smiling and looked at Silvenia. She looked back.

Kratos laughed. "Depends what it is, King Dymondo. I hope you are not going to ask your brother for his land!" Yatus and Kratos laughed loudly.

"Ha-ha! My brother loves me more than this piece of land," Dymondo said. "He has such a magnanimous heart. If Brother Grygerious or I asked for his Kingdom, my brother Shilathaar would give it to us without flinching. He loves his brothers more than anything in this realm."

Shilathaar's heart filled with compassion, and Silvenia was shocked to see such emotion in his eyes. She gave Shilathaar a stern stare as Dymondo continued addressing Kratos.

"But, nevertheless, great warrior Kratos, both Brother Grygerious and I know that there is but one great ruler in the entire realm! That is my brother, King Shilathaar! Brother Grygerious and I just happen to look after our pieces of land. But the true King of Kings is Shilathaar! And we respect and love him as such. I hope you will remember that before interrupting us brothers ever again."

Silvenia was cross with Dymondo for speaking to Kratos like that. Kratos was too astounded and embarrassed to reply.

Shilathaar found his smile again. "Kratos merely jests with you, Dymondo. Tell me! What would you like, Baby Brother!"

"May I take Gracia with me?"

Shilathaar laughed. So did Silvenia.

"I shall have an entire cart of Gracia wine loaded onto your ship right away. Guards!" The guards ran to fetch a cart of wine.

"Ha-ha! Gratitude, dear Brother." Both laughed and Dymondo walked up to his brother and tiptoed to bring his mouth near Shilathaar's ear. Shilathaar lowered his head and brought his ear closer to Dymondo's mouth.

"I meant Gracia…her…but since you have already given it, I shall take the wine as well," Dymondo said and winked at his brother.

Shilathaar threw his head back and roared with laughter, then came close and whispered to Dymondo. "Good, was she?"

Dymondo acted shy and looked away, scratched his head and smiled. Sterferep did not look pleased. Kor had a playful smile on his face and looked at Dan.

"Gracia! Come hither!"

The timid young woman walked up to the great King. "From now onwards, you are free from my services. You shall serve Dymondo now. You are to travel to Gammafor with him, and you will do as my younger brother commands from now onwards."

Gracia bowed and stepped behind Dymondo. Silvenia walked up to Dymondo and whispered in his ear.

"So you took her? Well done! A recommendation…Fuck her on the ship back home…its especially fun when the vessel rocks," she winked. Dymondo just smiled and nodded.

The cart of wine arrived and Sterferep lifted it into his arms. The tassels upon his shoulders got caught in the attempt, and his shoulders were exposed, and so was the mark. Shilathaar did not notice, but Silvenia and Kratos did and exchanged shocked glances.

The brothers embraced and Dymondo stepped onto the deck of his ship with the sun high above him, the ocean and the deck baking in its rays. With that, he set sail.

Silvenia rushed back to the palace with Kratos hastily following. Yatus and Shilathaar did not know why the siblings were so agitated and just smiled at one another as they headed back at a more leisurely pace. After bidding farewell, Shilathaar headed to the training ground and Yatus to his sister's chamber.

Yatus knocked and entered to find his siblings in a deep, heated argument.

"…And what can we do about it?!" snapped Silvenia.

"I do not know!" replied Kratos.

"What is going on here? Are you alright?" asked Yatus.

"Does it look as though we are alright?!" Silvenia asked sarcastically.

"Alright, alright. So I don't know what happened. Would someone like to tell me?"

"You tell him!" Silvenia commanded Kratos.

"The mark! Our mark!"

Yatus looked at his shoulder. "What about our mark?"

"It is upon that Lance's shoulder!"

"The Lance that came with Dymondo?" asked Yatus.

"Yes!" screamed Silvenia.

Now Yatus was horrified. "So…he bears the mark, too?"

"He does, Yatus, and we are trying to work out how," Kratos explained.

"There is only one explanation," Yatus said.

"No! There must be another!" Silvenia shrieked. Her eyes rarely displayed such fear. She ran up to Kratos and held his strong shoulder tight. "I'm scared, dear Brother."

Kratos put his arm around her to comfort her. "There now, nothing to be scared of, dear Sister."

Yatus despised the distress in Silvenia's eyes. Yet he too walked up and held her hand in support.

"Do not be worried. Your brothers yet live, and as long as we are alive, nothing can harm you, dear Sister," comforted

Yatus.

"Kill him…" she demanded.

"No dear Sister, we cannot act in haste."

"He may not even know what it is."

"That's true, But…"

"But what?" Silvenia implored them.

"If the Lance indeed bears the mark, only we can kill him, even you know that dear Sister… but it also means he can kill us."

No one spoke after that.

***

Dymondo stood smiling on the deck looking into the blue, clean water as the mighty ship sailed towards their destination. Gracia had been given a cabin and was below breathing her first air of freedom with Sterferep attending to her comforts. After the Lance did his duty, he went onto the deck to speak to Dymondo.

"Why did you bring her along?"

"She was sent to please me. I would not take her. She told me if I refused, then Shilathaar would put her to death as she is a virgin."

"She could be a spy, Dymondo, an assassin!"

"No, I doubt it very much."

"How can you be sure?"

"I'm not sure. I just feel she is a good, young lady."

"She could be a poison damsel, my King."

"I doubt it. She would have tried to ensnare me in her trap by now."

"You are becoming too generous," said Sterferep.

"That is why I have you to keep an eye on her," said Dymondo.

"Is everything good between us?"

"Well, you tell me dear Sterferep…is it?"

"My King?"

"Show me that mark on your shoulder."

Sterferep hesitated, slumped his shoulders and lifted his tassels. Dymondo beheld the Cecrops, half man/half serpent!

"My! Silvenia, Kratos and Yatus bear the same mark!"

Sterferep did not say anything, but they both knew he'd seen it too.

"Why did you not say anything about it to me?" Dymondo was hurt. Sterferep lowered his eyes.

"I only found out Silvenia bore this mark when Zircornia told me the other night. She had noticed it on our first night together, but only said something recently. I did not know what it was. I still don't completely understand."

"You must find out then."

Sterferep covered his arm with the tassels again and looked out over the ocean.

"I shall."

Dymondo nodded.

"My King, think about the task that lies ahead. Do not let these distractions impede your concentration."

"It is difficult. But you are right."

"Is there anything else that bothers my King?"

"Am I a good King, Sterferep?"

"Yes."

"That was convincing," scoffed Dymondo.

"My King, you are definitely worthy of the throne—not just of Gammafor and Fourtfor, but of all of Landsfor.

Dymondo was about to remind Sterferep that no one called it that anymore, but decided against it.

"But…"

"But what, Sterferep?"

"Haste! You need to think before you act, yet you need to be assertive and control your emotions. You at times display great courage and confidence then at other times seek advice for the most trivial matters. Maintain balance, my King. Confidence is good, but try not to let your ego lead you to arrogance."

Dymondo nodded. "You are right. But you must admit, I am improving."

"I am your friend, Dy. My praises are worthless."

"So am I not?"

"The King of Haask sent you a gift. Why? Because he respects you. The Gods have chosen to entrust *you* with the divine weapon. Why? Because they think you will uphold the banner of righteousness and use the weapon only for the welfare of humankind."

Dymondo's eyes lit up with confidence and his chest broadened upon hearing this and Sterferep was quick to defuse this.

"Balance, my King," he reminded him. "Remain positive and all shall be well. Never for one minute let arrogance get the better of you. You are headed in the right direction, but you have far to go."

"But will I be able to do it?"

"What you do think?"

Dymondo nodded and resolve came into his eyes as he looked out at sea.

"Good." smiled Sterferep.

They did not speak after that. Many hours passed and Dymondo remained on deck. The setting sun melted into the deepening blue sea, spilling magnificent colours over the deck.

Dymondo desired sleep and went down to his cabin where he found Gracia at his service.

"Gracia, my dear, please can you step outside? I shall be fine. Please return to your cabin."

Gracia did as she was told. Dymondo collapsed onto the bed and closed his eyes and fell asleep, but his dreams returned. He saw it all again. Dymondo and Grygerious running after Shilathaar. Grygerious applauding Shilathaar and relishing the murder in his brother's face. But it was not Shilathaar. It was the devil. Dymondo saw the devil walk up to Syterius and strike him and Syterius fall to his death. All the while, Dymondo was helpless to stop it.

"No! Stop, Brother!" he saw himself shouting again and again, but it was no use. The two demons only laughed louder, their laughter growing more and more terrifying.

Dymondo fell off his bed and jolted awake from his nightmare. The ship was fighting large waves; a rough part of the sea. Dymondo found himself breathless and wet with perspiration. He ran his hands through his thick, wet hair slicking it back with his fingers and taking deep breaths to steady his pulse before getting back up. He returned to the bed, lay his head upon the damp pillow and put his arm upon his forehead...*At least it is over for now,* he thought.

CHAPTER 11

JOURNEY TO THE AQUACAVES

The next morning, Dymondo brought out the map and showed it to the captain. The captain set course for the area of the map showing the Aquacaves, and the ship sailed and sailed until the jaw-dropping circular sinkhole came into view.

"Drop the anchor! Come about!" a crewmember shouted hysterically from atop the mast. He climbed down, looking petrified as though he had seen a demon, and ran up to the captain and the King.

"Cap'n, we have to stop now!"

"What is it?" asked the captain.

"That large blue circle. There! Do you see it?!"

"Drop the anchor!" shouted the captain.

"But Captain! That is where we are headed," King Dymondo objected.

"No, my King. It's too dangerous. That hole will swallow us. We must turn back!"

"Hole?" asked Dymondo, approaching the helm. The rest of the crew gathered round as the ship slowed and lurched to port under the strain from the anchor.

"The light blue water surrounding it is shallow, but that dense blue abyss has no end! These water caves sometimes appear near coasts. We must be near Doosranfor."

"There are rocks around it, too," Sterferep pointed out.

"He's right. Can you see the contrast of colour between the ocean and the hole itself? It is a chasm of death! Animals linger in its depths—large fish with sharp teeth—demons of the deep!"

"Captain, you are not on stage right now, and we are not enacting a play, so spare the monologues!" said Kor rather annoyed at the captain's dramatic descriptions.

"You think I jest? No Lance Kor, I do not. He who plunges in never returns."

"A hole in the water? Amazing!" Dan swooned.

"It looks as though the surface has given way," added Dwarpal. "That must have taken eons to form—for the rock to just crumble away like that and create a hole in the water?"

"True, and the level of the water has risen since then," added the captain. "Let's sail back, my King! I beg of you!"

"How come this was never discovered before?" asked Dymondo.

"King Grygerious neglected this part of his waters," the captain explained.

"By keeping his face between a pair of tits, day and night," quipped Kor to the entertainment of the crew.

"I hear his ministers are sharp, King Dymondo," warned Lance Sterferep. "They will be keeping an eye on their borders. We must be careful. The captain is right; we mustn't sail into Doosran waters."

Dymondo eyed the cave now at starboard and wondered how his father, King Balathaar, never braved these waters.

"I'll swim to it," Dymondo finally said. "Captain, bring the ship nearer to the edge and drop the anchor there. I will jump into the abyss, and once done, you will sail back here to this position."

"But King, what if the weapon is hidden somewhere deep?" Sterferep objected. "How will you breathe? You will have to keep returning to the surface for air. You have no idea how deep the cave goes."

"I cannot see any choice but to take the risk," said Dymondo.

"We cannot risk your life. Let one of us go in your stead," said Kor.

"No, it must be me. No one else."

"But King, it's suicide!" shouted Sterferep.

"The great bird said if I get stuck in the cave, then I must pray to God Aquinious. He will come to my aid. I must have faith, dear Sterferep."

Sterferep walked up to him and spoke quietly. "This is exactly what I spoke to you about, Dy."

"And I heeded your words, Ster," Dymondo responded in an equally low voice. "This is not a hasty decision, but one born of necessity. This is confidence, not arrogance."

"Very well, my King. Then persist assertively absent aggression and remain calculated."

Dymondo nodded and both embraced. Dymondo removed his armour and boots. He removed his heavy sword, picked up a lighter, finer, sharper sword and tied it around his waist. Then he mounted the plank in just his white cotton shirt and dark trousers now rolled up to his ankles.

"Hail God Aquinious!" he prayed aloud and dove into the blue blanket.

The sun had warmed the water slightly, but it was still bracing. He dealt with the shock by floating for a moment on the surface, then swam from the shallow part up to the sink hole where it was colder still. He could feel the difference immediately.

As he entered the sapphire surface of the abyss, he dove deeper, swimming down and down, looking here and there for anything out of the ordinary. He saw nothing but darkness, and in no time, the pressure and his need for air overwhelmed him. He retreated upward and gasped for air as he broke through the surface. Everyone on the ship sighed in relief, seeing their King resurface in the distance.

Dymondo continued like this futilely, taking ever larger breaths and pushing himself further into the deep. On one attempt, his vision left him completely, and uncertainty sank in.

Yet he pressed on, ignoring his body's need for air. The pressure grew greater and it felt that is ears would cave into his skull. It was too late to turn to the surface. He would never reach it in time. In a last desperate effort, he called to God Aquinious, just before he went unconscious and fell deeper into the chasm.

When Dymondo opened his eyes again, he was lying in the palms of a giant who was himself standing in the great hole. The giant's lower body was below the surface, while his upper body was visible above the surface of the water. Everyone on the ship beheld this enigmatic, super divinity holding their King in his hand, and they all bowed and knelt in reverence.

Dymondo coughed up the excess water from his lungs and struggled to catch his breath. Then he rose to his feet and stood upon the great giant's palm, looking into the face of his saviour. Indeed it was God Aquinious. His long hair and beard were brilliant white. His crown shone gold. His physique was impeccable, bearing invincible strength, yet he wore an angelic smile. He was perfection.

"O great God Aquinious, I bow before you!" proclaimed Dymondo and bowed and knelt before him.

"Long may you live, Dymondo!" proclaimed Aquinious in return. "You have shown great faith in me. I shall grant you divine vision and the ability to breathe under water so that you may be successful in your mission. Remember, these powers will return to me once your mission has been accomplished. Go Dymondo. May you be victorious!"

The divine voice boomed to the heavens as God Aquinious placed Dymondo back into the water and then disappeared.

A momentary pain shot through the sides of Dymondo's head and the King shouted in agony, feeling behind his ears. *Gills*, he realised, *just like a fish*. A bright flash shot across his eyes and his vision became astoundingly sharp. With new confidence, Dymondo plunged back under the surface.

All on the vessel cheered this time as their King dove under the water for they had witnessed this marvellous sight and heard the great booming voice. They were no longer concerned for their King. They knew that God himself was with him.

101

And he was. This time, Dymondo was faster and sharper. He could swim with ease and see a great distance underwater. Not only he was able to use his divine vision to scan the ocean cave in no time, he could even hear himself talk. He was swimming faster than ever and breathed as if were walking casually on land.

Still, there was no sight of the divine weapon or anything remotely resembling it. The waters only grew deeper and denser. Hundreds of tiny fish swam by as Dymondo grew mesmerized by the beautiful stones, rocks, plants and coral glinting in the sun's defused rays in this submarine cathedral.

Dymondo swam on until something made him stop and look around. He was not alone. Something had swum swiftly just behind him, and whatever it was had just as swiftly camouflaged itself. Dymondo whipped around, looking in all directions, when suddenly a sharp needle-like object slashed his back. It did not cause a deep wound, but Dymondo cried out in pain. That's when he spotted the enormous fish with its long, sharp snout.

Dymondo drew his sword from his waist in preparation for another attack. The fish swam a distance away only to turn back towards Dymondo and accelerate directly towards him. This time, Dymondo parried away the blade-like nose while inflicting a minor injury on the large predator. He also got a good look at his enemy.

It was a gigantic fish—a fish capable of swallowing an entire person whole. The only thing more terrifying than its long, sharp snout was its vicious, razor-sharp teeth. The creature had large, deathly eyes and a great fin on its back. It travelled with tremendous velocity and agility.

Dymondo had read of a macro, predatory fish known to be found in deep waters. These fish tended to have dense rows of serrated, brittle teeth, large conical snouts and great fins. This fish had all those features, along with one more: a long, flat bill. Dymondo was facing an unknown species.

At its next pass, Dymondo realised the fish was not attempting to spear him but to slash him. Without his blade, Dymondo would have been in grave trouble. The fish came again and again, turning and cutting Dymondo with each onslaught. Dymondo too managed to strike the fish a few times, but the fish had large, thick scales, making it difficult to do much damage.

The underwater battle continued and blood began to muddy the crystal, blue waters. The fish was beginning to get the upper hand, and it could sense Dymondo was getting tired. On its next turn, the fish tried a new tactic. Instead of going in with its long snout, it opened its mouth to exhibit its deadly teeth and swam straight at Dymondo, intending to devour him.

Dymondo escaped the first attempt, slashing the fish's inner mouth. As the fish retreated, Dymondo got an opportunity to cleanly swing his weapon, nearly severing the fish's spiked fin and throwing the fish into a thrashing, anguished rage.

That's when Dymondo saw it—something emerging from the depths of the cave, a great, large, blue bear. *How could it be?* Dymondo thought.

Before he could react, the fish came lunging towards him once more. With that, the bear surged upward, grabbed the fish by its long bill and snapped it off. The fish writhed in agony, launching itself towards the bear, only to meet its end. The bear grabbed it again by the snout then forced his strong hands inside the fish's mouth, getting a firm grip on the upper and lower jaws to keep them from snapping shut. The fish violently shook its head in an attempt to escape from the bear's mighty clutch, but it was no use. The bear applied more pressure and tore the fish apart at its mouth, completely ripping the fish in two from jaw to belly. Blood and viscera exploded around the carcass, creating a feeding frenzy for the smaller fish nearby. The bear let the rest of the fish drop into the endless abyss.

The bear treaded water for a moment before swimming closer to Dymondo. Dymondo clutched his sword, preparing for another attack.

"This place is not safe for humans. Don't tarry! Go! Now!"

"You can talk?" Dymondo said, lowering his sword. Bubbles came from his own mouth as he spoke.

"And so, can you! Great observational skills! Now go! That fish was nothing; more fearsome creatures await you in the depths. Much human blood has been split here. These creatures already have a taste for it. So, you must…." The bear stopped speaking when he noticed Dymondo's gills. The bear drifted closer, then suddenly his face exuded reverence.

"God Aquinious, you are he! The one I've been waiting for!"

CHAPTER 12

BAAZALI

Dymondo asked, still treading water as the large, blue bear bowed to him and folded his hands wearing a long, white, tatty tunic that went down to his knees. "Can you tell me who you are?"

"I am Baazli, the great blue bear. I served the King of Landsfor as his mount until the day of the great misfortune—a wrongful deed committed by my hands. I have the boon to live as long as I wish—to live through water and fire, but I had to be banished from the Kingdom, so I was happy to see out my worthless remaining days here in the Aquacaves. Still, I could never forgive myself, so I sought an audience with the King. I made request after request. After many moons, he bestowed upon me the pleasure of beholding him. I begged him to release me from this sentence, but the King lowered his head and told me that once word left his mouth, it could not be retracted.

"He asked me to pray to God Aquinious. I prayed for years and then the God of water, Aquinious, manifested before me. After greeting and saluting him, I leapt at his feet and wept. He then told me when my penance would end. But first, he asked me to safe keep the divine weapon and to steer away any thieves, which meant I must remain in the Aquacaves. Till this day, I have honourably fulfilled this task."

"The divine weapon?" Dymondo asked excitedly.

"Yes. He said that one day the true King of Landsfor would come searching for the divine weapon, so that it may be used for the welfare of humankind. He said this man will be able to breath under water and will attempt to cause me no harm. God Aquinious told me, on this day, my penance will be rendered complete. I shall have the opportunity to serve my new King, to once again become his mount and help him in his quest to restore peace in the land. And now, my King...you are here before me!" exclaimed the bear with a bow.

Dymondo had never met such a strange creature. He wasn't sure he could trust him. Nevertheless, Dymondo decided to tell him of his quest.

"Great creature, I respect your words. You must be a magical and powerful animal. I have not met a single bear who can converse in my tongue. Indeed, I have come to retrieve a divine weapon."

"Yes, you have come here for the Emispear—the ultimate weapon of Frozenfire. You seek it, so you can use it for the welfare of Landsfor," replied Baazli.

"You said you were the mount to the King of Landsfor. My father had no mount! Certainly, not a bear!"

"Not your father. Your great-grandfather, King Solothaar. He was a great King, powerful and strong yet just as compassionate—everything a King should be! Sad to say his son, King Komodothaar Rain, did not possess his qualities. Word has come to me that neither was Komodothaar's son Balathaar Rain any good. But you...You seem to possess something special!"

"There is no need to speak ill of King Komodothaar Rain or of King Balathaar Rain. Rightfully, in their own ways, they were good Kings. Komodothaar Rain was my grandfather and Balathaar Rain was my father."

"I beg your pardon, my King."

"You said the King of Landsfor will come here looking for the divine weapon. I am not the King of Landsfor, but only of Gammafor and Fourtfor."

"I was the mount to your great-grandfather, my King. Everyone knows you are the rightful heir and worthy King of Landsfor."

"Very well. In that case, where is the Emispear? Where is it kept?"

"The honour will be mine to hand it over to you, my King, when the need arises."

"The need has arisen, great Bear. Give me the weapon. Besides, I must get back. My men will surely be worried. Once you give me the weapon, you will be free and will not need to confine yourself to this watery chasm. After you have given the Frozenfire to me, you will be free to walk on the soil of my Kingdom and live wherever you wish—land, sky, soil or water— as long as you live in peace and cause no harm to others!"

The bear looked bemused and a small grin developed under his snout, which did not please Dymondo. "I seek pardon for my chuckle, my King, but my life's purpose is to serve you now, as per the prophecy by the God of Water himself."

"That is not required at this moment. I shall call upon you only if I need you. Now the weapon... if you may..." said Dymondo extending out his strong hand.

"My dear ruler of Landsfor, again forgive my audacity, but that weapon is *within* me...!" Baazli said softly. Dymondo was shocked.

"The weapon exerts upon the enemy the flawless power of the Frozenfire. It is a combination of four parts: one of the elements which is within me.

The other element, which I am guarding, is the fire. It used to reside inside a great red bear but misfortune ensued. He is no longer the guardian and keeper of it. If this weapon is to be invoked, then we must work together. One element is worthless without the other parts. So, my King, that means you must accept me as your mount."

Dymondo, unconvinced by all this, became very angry. "You're knitting a web of lies, great Bear! I am grateful to you. You took down the water creature, but—"

"Sharpfish."

"Whatever that wretched creature was! You may have been safeguarding the weapon up till now, which is good, but I demand you hand it over to me! Stop deterring me from my path! Give me the weapon right now, Bear!"

"I speak only the truth! The great blue bear is a righteous creature! You must believe me."

"Rubbish! I don't believe you! If you were righteous, then why this punishment to linger in the Aquacaves for two generations? Move from my path or I shall use force!" Dymondo said.

"Come with me," said Baazli and swam further down, manoeuvring into an inner cave.

Dymondo sighed and followed.

They swam further into the cave until the bear stopped and pointed to a large, red glimmering staff seated on a rock pedestal in the distance. The bear moved aside and bowed his head as Dymondo came forth and swam past him into the inner cave. He grabbed the weapon from the rock pedestal. It appeared to be a small red rod. As soon as he held it, the red staff began to glow intermittently. The bear stood tall. Dymondo noticed a similar sized rod glowing blue inside the bear's belly, shining through his tunic.

"Magical illusions, eh Bear? But no! I am leaving, and without you! But first you shall hand over the blue rod!" Dymondo shouted. Baazli did so and Dymondo began to swim towards the exit. The bear slumped down to a sitting position inside the inner cave, lowered his head and began to weep.

Suddenly, before Dymondo could exit, the God of Water, Aquinious manifested before him—this time in a smaller form. Dymondo came to a halt, and immediately bowed and knelt in reverence. The bear stood up promptly and bowed to the Water God.

"Dymondo," spoke the God. "This bear is no conjurer. He is your ally. What he speaks is the truth."

"The truth is you need him more than he needs you. He is humble and does not say this to you directly, as you are King and he is modest. You are a good man, Dymondo. You can see right from wrong. Why do you fail to recognise it this time?" His voice was heavenly.

"I seek your pardon, my Lord. Current events in my life have clouded my mind. I cannot fathom what the truth is and what is a lie."

"This bear is much wiser than you. To have him as your mount will be beneficial for you…honourable!" Dymondo did not reply but stood bewildered. God disappeared and both Dymondo and Baazli bowed as he vanished. Dymondo turned to Baazli. Baazli stood there with his head down.

"So… I guess…Baazli…we are a team?" said Dymondo, slightly nervous and embarrassed.

The bear looked up, still looking wounded. Dymondo understood the creature wanted to be consoled and he smiled with affection and embraced the creature.

"Forgive me, friend. I failed to recognise you."

The bear wept more and replied, "No, my King, please do not say that. I am always here for you."

The bear's weeping brought a tear to Dymondo's eye and he cleared his throat. "Right!" he said firmly, yet positively. "Bear! We have a journey to complete and perhaps even a war to wage! Are you ready?"

"Yes, my King!" replied the bear, standing up straighter with a focused look.

"Good! Then come with me."

"This divine weapon has the power to slay anyone. It is ever so powerful. You will need this in the war against your toughest opponents: your brothers."

Dymondo placed his hands on his hips and gave Baazli a stern look.

"How do you know about this?

"I know you do not wish to hear such words, my King. Jump on my back and let us leap out of the Aquacaves. I shall explain everything afterwards."

With the second and third element of the divine weapon retrieved, Dymondo mounted Baazli, and the bear swam out of the inner cave then launched himself upwards. Within moments, they surged out of the underwater sinkhole and exploded through the surface of the sea. Baazli remained treading water with Dymondo on his back. Dymondo's gills disappeared along with his ability to see and hear underwater.

"I have a ship waiting," said Dymondo pointing across the water.

"Then we shall waste no more time! I will run across the water as if it is ground and get you to your ship. But, you must remember…"

"What is that?"

"The weapon is yet incomplete."

"Incomplete?"

"Yes… a red staff and blue staff. These two you have. The third part is a golden feather, like a spearhead. And the fourth part we shall find in a shrub."

"A shrub?"

"Yes… it has a bad habit of launching its red berries."

Dymondo wondered if the shrub talked like the other creatures. "I have the golden feather," he finally said.

"Do you have it with you now?"

"I do. Look here."

Dymondo pulled down his cotton shirt to reveal a thick black thread tied tight around his neck with a white pouch hanging from its end.

"My Queen tied it around my neck. The feather is inside this pouch."

"I beg your pardon, my King, but you took a great risk. You could have lost it. You must check to see if it is still there when we get on your ship."

"I have been doing so from time to time on my journey. My Queen thought it best that I keep the feather with me, in case I found the other parts of the Emispear."

The bear thought for a while. "Yes, I can understand her thoughts. But still we must keep these elements safe."

Dymondo nodded.

"So, you met Quilliblade?" asked Baazli.

"Yes, how do you—?"

"Plenty of time for explanations later, my King. For now, we will head to shore so we can find the shrub."

CHAPTER 13

SON OF GOD

It was a true marvel for the men on the deck to withhold their monarch mounted on a giant blue bear galloping across the deep ocean as though it was ground.

"Look over there!" shouted Kor.

"Great valour!" gasped Dwarpal.

"He is our King after all!" cheered Sterferep.

As Baazli ran closer to the ship, he leaped in the air over the heads of Dymondo's men and onto the deck, gently rocking the ship with his smooth landing.

"Woo! That was marvellous, Baazli. Bravo!" praised Dymondo as he got off the bear's back and Baazli stood to his feet.

"My pleasure, my King!" replied Baazli to everyone's disbelief.

"King Dymondo, how do you fare?" asked Sterferep, advancing to embrace him. Dymondo greeted Sterferep, then Kor, Dan and Dwarpal.

"Right, my men! This is Baazli! A true friend! Without his aid, I would not have survived nor come into possession of this divine weapon!" he said, showing them the red and blue staff. All the men bowed to the great bear.

"He is the great blue bear. He possesses great strength and is skilled in warfare. He will be a true ally."

112

"He talks!" mentioned Dan.

"Yes Dan, like you and I and everyone else, Baazli speaks and understands our tongue. I used to believe that the days of talking animals had long passed, but I was wrong. Recently, I have witnessed many animals speak. Who can forget the great bird perched on the gate of our Kingdom?"

"Good to have you with us, O great Bear," said Sterferep. "We need allies. For a long while now the number of our enemies has been on the increase. To finally gain an ally is quite refreshing."

"The pleasure is mine," replied Baazli.

"This is Kor, Dwarpal and Dan, and I am Sterferep," he said.

"Pleasure to meet everyone. Like yourselves, I now remain in the service of the great King Dymondo!"

After pleasantries were exchanged, Dymondo commanded the captain to set sail towards Gammafor while he and Baazli had their wounds from the battle tended to. When no one was looking, Dymondo checked the pouch for the feather. It was there. Dymondo sighed with relief.

It was midday when the bear, the King, his men and Gracia finally set foot on land. Dymondo squinted into the hot sun and took a deep breath as he strode onto the sandy beach.

"Always great to be home!" he exclaimed.

"My King, we must head to the shrub," reminded Baazli.

"Yes, that we must! Sterferep, I would like you all to head back to the Kingdom, I must go with Baazli to retrieve the last piece of the Emispear."

"But, King, let us come with you," said Sterferep.

"No Sterferep, you go on ahead. I shall ride back with Baazli."

"The ride is long, great Sterferep," explained Baazli. "I can take the King there in less time. It will be difficult for you all to keep pace with us. You must do as your King says and head towards the Kingdom,"

Dymondo's men looked at one another.

"May we at least wait for you at the entrance to the Kingdom?" asked Kor.

"No need. Baazli is with me," assured Dymondo.

Baazli smiled. He appreciated the fact his King had so much confidence in him. Sterferep was less pleased. He did not fully trust Baazli yet.

Despite much persistence by Sterferep, Dymondo finally cajoled his men into proceeding towards the Kingdom's gate. Baazli went onto four feet, and Dymondo strapped his sword belt tight and mounted the large bear. Sterferep handed Dymondo camping supplies and equipment which the King also secured. Without warning, the bear took a boundless starting leap which eventually materialised into the fastest sprint ever witnessed by man. The bear and the King were out of sight in no time.

"Do you trust him?" asked Kor to Sterferep.

"The bear?"

"Yes, the bear."

"I have no reason not to. At least not yet."

"What shall we do?" asked Dan.

"We cannot follow them, that's for sure," said Dwarpal.

"We have to be patient. Let us wait at the entrance to the Kingdom. The crew is with us and so is Gracia. When we get to the gates, one of us will show Gracia to the servant chambers, and the crew can return to their homes."

"I'll take her," said Dan. "But then I shall return to the entrance once I have done so."

Gracia smiled at Dan and he smiled back at her.

Sterferep nodded in agreement.

"We'll give them three days. If they do not return, then we'll go seek them out," said Sterferep.

"Where are they headed? Did he say anything to you on the ship?" asked Kor.

"He did. They are heading into the desert, across Sent, the gargantuan battlefield."

"But that place is cursed."

"Yes, Kor. Many eons ago a revered sage cursed a former monarch of the Rain dynasty for his crude behaviour."

"What was the curse?" asked Dan.

"That a time will come when the entire battlefield will be soaked in the red blood of his family line—so much blood that the ground will remain red for eons."

"I guess a great war is on the horizon then," said Dwarpal.

"At least we have our King. He returns with much more confidence, doesn't he, Sterferep?" asked Kor.

"He does no doubt. But there are a few more lessons he needs to learn."

No one else spoke after that. Everyone headed towards the Kingdom, heeding Dymondo's orders.

Dymondo and Baazli travelled for a distance across the barren, dry, white lands in the scorching heat. The sun was high in the sky, and sweat drained from their bodies. After a time, they reached the vast battleground enclosed with large mountains and trees. It had lain dormant for many years, and there was much gravel on the ground. Eventually, they cleared the battlefield and reached the desert. It was a large stretch of land, wide like an open mouth, surrounded by cacti, tumbleweed and shrubs.

"Where is it?" asked Dymondo, looking for the shrub Baazli had told him about.

"I'm tired now, Dymondo," said the bear. "I need water!"

"Fine," said the King.

They continued to look around when suddenly, on Baazli's blue fur, Dymondo noticed a soft red liquid. "Baazli, you're hurt!" said Dymondo.

"Can't be! I'm in no pain."

"Then what is this?" asked Dymondo pointing to the runny goo on the beast's fur.

Baazli touched the spot in question and found it to be a sticky red juice. As he rubbed it in his hand, his inner paws too got stained. "It's a berry!" he shouted. "We're not far!"

Encouraged, the two ventured forward until, behind a large rock, they came upon the shrub they were searching for. It was just as Baazli had described—a small shrub that had a habit of launching its berries. Both were astounded as it seemed the shrub had appeared out of nowhere.

Dymondo approached and a full bunch of red berries came flying at him, hitting him hard on his face. Some bounced off and landed on the ground, but one or two burst, marking his face with the red juice.

"Ouch!" he shouted.

"Don't get too near, Dymondo. Those berries could be poisonous," warned Baazli.

"Poisonous!" The plant spoke. "How can they be poisonous? Really, you both say the most ridiculous things. It pains me to hear such stupid words from such clever, great warriors. Baazli, you of all creatures should know better." The shrub's voice was effeminate and patronising. Dymondo made an attempt to introduce himself.

"I am——"

"I know who you both are! No need to tell me. You are Dymondo and you are Baazli," said the disembodied voice.

"Great! He knows us!"

"He? Great Gods! From which angle, do I look like a 'he?'" asked the shrub.

"She?" asked Dymondo.

"Come now, Dymondo, you are not so stupid. So please do not act so. I am a shrub, a plant. If you must talk about me, then refer to me as 'it'," scolded the shrub.

"You have not changed have you? Greetings by the way," said Baazli.

"No I have not. Greetings to you, too, Baazli."

"You have something to give me or tell me?" asked Dymondo, already fed up with the exchange.

"Yes, Son of God, I do have to tell you something."

Dymondo placed his hands on his waist. "Why do you call me Son of God?"

"Because you *are*! As your mother, Queen Ohio told you, Balathaar is not your father! You were all born with the blessings of the deities."

"You know?" Dymondo asked, thinking back to the troubling revelation his mother had given him before her death.

"That's correct, Dymondo. His seed could not impregnate

116

your mother for years, which he and your mother hid from the world. But your mother is a pious woman. She invoked the Gods through her penance and the Gods appeared before her—not once, not twice but thrice—and she was blessed with three children. You brother Shilathaar is the son of Terradeus the God of War. Your brother Grygerious, is the son of the God of Love, Ishq. And you, Dymondo, are the son of the King of the Gods, Topus! But of course, you already know all this, don't you?"

Dymondo lowered his head in acknowledgement of the troubling implication of the shrub's words.

"They are not your brothers, Dymondo! They do not love you, and that is the bitter truth! The only sibling that loves you dearly is your sister, Nilharia, but I'm afraid…" There was a long silence.

"Afraid of what?" asked Dymondo sternly. He cared for his sister too much to be played with in such a way.

"Let me explain first. I shall get to that," said the shrub.

Dymondo calmed himself. "Do they know this?" he asked.

"That you are not brothers? Well, you have kindly blurted it out to them. What do you think?"

"No. That they are demi-Gods."

"No! And they must never find out! But no need to worry. They will never attempt to learn such a thing! The eldest is just a power-hungry beast, and the golden boy gets his ministers to think for him! You on the other hand always use your head. You think about things yourself and are clever! So, I was thinking, out of all them, *you* must understand as only you have *any* potential of bringing peace, joy and prosperity to this land."

"Understand what?"

"Must I spell out everything?"

"Shrub!!!"

"Calm!" the shrub barked, and Dymondo took a breath.

"To understand your brothers have always been conspiring against you. They despise you because they know you are the best of them. Hence they want to overthrow you."

"They conspire against me, *together*?"

"No! Shilathaar wants it all to himself, and to be perfectly truthful, he can gain everything because he is that powerful. In a duel between you both, he would surely emerge victorious!

"That most certainly is not true!"

"It is."

"But—" Another bunch of berries hit Dymondo's face, this time harder than before.

"Be quiet! I have not finished... Son of God!" The shrub was truly testing Dymondo's patience.

"Now where was I?" spoke the shrub. "Ah yes! Believe me, he can beat you. That is a fact, unless you use unrighteous tactics in the duel." Dymondo and Baazli looked at one another. The shrub huffed. "But of course you won't. You still have honour."

"So what can I do?"

"Shilathaar has strong men in his army. He has strong allies. If you were to wage a war against him, then you must gain more strength, which means allies and a vast army like his. Shilathaar knows he can remove Grygerious from his path whenever he wants. But he also understands removing you from your throne will not be an easy task. Therefore, day by day, he is gaining strength and allies. Surely, you must be aware of this."

Dymondo could not dispute it. He had seen the armaments and heard of the recent alliances with Orakray and Blee.

"And Grygerious?" asked Dymondo.

"Answer me first! Am I correct?"

"You are," sighed Dymondo.

"Grygerious! Ah him! The most dangerous foe of all! He will cause you great harm, if he hasn't done so already. But how can Grygerious cause you harm, you must be asking. After all, he has no strength, and he is thin and weak. Correct?"

"Perhaps."

"Not Perhaps! He is! So, in a duel, you will be able to beat him in moments. One strike of your clenched fist would be enough to knock his head clean off his body. Ha-ha!" laughed the shrub.

Again, there was an awkward silence. The shrub stopped laughing and noted the tension.

"Err...right... perhaps that was a bit a too graphic.

118

Apologies! But I speak only the truth. Grygerious too wishes to overthrow both his brothers, but his heart is filled with covetousness as he is not skilled in warfare. He does not possess strength or have allies enough to beat either of you in a conventional war, and for him, a duel is futile as he knows his defeat would be inevitable. But make no mistake, Grygerious is the most malicious of your brothers, and he is likely to strike you at your weakest point. He is conniving and treacherous, and once he has figured out a plan to harm you both, he will strike. Since he has no honour he is not above any tactic. He may use assassins, poison, anything! So, beware!"

"So, this is all happening as we speak?" asked Dymondo.

"Yes!" the shrub answered in an exasperated tone. "You yourself have seen what is happening in Forprimiera, yet you ask?"

Dymondo nodded.

"May I say something?" asked Baazli. "The three brothers have their own Kingdoms and they all have been Kings of their own islands for many years now. No one has attacked anyone to gain more land, so why now?"

"Ambitions and water have similar characteristics, great Bear. They yearn! They can never remain still and be content. Human desire grows with every rising and setting of the sun. There is no man or woman who can accept what they have. They always yearn for more. Dymondo, if there must only be one King of Landsfor, then it should be you. You were destined to rule, but you are losing valuable time."

"You are a fortune teller as well now?" mocked Dymondo.

"I said you *should* be King of Landsfor; I did not say that you most definitely *will* be King."

"No one calls it that anymore, shrub."

"Well… all those people are idiots. It *was* called Landsfor, it still *is* Landsfor and it shall forever *be* Landsfor!" said the shrub passionately. "Why should it be called by four different names? Only because a fourth of it is dominated by a brute and the other fourth by an incompetent perfidious jackal?!"

For once Dymondo agreed. "So you are suggesting I declare

war on my brothers?" he asked.

The shrub threw another bunch of berries at Dymondo's face.

"Shrub!" Dymondo yelled wiping away berry juice from his face.

"They are not your brothers and I suggested nothing! Pay attention to my words… Son of God! A great war is heading your way, that I can say. Will you declare it, or will they declare it? Only time will tell. All I know is the battlefield will turn blood red and remain stained for eons. Your blood will flow, and so will Shilathaar's."

"I most certainly will not attack them!"

"And most certainly you should not, but you will kill them."

"Why would I kill them? How?"

"You will defend your land if they attack you…will you not?"

"I will."

"There we are. I suggest you prepare yourself then, for once he has gained strength, Shilathaar *will* attack you."

"But why would I kill Grygerious? Surely, he will not attack me. He cannot be that stupid."

"Ha-ha. You want to know the *entire* future now? Didn't I tell you, I am not a fortune teller?" laughed the shrub.

Dymondo was at the point of giving up. "I don't know why I even came here!"

"Ha-ha…Because you used your head, and you are wise! You cannot fight destiny. Your enemies are blinded by their greed and ambition, which will lead them to carry out heinous acts. Some deeds which you will not be able to forgive them for. Some deeds that are punishable by death," said the shrub.

Dymondo looked both baffled and worried.

"At ease, Dymondo. I will tell you. I have appeared before you to warn you of something and that I will do. I will speak the truth…but my dear Son of God…the truth is always bitter. Let me ask you, Dymondo… would you fight someone, if they challenged you?" asked the shrub.

"Yes."

"Would you fight someone with the intent to kill, to punish

them for a sinful and inhumane act?

"Yes, that would compel me."

"There we are. There are more reasons in the world to punish a man or woman by death if they carry out a sinful, wrongful and unrighteous act."

"So, you mean to say that I will be compelled to kill Grygerious?"

"You will kill them, but not without a strong reason. You are a good man."

"That doesn't answer my question."

"Some things are understood without being spoken in clear words. Let us just conclude with this. When the time comes for you to kill Grygerious, you will have a righteous reason to do so, and you will not regret your action. You will also long to kill Shilathaar before he attacks…again for good reason."

"And what of Nilharia?"

"Yes, she is your true sibling. She genuinely cares for you."

"So her birth was natural?"

"Yes! Your father's seed could not impregnate your mother *for years*. Listen carefully! He did eventually succeed. Nilharia is your sister, and she will not harm you in anyway…but…"

"But what?!"

"I'm afraid she will suffer a terrible fate, and her lifespan will be short."

"What?!"

"You cannot do anything about that. I can only recommend you attempt to keep her safe and give her as much affection and love as you can. That is all you can do. But Dymondo, you will not be able to overturn this fate."

Dymondo was shocked and grieved. He nearly broke down into tears, but he maintained his composure.

"There must be something I can do to stop this from happening. You must help me!" begged Dymondo, moving toward the shrub just before another bunch of red berries launched towards him. Dymondo closed his eyes to brace for impact, but this time the berries stopped in mid-air before they connected with his face. Dymondo opened his eyes to find the berries on the ground before him.

"It would have been wrong to hit you, but I had to brush you back. I tell the truth, Dymondo. Keep her safe if you can."

"But there must be some way to prevent…what is this act? Tell me."

"A man shall attempt to violate her dignity, and he will sadly succeed."

"No! Never! I will part him from his manhood and take his head before he lays a finger on my sister! Who is this man?!" screamed Dymondo.

"I am sure you will do exactly that to him, but only after he has committed the heinous act."

"I can stop it!" cried Dymondo.

"I am sure you will try and if you can stop this act, then do so Dymondo, because it would be horrendous if it happened," said the shrub.

"But why not tell me his name!"

"Truthfully, O great King Dymondo…I would, but I do not know who it will be. Even I don't know everything. I have told you all I know. Just keep Nilharia safe and keep your mother safe as well."

"My mother is dead!"

"Ah, so that calamity has already struck?"

"Aren't you meant to know everything?"

"I don't know everything!" The shrub was angry and annoyed. "All I knew was that an unnatural death awaited her, too."

"Unnatural! No! You are wrong."

"Someone took her life."

"No. She died in her sleep. She went peacefully."

"No, Son of God. Someone took her life."

"You are wrong."

"I am not. If you think she went peacefully, then you have more to learn about her death."

"Then tell me. I will kill—"

"I am sure you will! Take this!" the shrub yelled, and out from the shrub, instead of red berries, came hurling a gleaming, green shaft.

Dymondo caught it in his left hand. It had a sharp green glow that lit the skies as Dymondo clasped it.

"What is this?"

"It is the divine weapon!"

"Frozenfire!"

"Yes, Dymondo. This is the fourth and final element. The yellow feather which you possess, given to you by Quilliblade, is the spearhead which gives you the strength of the sun. Affix that feather blade atop the red shaft you already carry. (There is a story about the red shaft which Baazli can tell you.) It will give you the power of fire. Then the green shaft, the power of the earth and soil and the goodness it holds. Then finally the blue which will give you the speed of the wind, the greatness of the sky and the power of water. Once these shafts are set together, this will give you the ultimate power to defeat your enemies. The Emispear is invincible and can be invoked as many times as you wish."

"Gratitude, Shrub," bowed Dymondo.

"You cannot kill your brothers with just any weapon but only with the Frozenfire as they too are sons of—"

"Sons of Gods, I know."

"It is not that simple. But you know about the demonic intervention, don't you? However, I must now go. God is with you, Dymondo."

"No I have more questions."

"To which you will have answers soon."

"No, tell me, who killed my mother?"

"In good time, Dymondo, you will know," spoke the shrub and disappeared.

"Wait! No! Come back!" screamed Dymondo and collapsed to the ground.

CHAPTER 14

THE BOY AND THE BEAR

D ymondo and Baazli started back for Gammafor, stopping at various places along way upon exiting the desert. The sun was still in the sky and there was a sweet fragrance in the air. Eventually they heard the soft sound of the river and Dymondo suggested it as a good place to take a rest. When they arrived Dymondo laid the three coloured rods on the bank. He pulled the feather from the inside the pouch tied around his neck and laid it alongside the other pieces, gazing upon his treasure as if he felt unconquerable. Baazli did not like the look on Dymondo's face and knew he had to approach the King with subtlety.

"Beautiful isn't it?"

"Yes, it is."

"The power of the Emispear is truly sublime. Are you familiar with spear-to-spear combat?"

"I am, but Lance Kor is a natural with it. I must train with him when we get back."

"Great thought, my King. But do not train with the Emispear itself. The power of the Frozenfire is boundless. Precision and control are absolutely necessary. But there is more. You must possess calmness of mind, maintain sharpness in your eyes, and the speed of your reactions must come from the confidence within your heart."

Dymondo looked over oddly.

"You think I don't know all of this already?"

"My King, you are no doubt the correct man to carry this weapon, but are you not ready to wield it…not just yet," smiled Baazli.

Dymondo stood up and placed his hand upon his hips and faced Baazli. "I believe I am!"

"Ha-ha, with all due respect, that sounded more like arrogance and less like confidence."

"Fine! I shall show you confidence!" Dymondo got enraged and picked up one rod after another and assembled the shaft.

"My King, I strongly suggest you not put it together just yet. Let us return home and then we can do so in a more controlled environment."

Dymondo had the spearhead in his hand and was about to join it to the staff.

"Baazli, when I am in danger, I am not going to have time to judge my surroundings and see if it is a controlled environment. If I am to wield this weapon, then this place is as good as any other!" snapped Dymondo.

"But my King…"

"Enough!" and Dymondo and joined the spearhead to the shaft.

The spear trembled in Dymondo's hand and a magnificent bright white light emanated from the weapon that brightened the entire sky. The Emispear was truly powerful—full of energy—so much that it was difficult for Dymondo to control it, and he could not hold it for long, let alone wield it. At last Dymondo simply let go.

"What are you doing?!" shouted Baazli and walked over to the spear where it had landed on the ground. Baazli lifted it and hurriedly disassembled it. The bright light was gone.

"Did you see how bright the light was? That shows you are not ready. Why did you have to act like a boy?"

"I am not a boy, Baazli!" shouted Dymondo.

Baazli huffed and gathered himself and walked up to him.

"The light must be minimal. I said to you: mind, eyes and

heart. You had control over none of these."

"Then how can I control it?"

"I will show you, but when we get back. We should move on from here though and keep going until nightfall. After a spectacle like that, it would not be safe to stay around here anymore."

"Why?"

"Only the Gods know who or what might have seen us. The light was too bright. We have to keep this weapon safe."

Baazli chanted a couplet and the spear transformed into a medallion and dropped into Baazli's neck.

"How did you do that?"

"I will tell you later. We must go!"

Dymondo agreed and mounted Baazli's back to continue their journey.

***

Baazli's fears were correct. Many had seen the bright light.

Grygerious was awoken from slumber inside his shallow bathing pool. He was naked with Cresenia and other maidservants, and inebriated when he saw the Emispear's flash in the sky. It was as though the heavens had opened. All were in awe and shock at the light, but in his drunken state, he was unable to keep his eyes open, hence they all ultimately ignored the flash and fell back to sleep.

Across all four islands of Landsfor, and the surrounding islands to the north and south, priests in the various temples ran outside to witness the marvel and bowed before it as a miracle. "The winds are changing!" they said as they fixed their gaze to the brilliant white sky. Even in the window of the King's chamber, in the highest tower in the Kingdom of Haask, the drapes had been moved aside to witness the great beam.

Shilathaar too saw the bright light. At the time, he was at the banks of Lake Grit, deep in conversation with a giant talking snake. Only the snake's deathly eyes could be seen as the rest of its body was submerged under water.

"There it is..." hissed the snake.

"There is what...?"

"The only time I saw such a light was when the Emispear was wielded by your great grandfather."

"The what?" asked Shilathaar.

"A divine weapon. But it cannot be… because the Emispear was…disassembled and taken back by the Gods."

"Then what is it?"

"I do not know, but I will have to find out. It looks to be shining from Gammafor…"

"That means—"

"Your brother is up to something."

"How dare he move against me," sneered Shilathaar.

"*You* too move against him… you are here to ask whether my snake army and I will fight under your banner if there is a war. You have convinced the most powerful warriors in the land, Brog Sceptaro, Volglade, Hastinia Kral and Saji Miniscus, to fight under your banner already."

"Yes and they will. Will you?"

"You have my army of serpents on your side, King Shilathaar," hissed the snake. "I will support you."

"I need to you do me one task."

"What might that be?"

"Find out what this bright light is. Go to Gammafor and see what is going on and…" Shilathaar hesitated for a while. His heart stopped him from uttering the following words.

"And…?"

"If Dymondo is gathering armies or weapons, then ensure he is finished!"

"You mean—?"

"Yes."

"So be it!" the snake hissed and went under water.

Shilathaar watched the black ripples subside and headed back to his palace.

CHAPTER 15

THE SERPENT AND THE BEAR

Together, Dymondo and the bear journeyed back towards the Kingdom. They travelled across the dry land, through the forest, and reached the banks of the river Krool by evening of the following day. Baazli recommended they rest overnight beside the river as he was too tired to gallop back to the Kingdom.

So Dymondo and the great bear set camp beside the river bank. Under the black blanket of night brightened by the glimmering stars and a large full moon overhead, Dymondo sat in front of a small fire, in silence, digging his sharp dagger into the soil. The noise from the digging woke the resting Baazli who got up and walked over to Dymondo.

"What are you thinking?"

Dymondo sighed deeply and gave no reply.

"Thinking about what the shrub said?" asked Baazli.

"Hmm..." responded Dymondo.

"Yes, the truth is bitter, but it is still the truth," stated Baazli. That was not what Dymondo wanted to hear.

"Well I don't believe it! Why must I change my ways towards my brothers just because of the words of a shrub?!"

"Change nothing, my King but do not ignore it. Just bear the shrub's words in mind and be vigilant. Have you been to visit any of your brothers recently?"

Dymondo stared into the sky and then back at the ground. "I have. I went to Forprimiera, where my brother Shilathaar reigns as King. Why do you ask?"

"Did you notice anything strange? Any hostility or special preparations?"

"Preparations, yes." Dymondo thought of the large number of soldiers he had seen marching into the capital, the blacksmiths forging new weapons, the intense training, and the large cannons and catapults. "Gods...I have not seen so much iron accumulated."

"Kings do not prepare unless there is a reason?"

"It could just be routine."

"Or it could be preparation for war. We can't know. All we know is that Shilathaar is strengthening. You must do the same."

"I have already begun."

"Still, we have much work to do when we get back to your Kingdom. We need to be able to withstand a full attack if one comes."

"My brothers have done me no harm nor given me any cause to fight with them. I cannot say they love me, but they have not harmed me."

"Perhaps not yet. The shrub talked of the future."

"Ha-ha! Astrologers and philosophers cannot predict the future. How can a shrub?"

"I know...it does not sound possible, but it cannot be disregarded either. Take no action against your brothers, my King, but remember that you have been warned about them. Quilliblade warned you, too."

Dymondo looked at Baazli but said nothing.

"Just keep a close eye on them. When we return to Gammafor, we will strengthen your army further. Now get some sleep, my King. We have a long day of travel ahead of us, but we will be home by tomorrow evening," consoled Baazli.

"That story about my mother's death is baffling."

"I imagine that was tough for you to hear. You must investigate."

"What is the story of the red bear?" Dymondo asked, lying

129

down.

"The red staff resided in Baazla, the great red bear. The blue staff resides in me. The green staff resided with the shrub."

"Where is Baazla?"

"He turned unrighteous. He wanted to be the sole keeper of the weapon. He caused the shrub and Quilliblade harm in trying to obtain the elements from them. So the God of Fire, Ignio, withdrew the honour from him. He was no longer worthy to be the keeper of the red staff."

"Then? How did you get banished from the Kingdom? How did the shrub get to safe keep the green staff? Why was the red staff kept in the Aquacaves?"

Baazli went quiet.

"I realise I ask too many questions and that it is a sensitive matter. You can tell me in your own time, dear Baazli," said Dymondo and closed his eyes. Baazli too went back to sleep.

After a few hours, when the two were deep in slumber, the waters of the river Krool began to ripple and deep gurgling sounds came forth. Dymondo remained in a deep sleep and did not acknowledge the noise; however, Baazli stirred.

Out of the water, an enormous serpent's hood emerged—a hood so large, the entire river bank was under its shelter. Baazli woke up and stood immediately. He looked over at Dymondo who was still asleep, then turned to face the serpent hood, ready to engage in battle. The serpent's eyes were blood-red and its jet-black body gleamed under the moonlight. One could tell by looking at it that a drop of its venom would kill any living creature instantly.

"Baazli," hissed the serpent.

"Quiet! Go away!" spoke Baazli softly.

"Away?" said the shiny snake and brought its face near to Baazli's face, exhibiting its sharp poisonous fangs.

"Yes! Away! I have nothing to do with you anymore. You have caused me too much grief in the past! So go! Now!" whispered Baazli.

"Grief? What grief? We are friends, Baazli."

"It is because of you I trod on the wrong path. I and my

brother both. Fortunately, I realised in good time."

Dymondo gained consciousness and heard the voices, but he did not move or turn. He wanted to hear the conversation, so he listened closely, keeping his back to both the serpent and the bear.

"Baazli, Baazli," laughed the snake in his sinister voice. "I bring you a message from your brother, the great red bear, Baazla. He misses you!"

"No! He is not my brother anymore, and you are not my friend! Just go away, leave me to my chosen path!"

"Path?! You are nothing but a donkey to that man. His mount! If you wish, you can tear that man to shreds within moments. You are nothing but a slave to him."

"I am his mount, and for me, this is more honourable than standing beside my brother in wrong deeds. In dreams, I see the both of us standing on opposite sides of the battlefield!"

"Ha-ha! Baazli, you are a bear!—a carnivore and a warrior. Why must you act like an ass? Come with me. Your brother awaits you. Together we can achieve everything! Do you know that King Shilathaar is gathering an army to wage a great war?"

Baazli remained silent.

"Baazla and I have given him our word that we shall stand beside him. I have come to fetch you. Join us."

"What is this great war? Whom does Shilathaar wish to kill?"

"Ha-ha! I am not stupid, Baazli. First give us your word that you will stand with us, and then you will know all!"

"No! I have left that life behind! I will not give you my word. I want none of it!"

"Stupid fool! Kill that man and come back to us!"

"I will stamp on your hood and snap your fangs, Sanpsarp, if you don't stop your nonsense! You know I am capable of that! Your venom cannot harm me. So slither away now before you anger me more."

The snake hissed in discontent.

"And if a drop of your venom poisons this river, then I promise I will hunt you down, and kill you! Animals of this forest drink from this water!"

"Just as they do in Lake Grit."

"So that is where you reside… in Forprimiera. How did you get here?"

"I witnessed the beautiful lights in the skies. They came from Gammafor."

Baazli did not reply.

"Did you see them?"

"I did."

"Do you know what caused them?"

"No," lied Baazli. "And even if I did, why would I waste my time talking to you about it."

"Temper, temper!"

Baazli remained silent.

"Fine don't tell me!"

"That light happened just today. How did you get here so fast?"

"*You* know *I* am capable of that."

"Right…I forgot."

"Join us, Baazli," the snake tried again.

"Leave!"

"Very well, Baazli… the great blue bear…have it your way. I guess I should stop calling you the great blue bear as there is only one great bear, the red bear, your brother, Baazla!"

"Away with you…now!"

"Before I go… I want you to know something…"

"Hiss it out and be gone."

"That human. Is that Dymondo? Shilathaar's brother?"

"What is it to you? Be gone!"

"I knew his father… Balathaar was it not?"

"How do you know him?"

"So, it is he, eh? His father had me do a task… when that boy was a baby."

"What did he have you do?"

"Interested, now are we? Ha-Ha!"

"Sanpsarp!" Baazli clenched his thunderbolt-like fist.

Sanpsarp gasped in fear. "Alright! He asked me to kill his wife's brother and the royal physician. In return, he gave me gems! I think their names were Marahud and…Ramos."

"King Balathaar is dead—"

"I know, you fool."

"Why do you tell me this…so I can tell him?"

"Yes," the snake hissed and smiled.

"Why?"

"Fine… don't tell him… I am going."

"Tell me, Sanpsarp!"

"They knew King Balathaar's secret! They were the only persons who knew"

"What secret?" Baazli asked, feigning ignorance.

"How would I know, you fool? Balathaar never told me, and neither did Marahud or Ramos before they died."

Baazli nodded.

"One more thing."

"Just hurry."

"I am concerned for you. If you stand with him and Shilathaar comes, then neither of you stand a chance. Shilathaar's army is gigantic—even bigger than Haask's army."

"I doubt that."

"Orakray sides with him. Blee sides with him. Baazla will side with him. I will side with him. And—"

"And?"

"Brog Sceptaro, Volglade, Hastinia Kral and Saji Miniscus will too."

Baazli now looked worried.

"Yesss…those names send shivers down your spine, don't they?"

"Only the name of Haask worries me."

Sanpsarp smiled at Baazli's attempt to look calm.

"All I am saying is…" the snake continued, acting humble, "…I respect you. You are a great warrior. But even with you, he will not be able to defeat Shilathaar. Dymondo doesn't have an army that compares with Shilathaar's. Join our side. Or else you will lose."

"Gratitude for the respect, Sanpsarp, and the offer, but I stand with Dymondo."

"Your loss," hissed Sanpsarp, lowering into the water.

"Watch the water, no poison!"

"Yes, yes," hissed Sanpsarp and submerged into the river.

Baazli sighed in relief. He looked back over at Dymondo to make sure he was still asleep then lay down and closed his eyes.

Dymondo did not sleep a wink after that.

CHAPTER 16

THE TEST

Afterward a restless night, Dymondo was very tired. In the early hours of the morning he managed to fall asleep, but only to be haunted by his same nightmare.

He saw himself and his brothers playing their game with Syterius and Syterius defeating Shilathaar many times, thus enraging him. He saw Shilathaar grabbing Syterius by his neck and pushing him toward the cliff of the mountain. He saw himself and Grygerious running after him with Grygerious inciting Shilathaar and Dymondo again shouting... "No!" "Stop, Brother!"

But then he saw something different. This time in the dream, Dymondo grabbed Shilathaar's shoulder and was able to pull him back slightly. But Shilathaar was too tough for him and still managed to push the poor boy to his death.

Dymondo rose instantly from his sleep panting and sweating. Baazli ran over to him.

"Are you alright? What happened?"

Dymondo still in shock did not answer.

"What happened?"

"Nothing."

Baazli was concerned. Dymondo had overheard the conversation between the bear and the other voice, which sounded to him like a large talking snake, and though he no

135

longer felt surprised by talking animals, he now felt cautious toward Baazli. Fortunately, the sun was shining brightly and the morning air had a beautiful, fresh scent as it blew gently across the water. Baazli went back to packing up the camp. Dymondo rubbed his eyes and stretched his arms high in the air. Then he stood up and headed towards the river. Baazli hurriedly walked up to him and offered Dymondo water from a sack.

"Best use this, my King. I drew it earlier."

The King was still half asleep and stared at the bear. He looked around, then put his hands together and allowed Baazli to pour. He washed his face and eyes before drinking some, then turned to gather his belongings. Baazli sensed the tension between them and decided to come clean.

"Someone paid me a visit last night...whilst you were sleeping."

Dymondo stopped packing and turned towards him. Baazli had his full attention.

"Difficult to believe, but it happened to be a large snake...from the river."

No reply from Dymondo.

"The serpent tried to incite me against you. He told me to leave your side, but I refused." The bear finished and turned back to gather their items.

"Why?" Dymondo enquired.

"For various kinds of bribes."

"No, I mean, why did you refuse?" The bear stopped working, but did not turn around to face Dymondo.

"Another splash of water perhaps, my King, to awaken you from your sleep completely? Maybe then, you will start asking some questions that make more sense."

Dymondo had no reply. They finished packing and set on the path to Gammafor. After a time, they came to a large stretch and Baazli picked up speed. Neither of them spoke much during the journey.

For some strange reason, the return journey felt longer after the morning turned to midday, the two stopped for another break. Dymondo was still wrestling with his thoughts. The journey had been not only physically, but mentally and emotionally exhausting. However, it certainly had made Dymondo a tougher person than before he started. But still, there was too much to digest in such little time. Baazli knew this and chose to only answer when spoken to.

"It was wrong of me to assemble the weapon," said Dymondo.

"Yes it was. It was too early."

"Can I practice now? There is no one around."

"It doesn't matter. The light which emanates from the weapon is too strong if is not controlled."

"Then how can I control it?"

Baazli sighed. "Alright. Bring out the elements and slowly build the staff."

Dymondo did so.

"Now, before you attach the spearhead, clear your mind of any thoughts and focus on the spear and the power of God."

Dymondo followed the instructions, then slowly attached the spearhead. Again the spear shuddered and another bright beam was about to shoot up to whiten the skies. But before it could, Baazli took the weapon from Dymondo's hands and removed the spearhead.

"It is no use!" snapped Dymondo.

Baazli thought for a moment.

"Seek its permission."

"Seek what...?"

"Permission. Remember this is a divine weapon. A weapon of the Gods. Your birth may be divine, yet you must be humble. Seek the weapon's permission for it to allow you to wield it and to give you strength to control is insurmountable powers."

Dymondo did not argue. He decided to listen to his mentor, and humbly took the weapon from Baazli.

"O great weapon! Bestow upon me your powers and give me permission to wield you against evil and all the dark forces that threaten righteousness! Give me the strength to control your power!" said Dymondo to the weapon before re-assembling the spearhead.

The experience was different this time. The light still shone from the weapon, but not as bright as before and no longer irradiating the sky. The weapon was still difficult to control, but it didn't vibrate like before.

Baazli's face lit up with joy.

"Yes!"

"It's working…!"

"Yes it is, but remain calm! Now slowly swing it in the air. Slowly!"

Dymondo did as he was told. As he rotated it, the spear slicing the heat and dust in the air, making noises as it moved. But it was still difficult to control. It was just too powerful.

"Steady on! Focus. Keep your eyes fixed upon your target. Focus on that large rock," said Baazli pointing towards a large boulder next to them on the ground.

Dymondo focused and swung the spear across the rock. He was able to cut into the rock with the weapon as though it was warm butter, but midway, it got lodged.

"Don't lose focus, do not take your eye off your target! Concentrate!" shouted Baazli.

Dymondo nodded, regaining his focus and was able to glide the weapon the rest of the way through the rock, cutting it in half.

"Amazing! It cut through the stone!" Dymondo could not believe his eyes.

"Now thrust the spear into one of the halves of the rock."

Dymondo again followed Baazli's instructions. At the first attempt, the spear just ricocheted off the rock and caused Dymondo to fall backward. The spear made an enormous clashing sound as it threw him back.

"Focus! Believe in who you are! You are the Son of God. Focus on God." It was as if Dymondo could hear both Baazli's voice and the voice of the shrub at the same time.

Dymondo nodded, brushed himself off, cleared his mind and tried again.

At the second thrust, the rock shattered into pieces.

"Astonishing!"

"Isn't it just?!" Baazli was very excited. "Now put it away."

"A little more," Dymondo asked, lost in his own excitement.

"Alright, then, hurl it at the other half of the rock," instructed Baazli.

Dymondo obeyed and the spear pierced straight through the rock.

"That was better," praised Baazli. "Now when you remove it, again focus, as the spear is lodged deep into the stone."

Dymondo walked up and waited, looking at the weapon. He closed his eyes and bowed his head.

"Yes!" whispered Baazli to himself.

Dymondo pulled it out with one hand.

"Bravo!" shouted Baazli. "Now let's put it away."

Dymondo nodded, but still kept on practicing his swing and thrust.

"I am going to gallop ahead, atop that large hill," said Baazli, pointing. "I need to see our path ahead. It is taking us longer to get back than expected, so I want to determine our route. I shall collect more water on the way back. Will you be alright for a few moments?"

"Of course, go on ahead."

"Put the spear away now, Dymondo."

"Yes, I will," Dymondo assured him, but as Baazli left for the hill, Dymondo kept on swinging his new weapon and continued practising.

Suddenly, he was encircled by ten masked men. They emerged from behind hills, trees and rocks, surrounding him from all directions. They approached and began jumping, kicking and somersaulting in the air around him, displaying their acrobatic skills.

"Who are you and what do you want?!" asked Dymondo sternly.

"We want that glowing rod, the one you hold in your hand. Hand it over, now!"

The ten men attackers all unsheathed their daggers from their waist belts and moved in gradually.

"Hand it over and we will not hurt you…much!" They all

laughed.

"You don't know how powerful this weapon is. Back off!"

"Then show us it's power!"

Dymondo got angry and as he did, the spear began to tremble again, making it difficult for him to swing or thrust it. He tried a few times and missed the men completely and in return received two punches to the stomach and one stiff one across the face.

"Powerful is it?" They laughed. "Hand it over…boy!"

"I am not a boy!"

Dymondo's face was blue from bruises and red blood appeared on the side of his lips. He realised he needed to clear his mind, remain calm and focus. He remembered Baazli's words and focused hard. The first two men came forth towards him and he swung the spear across their bellies, halving both of them. The other eight men grew frightened and all of them stepped back.

Still, two mustered the courage and came forth once again, but only to receive a thrust each from Dymondo's spear to their chests. The two men went down and the spear shook even less. Dymondo was relaxing. Two more approached and with one swing Dymondo parted their heads from their bodies. The next two changed their tactic. They approached in a line; one behind the other. Dymondo hurled the spear straight through the first man and right through the second, pulling it out of them before anyone else could get their hands on it. The two collapsed to the ground.

With confidence, Dymondo turned to the last two men. "Be gone unless you want to meet the fate of your friends!"

One of the remaining attackers sneered at Dymondo. "You thought there were just ten of us? Ha-ha!" He whistled loudly and it echoed across the hills.

Within moments, more masked men appeared from behind the tress and the rocks. They were too many to count. All sprung onto Dymondo like a pack of wolves, but Dymondo held tight to the spear. He could not lose it. Dymondo could not fathom where the strikes came from. He took many hits to his face, his chest, his stomach, and legs. His breast plate was now mangled and blood started flowing from his wounds. Bile from his mouth spurted out. His grip, however did not loosen on the weapon. Still, the pain was becoming too much for him to endure. He curled into a ball on the ground and the men kept kicking and hitting him. Some of the men tried to snatch the weapon from him, but he held fast to it.

Amidst the beating, Dymondo saw a vision from his nightmare in broad light: how he was not able to stand up to Shilathaar and save Syterius. Again, he saw the boy fall off the cliff to his death. He felt sick. Then Baazli's words began to drum into his ears.

"Focus...Believe in who you are... You are the Son of God...You are the Son of God!"

He cleared his mind and began to relax and focus. Gathering his strength, he swung the spear fast in a great circle. The ten or twenty men that had been kicking him now all wailed in agony as the swing of Dymondo's spear had cut off their legs. Blood spurted from their severed limbs, turning the dry ground red.

Dymondo rose from the ground and let out a battle cry, and without aggression he stood still awaiting the next attack. There were many other masked robbers still around him, jumping and kicking the air, but no one dared come forward.

"Don't let him regain his confidence!" shouted what seemed to be the leader of the pack. "Without his confidence, he is nothing! You are no match for all of us put together! You will fall!" he roared and all the other masked men laughed.

Dymondo's heart sank as his head heard those words. The spear began trembling again. He looked up at them again and as they laughed at his helplessness, he saw Shilathaar and Grygerious in all of them. Dymondo clenched his eyes and again recollected Baazli's words.

"Focus...Believe in who you are...You are the Son of God!" He shut his eyes and again his nightmare appeared. *No!* He thought, *I am not going to let him die again!*

This time in his vision, he saw himself do something that he thought he'd never be able to do. He managed to pull Shilathaar back with an unknown strength, sending him crashing into Grygerious and eventually to the ground thus saving Syterius from the fall. He then saw himself standing over Shilathaar and Grygerious, both lying on the ground looking up at him with fear in their eyes, and he spoke. *No! I will not let this happen!*

He opened his eyes. His heart was at ease and he was content. He had saved Syterius. He was no longer helpless against his unrighteous brothers. He had stood up to them. And he no longer saw Shilathaar and Grygerious in his enemies.

"You are wrong, you filthy bastard! You are no match for me! Let's fight!"

Dymondo leapt upon them like a battle lion. Not one of them could get close to him after that. They had no answers for his controlled swings and his low and high lunges. He parried their daggers with ease, spinning the spear in mid-air, displaying great spirit and deadly technique. One by one, all the men went down save for their leader.

Dymondo walked up to him slowly.

"No confidence, eh?"

"Forgive me, let me go!" begged the man.

"Fuck you! Tell me who sent you to attack me?"

By the time Dymondo put the question to him, Baazli had galloped down the hill and found the ground filled with bodies. Severed heads and limbs were scattered everywhere, and the soil was caked with blood.

"I cannot. Spare me, please," the man begged again.

"Never."

"What on earth happened here?" enquired Baazli.

"Speak!" Dymondo was too busy interrogating his captive to notice Baazli's return.

The mercenary went down on his knees and begged for mercy.

Dymondo used the tip of the sharp spear to leisurely cut across the man's belly. The masked robber screamed in agony as he tried holding his inner organs inside with his hands.

"Please, please, kill me! I can't bear this pain!"

"No not until you tell me. I am happy to wait."

The man screamed and cried, finding it hard to keep his inner organs contained. Blood gushed everywhere.

"The choice is yours. I can wait and watch you suffer, or you can tell me and I can make it a quick death for you."

"I will tell you! But kill me right away!"

Dymondo nodded.

"King Shilathaar. He sent us a message by messenger bird to attack and kill you, then head to Forprimiera to collect our reward."

"You lie!" screamed Dymondo.

"I do not!"

"How did you know we were here?"

"The message said to follow the bright light and that you were last seen by the banks of river Krool."

"Sanpsarp," said Baazli.

Dymondo's eyes filled with tears upon hearing of this treachery, but he remained calm and lifted his head. He slowly placed the spear into the robber's open mouth and plunged it through the back of his head.

"Rather unfortunate news, King Dymondo," Baazli said after a moment.

"Yes." Dymondo was trying to keep his tears in. "It seems the shrub and Quilliblade both tell the truth."

"So it has begun,"

"Yes it has begun,"

"My King, do not make any foolish mistakes. This is an indirect attack not a direct attack."

"What difference does it make?"

"It matters much. We cannot react in any way. We *must* not. We certainly cannot launch an attack or even reply to this."

"I am not a coward! I *will* reply to this."

"We are not ready! We need allies!" roared Baazli.

Dymondo flapped his arms in anger.

"However…"

"However what?"

"*You* seemed to be ready," smiled Baazli, eyeing the Emispear. "Seems as though you've got the hang of it."

Dymondo smiled.

"More practice, I reckon," he replied.

The impressed Baazli nodded in agreement.

"But I suppose I cannot be carrying it around with me all the time now can I?"

Baazli nodded. "You're right. It cannot be out in the open."

"So how do I keep it safe?"

"What do you like wearing the most in terms of jewellery and trinkets?"

"What does that have to do with it?"

"It has everything to do with it. Just tell me."

"If I had to wear a piece of jewellery all the time, then I would prefer it to be a bracelet"

"Very well. Now I will whisper something into your ear and you have to then close your eyes and say those words in your mind—not out loud—and see what happens."

Dymondo agreed, and Baazli walked up to him and whispered the words. Dymondo closed his eyes and spoke them in his mind. He opened his eyes once he had done so.

The spear flew out of his hand, changed form from a spear to a bracelet, then floated back to him and went around Dymondo's wrist. The Emispear now appeared as a smooth, solid-gold bangle.

"That's easy to carry around, is it not?" asked Baazli.

"And if I want it to become a spear again?"

"Ah, yes I forgot! Then you say…" He again went close and whispered the words. Dymondo again carried out the instructions and the bangle became a spear again.

"Amazing!"

"After all, it is the weapon of the Gods. Now turn it back to the bracelet."

"What if I want it to be a medallion or a ring or—"

"I will give you those chants when we get back," smiled Baazli.

CHAPTER 17

BELIEF AND RELIEF

When they got near the entrance to the Kingdom, Dymondo asked the great bear to stop, and dismounted. Before he met his men, he needed to address his own insecurities.

"Baazli, I am finding it difficult to believe in everything that has happened in the past few days."

"I can imagine, my King?"

"Do you believe that I am honestly equipped to handle the responsibility of the Emispear, the Frozenfire?"

"No, you still need more practice with it. But you did well against those men," smiled Baazli.

"And the war?"

"You need more allies and more weapons to help you, then you will be ready."

"But do you believe I can prevail?"

"*You*...my King?"

"Yes me!

"No."

"You don't? I don't follow."

"*You* cannot my King...*We*, on the other hand, can."

Dymondo smiled. "Fine, you're right and I am wrong," he

agreed.

The bear stood taller and seemed upset. "I serve you and you must always remember that. No enticement can part me from my path. Please believe me. I have full faith and trust in you, my King. Do you have the same in me? If not, then we have failed already. You and I may have to face more incidents like last night in the future. If another situation arises, then will you cast your suspicious eyes upon me again?!" The bear's voice had built to a roar.

"Be calm, Bear!" snapped Dymondo.

"Pardon me, my King." His voice lowered, along with his head.

Dymondo too dropped his head and they both eyed the ground in silence.

"Baazli, I am experiencing many emotions at present, and I am having trouble knowing who or what to trust, but I do trust you. Otherwise I would not have allowed you to accompany me this far, and to spend so much time with you alone. But you must understand, the events of the past few days have been difficult to comprehend. My mind needs rest. We will talk at great length once I have cleared my head."

With that, Dymondo headed towards the Kingdom with Baazli following. The bear understood, but he was still ill at ease.

"My King I have to tell you something else."

"What is that?"

"The night when I spoke to the serpent, he told me something peculiar. He said—"

"I heard your entire conversation, Baazli. I was not asleep."

"You what?"

"Yes."

"Then why didn't you mention anything?"

"I didn't need to, Baazli. You came clean the following morning, and you have come forth of your own accord today to tell me the rest. If there was anything else for me to know, I knew you would have told me in good time. I have full faith that you will tell me everything when the time is right."

"I hope the King is not upset with me for the delay."

146

"No, Baazli. As I said, I trust you, so no need to be worried. I do however wish to know one thing."

"What is that, my King?"

"How did you know of Quilliblade?"

"There are four keepers of the divine weapon, my King. Quilliblade is the demi god who kept the spearhead. Likewise the shrub is a divine deity, and I along with the red bear, Baazla, was given the responsibility to guard the other two parts," said Baazli.

"Does that mean you too are a demi god?"

"No."

"But why—"

"That I shall tell you later," interrupted Baazli.

"You mentioned in the Aquacaves about using this weapon against my brothers. How did you know my brothers were planning to move against me?"

"Quilliblade, the celestial bird, came to meet me in the Aquacaves before coming to warn you about your brothers. He wished to behold the parts of the divine weapon before he sent you on your quest. Quilliblade mentioned to me your brothers were planning to move against you. That is how I knew."

"And what of your brother, the red bear?"

"When the time is right, I shall tell you about me and Baazla."

"Very well," smiled Dymondo.

But inside, Dymondo was battling, but also digesting. He had discovered much over the past few weeks, and it was overpowering. He needed time to rest his mind before putting together all the pieces. He thought hard as they moved towards the entrance. He thought about what he had discovered through Baazli's conversation with the serpent.

Sure enough, it was dusk of the third day when the King arrived at the edge of his Kingdom. Sterferep and the others bowed and kneeled as their King walked up and the Lance immediately sent for the King's chariot to take him to the royal palace.

"Good to have you back, my King," said Sterferep, shaking Dymondo's arm strongly, noticing a strange new confidence on his face as he came forth.

Awaiting at the gates were many Lances, the royal steed, the royal carriage and Dymondo's royal chariot.

When Baazli came into view, the lower-ranked guards recoiled and drew their spears.

"My King, please stand back, there is a giant bear behind you!" one said.

"At ease, men!" commanded Dymondo. "The great bear is my friend, and you must treat him as such. He will accompany me to the royal palace and be given one of the best chambers in the tower, near my chamber."

"As you wish, my King. Does this bear speak like the hawk did the other day?" questioned another guard.

"Yes, he does. He is humble and friendly. No one needs to fear him, and I would like this announcement to be made to all our citizens. This bear is to be treated like royalty and to be given the same respect that is given to my family, friends and guests. Any insult towards him will not be tolerated!"

"Of course, my King. O great King of Bears, you are most welcome. Please enter and grace our city with your presence," said the guard to the bear.

Baazli was speechless. After the tension of the morning, this gesture from Dymondo gave him some relief.

"Come, Baazli. Come in my friend," Dymondo added with a gentle smile.

Both Baazli and the King were given a hero's welcome as they crossed into the Kingdom, and the citizens continued to cheer as Sterferep, Kor, Dan and Dwarpal followed on their steeds. Dymondo kept quiet throughout the journey back to his palace. Instead of mounting his elegant horse, Badal, he confined himself to the carriage and drew the velvet curtains from inside.

Sterferep took charge and led the others on their journey back to the palace.

Dwarpal, rode next to Sterferep.

"The King?" he asked.

"He's fine," Sterferep replied.

"His curtains are drawn. I'm worried for him."

"Ha-ha! Don't be worried, Dwarpal! Kings go through many emotions in just one day. I wouldn't be so troubled." Sterferep's consoling words covered his own concerns. He was a leader. He could not trouble the minds of his men by feeding into their worries.

"Will he be well enough for court?"

"Fret not, Dwarpal! The King is fine. But I do not believe there will be an assembly just yet."

"Never know. Courtier Majesma may be waiting at the gate with his never-ending list of queries! Ha-ha!"

"He means well, Dwarpal. You must not mock him so."

"*He* is the mockery. The man is a jester! He cannot think straight!"

"You abhor him, do you not?"

"Abhor is a strong word, Sterferep. Let's just say I do not have any respect for him."

Sterferep smiled and said nothing.

Dwarpal then starting singing: *"He's nothing but a sack of flour, sack of flour, sack of flour. He's nothing but a sack of flour…one day which shall be dough!"*

Sterferep couldn't help but laugh out loud.

As they passed through the city, night fell, but the citizens remained outside, cheering and waving at the royal carriage. Upon entering the palace gate, the King emerged and set foot on the ground. Sterferep ran up to him before anyone else.

"My King, is all well?"

"Yes Sterferep, gratitude. I now wish to retire to my chambers. Baazli, please would you follow me?"

"Certainly," came the reply.

"Dwarpal and I shall accompany you right away. Kor, you help the men with the belongings," said Sterferep. Kor nodded and went to work.

Dymondo started walking inside, and Sterferep promptly gestured to Dwarpal to follow. They rushed in with the King, while the King walked on ahead, keeping quiet until he reached his chamber. Dymondo personally showed Baazli to his chamber, which was one of the largest and most beautiful chambers in the tower. It had high ceilings and all the comforts Baazli could ever imagine.

"You grace us with your presence, Baazli. Please rest now, and if you need anything, please ask one of the guards, and they will attend to you. For now, I must go for someone awaits me in my chamber."

Baazli nodded. "Gratitude."

Dymondo half-smiled and asked, "Is there anything else that will help you get a good night's rest?"

Dymondo knew the bear was content after the talk, but Dymondo himself wanted to make sure. Baazli saw this and replied, "No, my King. Again…gratitude."

Sterferep and Dwarpal looked on as Dymondo walked up to Baazli, held his arms out to him and embraced him gently. "You are my friend, Baazli, and I trust you. *We*, as you said, can do this and will do this," said Dymondo.

Baazli's heart was filled with joy. "That is all I wanted to hear. Rest assured, I am not going to leave your side that easily," he said with a relieved smile on his face. Dymondo too was relieved.

"Great to have you with us, O great Bear," said Sterferep.

Dwarpal, Baazli, Dymondo and Sterferep all smiled at each other.

"You both need your wounds tended to. I'll send…"

"Just minor scratches, Sterferep. Goodnight, my friend," he said.

"Goodnight, my King."

Dymondo walked back to his chamber with the belief that great accomplishments were on the horizon. Baazli rested too, relieved and delighted to have gained such a powerful ally.

"Thank you, men!" Dymondo said once Baazli had gone inside. "We shall meet in court!"

The men bowed. "My King."

Dymondo walked off.

"He seems…different," said Dwarpal to Sterferep.

Sterferep smiled. "Indeed he does."

As Dymondo entered his chamber, Mysteria was waiting for him. She had just bathed and was wearing a gorgeous, silk, red dress, complimented by a golden necklace. He found her half-reclining on the bed and staring out into the starry night through the chamber window. Her gaze fell upon him, and she slowly rose from the bed. Dymondo walked up to her and took her by her slim waist and brought her nearer to him. They gently kissed for a long time and softly withdrew.

"I missed you, my King," she whispered.

"I missed you too, my love," he kindly replied.

"You were gone so long, dear," she said.

"I must bathe, for I carry the dust and filth from the journey…but you smell wonderful."

"O, my King, I have longed to be in your arms for days, and now you want to keep me from you longer?"

"Mysteria—"

"Be silent, O ruler, and just take me in your arms. Your scent does not repel me but draws me towards you. I cannot resist it. I forbid you to leave for the baths," she whispered.

Dymondo could not resist her either. He was mesmerised by her beauty and her passion. "So be it."

"Uh-uh!" She stopped him from coming nearer. "No garments permitted my King. These are the Queen's orders," she said passionately.

"Dymondo brought his lips near to hers. "A good leader follows her own rules," he mischievously answered.

She slowly stepped back and unclipped the golden broach holding the dress to her shoulder, and the silky dress dropped to ground revealing her beautifully shaped body. She stood completely unclothed before him. He swiftly removed his own garments, and as soon as she saw his strong chest, she moved toward him, pressing her breasts and pert nipples tight against his skin and letting out the largest sigh of relief:

"O, you cannot imagine how much I missed this!" she exclaimed.

He stared into her intoxicating eyes and they gave each other a passionate kiss as they fell onto the soft bed. After they kissed, Dymondo rose from the bed to snuff out the lamps in the chambers. The only light that entered now was the sinking sun and the mounting moon, which shone straight through the window and onto the bed, where the Queen lay waiting. She looked stunning. Dymondo returned to her caring arms and on top of the warm sheets, they made love before falling into a deep and peaceful sleep in each other's arms.

CHAPTER 18

THE MEETING

Three days had passed since Dymondo had returned from his journey, yet he had taken no great action. Dymondo spent the time with his Queen, trying to understand his findings. He thought hard for three days. Then, on the fourth day, he convened his court.

The Gammans were both shocked and excited to see Baazli in court that day. During the King's initial announcements, the courtiers could not take their eyes off the great blue bear. Great foods were prepared for the special guest, and Dymondo ordered a special chamber constructed for Baazli which would allow for plenty of room for movement. Baazli was gratified.

After a lengthy court session, Dymondo sent for his ministers and trusted friends and called them into a large discussion hall. The chamber was a discrete space draped in red and pink curtains with a large silver throne flanked by comfortable silver seats. No man could enter unless they had a special scroll signed and sealed by the King himself. Lances guarded the chamber and would only let those in possession of the scroll inside.

Dymondo rarely held meetings in this room, but when he did, all attendees knew that a grave matter was to be discussed.

Prime Minister Kriptus Magnus was the first to enter, supporting a clean-shaven look. He took his seat and waited. Majesma Lahall and Olivious Herrerous followed shortly after and the three greeted each other. A few moments later, the weak chief researcher and scholar, Lorca Loray, hobbled in with Defence Minister Urayu Dero. Olivious went over to Lorca and put his arm around his shoulder—a gesture that was well received as everyone respected the old scholar. Olivious helped him to his seat and went back to his own. After some delay, Lance Sterferep Unknown and Lance Kor Grayish entered, along with Dan Smoten and Dwarpal Kentish. All the courtiers greeted the four strong men, who returned their gestures. The Lances had come laden in their best armour with their finest blades at their sides, as did the guards.

Kriptus was the only one not pleased to see them. He expected only courtiers, ministers or people of proper standing to attend the meeting and gave Sterferep an evil glare.

"What is taking the King so long?" asked Kriptus, fidgeting.

"The King is never late! We are early, my lord," replied Sterferep.

"Yes, of course!" said Kriptus avoiding any further conversation with Sterferep.

"I wonder what this will be about." Majesma said to change the topic.

"My dear lord, Majesma, have patience. You worry too much," jested Dwarpal as he and all others took their seats. Majesma chose not to respond. He found Dwarpal to be very sarcastic and outspoken. Majesma was a simple man: soft spoken. Dwarpal did not believe he was qualified enough to be a fundamental courtier, yet he still enjoyed engaging in conversation with the plump, bald man.

Shortly after, the respected Commander-in-Chief of the Army entered, Hitius Opecious.

The Lances and the guards stood up for him and greeted him. A powerful figure, Hitius was a middle-aged man with the great responsibility of protecting the borders of Gammafor and Fourtfor, hence he was ridiculously busy. Sterferep admired the man, but Urayu the defence minister and Hitius did not see eye to eye.

"How do you fare now, Scholar Lorca?" asked Sterferep.

"I...I am as well...as I can be," stuttered Lorca. His voice was weak and there was whistling sound coming from his chest. He seemed be deteriorating at an accelerated rate.

"I'm sure he is fine, Sterferep, especially after his evening of entertainment," laughed Kor.

"I merely chose to rest during my time off," clarified Lorca abruptly.

"I wish you the very best of health," said Sterferep.

"Gratitude, Sterferep... you...you are kind." Lorca's eyes were drowsy and his neck drooped to one side. Everyone empathised with him.

Dan was on his best behaviour, sitting up straight and alert, patiently waiting for the King. Sterferep noticed this and put his arm on Dan's strong young shoulder and shook him out of his tension. They both exchanged smiles.

Baazli entered last with Puyol, ducking his magnificently large frame under the doorway. His blue fur shone after having been bathed, and he was dressed in a large, white tunic which went down to his knees and came laden with a golden breastplate. He looked like a warrior. Everyone greeted him in awe and he pleasantly returned their greetings.

Shortly after, King Dymondo entered and all stood up. "Greetings everyone, do remain seated," he said and walked up to his throne. He turned to his assembly and everyone sat down after him.

"I have called this meeting after much deliberation. I wish to both inform you and warn my most trusted advisers of the coming dangers we may have to face!"

"What dangers, my King?" asked Majesma.

"Worried already, courtier?" chuckled Dwarpal. Majesma gave Dwarpal an evil stare.

"Worried we all should be," corrected Dymondo.

"Apologies, my King," replied Dwarpal. Majesma looked at Dwarpal in disgust and then at the King.

"I admire your courage, Dwarpal. No danger worries you. But complacency can also be foolish. We need to be vigilant…all of us!" Sterferep gave Dwarpal a look and Dwarpal lowered his eyes.

"While there has been no direct indication, I fear Forprimiera is preparing for war!"

Several looks were exchanged between the others.

"I visited Forprimiera with Sterferep, Kor, Dan and Dwarpal and while we were there, my brother, King Shilathaar, showed me the strength of his army. He has accumulated quite a force and great deal of weapons. King Shilathaar's soldiers were training as if war is upon them. I observed weapons being tested, catapults and cannons at the ready, arrows being dipped in poison and blades being sharpened!"

"Forgive me, my King, but that could have been routine training. We do such practice here in Gammafor all the time," spoke Hitius.

"I understand, Hitius, but this was different. No doubt we are prepared and we carry out training exercises, but this was not typical training or preparation for national defence. This was preparation for an attack! Therefore, I believe we may be invaded soon, and we must strengthen accordingly. I will not launch an attack on anyone, but I will most definitely not leave us vulnerable to one!"

"Make no mistake, gentlemen. King Shilathaar is preparing for war. He is surely plotting something," continued Sterferep, "We must prepare if we're going to face this onslaught."

"But my lord, King Shilathaar is your brother! Why would he do such a thing?" asked Olivious.

"Please, Minister Olivious, do you truly believe both Shilathaar and my brother Grygerious are content that I have two islands of Landsfor under my control?"

"My King…no one—"

"Yes, Prime Minister Kriptus! No one calls it that! I know!"

"My King…the preparations?" interrupted Majesma.

"Yes, I have already given orders to strengthen our walls and sharpen our weapons. But I am worried. Are we powerful enough to withstand such an attack if they do indeed launch one?"

"Why do you ask this, my King?" asked Baazli.

"Shilathaar has sought help."

Everyone gasped in fear and murmured amongst themselves when they heard this.

"Then we are doomed!" cried Majesma.

"I will not entertain negativity!" shouted Dymondo.

"Apologies, my King," replied Majesma.

"Pathetic!" said Dwarpal under his breath, but Sterferep heard him and gave him a reprimand.

"Nevertheless, he has the armies of Orakray with him. They have great generals such as King Orayus Laaris himself, Crown Prince Kratos Laaris and Prince Yatus Laaris, and four of the most invincible warriors: Brog Sceptaro, Volglade, Hastinia Kral and Saji Miniscus. They are brutes! Shilathaar also sought aid from Blee. So, he has the backing of brother Grygerious, King Pharose Godsay and his son, the Crown Prince of Blee, Helemanen Godsay, not to mention the entire the army of Blee: a ferocious force in its own right. And there is one more concern. If there is war, then the great red bear, Baazla, and the mighty serpent Sanpsarp may too fight under Shilathaar's banner," announced Dymondo. Everyone looked terrified after hearing the line-up of warriors.

"Baazla has no army! I will crush his head to the ground!" shouted Baazli. "If they have the great red bear on their side, then King Dymondo has the great blue bear on his side!"

"But Sanpsarp can gather an army of serpents to fight, can he not?" asked Dymondo.

"My King, I have an answer to that," stated Baazli. "But first let me clarify something. I agree that Shilathaar is perhaps gathering an army. But you have sung too many praises of their warriors. You too have the greatest fighters in the realm. And you, yourself, are a tremendous fighter. And what of your Lances?! They are the finest fighters in the entire realm. One of your Lances is easily equal to three of their soldiers!"

"Hear hear!" Sterferep and Kor interjected.

"And let us not forget, we have God with us and righteousness is on our side. If there is a war, we will win!"

"I also have you, do I not, Baazli?"

"Of course, my King."

"My King, we are ready to take anyone on!" shouted Dwarpal.

"Wait!" interrupted Baazli. "Not quite yet," Everyone looked over at him.

"What is it, Baazli?" Dymondo asked.

"We are a great force, yes, but to battle some of the warriors, we too need allies! I know of a way to handle Sanpsarp's army. I speak of the Nevala warriors."

"Who are they?" asked Dymondo.

"Nevala are honourable creatures. They will side with you."

"But how can we be sure they would join our cause?"

"Because you are a righteous King, sire!"

"Creatures?" asked Kor.

"Yes, they are animals belonging to the Herpestes family. Grey in colour, with tails that are as long as their bodies. They can walk on two and four legs. They have long faces and long bodies with small rounded ears, short snouts, and oval eyes. They are covered in thick coats of fur and have long claws. Only the Nevala can fight and kill the serpents in Sanpsarp's army. They reside in the east."

"Why only the Nevala?" asked Sterferep.

"Venom. Sanpsarp is a hooded snake. He is highly venomous as are his snakes. We require an opponent that is invulnerable to venom and knows how to kill serpents. The Nevala are such creatures."

"But are you not insusceptible to venom?" Dymondo asked.

"True I am! And I can kill Sanpsarp singlehandedly and I can perhaps kill ten maybe fifteen snakes at one time, but what of the others? They will attack in force and our soldiers and Lances will be fatally injured. We need an entire army of creatures that can deal with the onslaught. And—"

"And?" asked Dymondo.

"Snakes are afraid of Nevala! Sanpsarp especially despises

158

Abariswidth Atiliax, the King Nevala, so you must become friends with him. Abariswidth is an honourable creature. If Sanpsarp has decided to side with Shilathaar, then Abariswidth may be encouraged to ally with you. He will never fight on the same side as Sanpsarp."

"Very well. Then I must find these warriors. Where can they be found?"

"They reside near the forest, in a cave," replied Baazli. "I can show you the way. But there is more."

"What, Baazli?"

"You speak of four great warriors. We need our own great warriors to match them, my King. I know of such fighters. Lansai is a great spear fighter and will challenge Hastinia Kral in spear combat. Arci is a bowman who can duel with the archer, Saji Miniscus. Lamino can face Volglade's sword, and Scipio's mace will answer Brog Sceptaro's flail. We need to get these four to fight for us."

"Great! Where can we find them?"

"In Haask."

Everyone murmured among one another and looked worried. Dymondo saw this and rose from his seat, causing the others to follow suit.

"Then Haask it is!" proclaimed Dymondo. "I, Dymondo Rain, the true ruler of Landsfor, take this pledge, that I will not allow any enemy to intrude on my land and disturb the peace of my people. With Baazli and with the help of all of you, I shall go to Haask, and not only seek out the four brave warriors to fight on my side but also extend the hand of friendship to the mighty King of Haask. I will convince him to join forces with us in this battle against unrighteousness!"

"Splendid!" said Puyol, accompanying the cheers of the others.

"But my King," said the pessimistic Majesma. "Haask has never accepted an alliance with any foreign Kingdom."

"Majesma this will be your last pessimistic remark. Although I appreciate you narrating the past to me, this is the present and we must fight for it and for our future!" announced Dymondo.

159

"I cannot do this alone. I need support from you all. The advice of the ministers and courtiers and the strength and power of my men. What has not happened till now, will happen in the future. Haask will become our ally!"

"So you're not capable of doing this by yourself?" asked Kriptus with a smile.

Everyone paused and gave a stern look at Kriptus.

Dymondo looked over too and smiled back and nodded.

"Perhaps I am, perhaps I'm not. Who can truly say, Prime Minister Kriptus? But I can say for sure that if we work together as team, then we can certainly do it."

Kriptus smiled. He lifted his head and closed his eyes and began to nod as though he had won something. Everyone applauded, including Kriptus.

"Hail King Dymondo ruler of Landsfor!" everyone shouted.

As Dymondo walked out amidst the applause, the others remained and absorbed the vitality that Dymondo had spread throughout the chamber, enjoying its effects. Baazli said nothing and just smiled and nodded at Sterferep who too breathed a sigh of relief.

"Well, Minister Olivious, what do you have to say now?" asked Puyol.

"I feel ten years younger, Minister Puyol."

"Still room for improvement?"

"There always is, isn't there?" They both laughed.

"But seriously now what are your thoughts?"

"Our boy has become a man!"

"But many stern tests yet lie ahead for him, my learned men," added Baazli.

"And our King is ready to face them!" exclaimed Puyol.

Baazli bowed to him and left.

CHAPTER 19

WE MUST STRENGTHEN!

D ymondo was now focused on the task ahead, but strangely enough, after the meeting, what he longed for most was an embrace from Mysteria. Before she became his Queen, she had been his friend, and before he set off on his journey, he wanted to be in her arms.

He marched to his chamber in his marvellous clothes and armour and opened the door. There she was. Though now a Queen, she was a simple, young woman and remarkably beautiful. Mysteria's face lit up and widened into a smile as she beheld her man's loving gaze. Dymondo slammed the door shut behind him, walked up to her and grabbed her from the waist and kissed her. Though he had seen her just that morning, he had pined for her all day. He had missed her warmth, her scent, and her gentle touch. They passionately kissed for a long time.

"My, my!" she said. "Did you miss me, my King?"

"I did. Can you request the other maidservants to prepare some hot water? I desire a bath."

"Of course, my King."

"I would have you join me."

"Is that a request or a command, my King?" she spoke in her sweet, strong voice as she raised her head and looked him straight in the eyes.

"A most humble request, my lady."

"Granted," she whispered in his ear and kissed him.

The bath was prepared by young beautiful maidservants with hot, clean water, Rose petals and fabulously scented oils. Once prepared, the other maidservants were asked to leave. No one else stood in the bathing chamber except for Mysteria and Dymondo. Dymondo removed his clothes and entered the bath. Mysteria waited on the side with her eyes lowered and a reticent smile.

Finally, she untied the trinket holding her dress and let it flutter off her magnificent body. She was perfect. Round breasts with hardened nipples. Her dusky skin glimmered as the oils in the water moistened it. Her flat, oval face suited her golden eyes. She swam straight up to him and placed her bosom against his strong chest and put her soft, thin arms around his shoulders. He grabbed her by the waist and brought her closer as she wrapped her long, toned legs around him.

"My King has never been so passionate before," she spoke softly and pecked his lips.

"Now that is unfair, my lady. You know I enjoy your touch and it sometimes makes me wild."

Mysteria was enjoying this seduction. She kissed him and he savoured her flesh with his lips and hands, playfully biting her neck and softly kissing her behind her ears which drove her crazy. He rubbed the oil from the water onto her torso which gave it beautiful shine and definition. He osculated her nipples and blew air onto them so they would reach maximum pertness. He embraced her tightly yet softly. Mysteria enjoyed his passion and the love he showed, and she moaned without hesitance during intercourse, releasing herself and melting into his muscular arms. She squeezed his hard thigh muscles and firmly placed her heels against his firm bottom, savouring the fantastic sex he gave her.

Both slumped to the seats inside the bath and caught their breath. Dymondo placed his right arm on the side and the left around Mysteria. She sat closely to him, panting, with her head on his chest and hand around his stomach.

"That was amazing!" she said.

"Indeed, my lady."

"My King, today was special and different, do you not agree?"

"I do, my love," said Dymondo and cunningly placed his left hand on her soft left breast and began gently running his fingers around her taut nipple.

"My King!" she laughed. "You are obsessed with them!"

"I am obsessed with you, Mysteria."

Mysteria stopped smiling and looked into his eyes. She adored these moments and slowly grabbed the back of his hair and brought his face nearer so she could kiss his lips. Yet behind all this, she knew that something was bothering him.

"What is troubling you, my King?"

Dymondo's head slumped backwards and he took a deep breath. "Your man is in a dilemma!"

"What kind of dilemma, my King?"

"My brother."

"In Forprimiera?"

"Yes. Shilathaar. He is strengthening his armies."

"Every King must do that. One must always be prepared for battle."

"This is more, Mysteria. He is preparing to launch an attack on someone."

"Is it possible it could be Doosranfor?"

"I doubt that very much. He shares a good relationship with Brother Grygerious and even though Grygerious is frail, Brother Shilathaar knows that his father-in-law Pharose Godsay, the ruler of Blee, and his armies would come to Doosranfor's aid."

"Even then, if King Shilathaar and his father-in-law join forces and attack, surely they would best the armies of Blee and emerge victorious, would they not?"

"Perhaps, but—"

"But you think they are planning to attack Fourtfor or Gammafor."

"Correct."

"We must strengthen!"

"I have already given orders to prepare."

163

"And what of your trip to Forprimiera and journey to the Aquacaves? Was it successful?"

"It was, my lady."

"You retrieved the weapon?"

"I did."

"I wondered. All I have heard was of the magnificent blue bear who returned with you."

"Yes, Baazli. He saved my life and has been a great help to me. Worry not, my love, you will meet him."

"But where is the weapon?"

"Do you see the gold bracelet around my wrist?"

Mysteria's eyes grew wide. "Is it—"

"Yes. But do not tell anyone. It must be kept secret."

Mysteria draped her legs over his thighs and played with his chest. "So you have your weapon and your men. What else do you require?"

"Allies, my love. Baazli suggests I journey to Haask to secure their aid, and to go in search of other fighters who may be able to help us."

"Will you go?"

"Yes, very soon."

"Then what is the dilemma, my King? You were given advice, you heeded it and now you will act. That is why you are the rightful ruler of Landsfor."

"My lady, you shouldn't say such things to me. There are many challenges we yet face. You can't let me grow too proud."

"Never, my King," she smiled mischievously and moved to lift herself above him. "Let us enjoy this moment for now," she whispered, gently kissing his lips. "We can talk more later."

The next morning, Dymondo assessed his Kingdom's readiness for battle. He first headed to the Lance training grounds to gauge their proficiency, then walked around his palace and castle to observe the security. After that, he went to court. He asked his courtiers, Lances and commanders for progress reports on the securing of the walls. Defence Minister Urayu Dero informed him that work had already begun to strength the walls with more iron and cement, and that the number of soldiers and Lances that stood guard atop the walls had also been increased with those on guard ordered to inform their superiors on anything or anyone that approached. Lance Sterferep announced that other Lances had been ordered to set camp atop mountains and high peaks to keep watch on the waters and on all lanes of approach. This was not only for Gammafor, but for Fourtfor as well.

Commander-in-Chief Hitius Opecious had already been sent to defend the northern borders of Fourtfor and the royal castle with a great number of Lances handpicked by Sterferep and Kor. Meanwhile, Dymondo ordered more soldiers sent to the northern border of Gammafor and promoted Dan and Dwarpal each to the rank of Lance. They had worked hard and had finally passed their Lance test. Now that they were promoted, they were given the responsibility to train more Lances and increase the training levels, focusing on hand-to-hand combat and advanced weaponry.

Though many Lances were being deployed to the far reaches of the Kingdom, Dymondo ordered Sterferep and Kor to stay with him at Gammafor palace and castle as they were his most trusted aids and who he relied on most for the safety of his family.

After receiving his briefings and making his announcements, Dymondo asked everyone to disperse expect for Olivious, Majesma, Urayu and Puyol. He asked Baazli, Sterferep, Dan and Dwarpal and Kor to remain as well.

"This must not become public knowledge," he announced, "but I will be embarking on yet another journey on which Baazli, Sterferep, Dwarpal, Dan and Kor shall accompany me. In a few days, we shall ride towards the east and be gone for five days. However, we will depart in the dark of night so that no other person apart from us here can know of the expedition. If anyone dares utter a word, then I shall have no choice but to part their tongue from their mouth!" Everybody looked at one another. Majesma spoke up.

"The east, My King. You mean you are searching for—"

165

"My good man! What did I just say?! I go east. That is all you need to know. However, if we have not returned within those five days, then you will send men to come and search for us in that direction. That too must be carried out in secret. I do not wish for any person to know the King is absent from his Kingdom."

No minister questioned the vague instructions of the King any further, which was exactly what Dymondo wanted. Dymondo adjourned the meeting and the courtiers dispersed to their respective homes or chambers.

Dymondo, Sterferep, Dwarpal, Dan, Kor and Baazli filed out of court, and once they were outside, Dymondo spoke up.

"Baazli, come and visit me and tell me where in the east these Nevala warriors reside."

Baazli nodded.

Sterferep spoke up and suggested Lance Tamaris should be recalled to join the flanks, but Dymondo still did not wish to discuss the Lance's future until he had spoken with him directly. Everyone was again told he was away due to personal reasons.

CHAPTER 20

NEVALA WARRIORS

With the four Lances following behind, Baazli accompanied Dymondo to his chamber and while the Lances waited outside, the great bear ducked under the door and entered the room. Mysteria gasped when she saw the giant blue bear and instinctively bowed before him.

"Up, my Queen, for it is I who should bow before you," Baazli said, bowing before her.

Dymondo chuckled and took Mysteria's hand to help her to her feet. "My love, meet Baazli, my new royal mount."

"A pleasure," Mysteria smiled, still stunned by the talking bear now standing in her bedchamber. "I have been hoping to meet you since your arrival in the palace," she said.

"And I am honoured to meet you, my Queen," he said in his heavy voice and bowed again.

"The honour is mine, Baazli. Dymondo says you saved his life."

"I only did what was necessary to serve the realm," bowing once more.

"Oh enough with formality," Mysteria said and went running to him and gave him a hug. She only stood as tall as his chest.

Baazli laughed and hugged her back, but being aware of his immense strength, he too held her gently and with care. She then took him by his large paw and they walked over to the large chair, where Dymondo was now sitting.

"Baazli! I am happy to meet you finally, but I can tell, you and my husband have much to discuss."

Dymondo and Baazli were both surprised and impressed by this observation.

"My King, I am grateful you have chosen such a knowledgeable Queen!"

Mysteria smiled and Dymondo did too, impressed by his life partner.

"Forgive me, my Queen, but yes…you are correct. There is a task at hand, and our King needs my advice."

"Then speak Baazli and the King will listen," answered Mysteria.

"As you wish, my Queen. The Nevala, my King. You asked of them."

"Yes, Baazli. What can you tell me?" Dymondo asked, leaning forward.

"As I mentioned, they are animals that belong to the Herpestes family. The King must meet with them soon if we are to defeat Sanpsarp. Otherwise, we have no hope at all."

"So they, too, can talk and walk on two and four legs like yourself?"

"Yes, my King. But more than that, we require an ally that can face the serpent army of Sanpsarp. Nevala are immune to their venom, so snakes are afraid of them! Sanpsarp despises Abariswidth Atiliax, the King Nevala, so you must become friends with him."

"Is he friendly," Mysteria asked.

"Yes, my Queen. Abariswidth is an honourable creature."

"Then we must pay him a visit," said Dymondo.

"Yes," Baazli's replied.

"Where do the Nevala reside?"

Baazli went silent.

"Baazli?" questioned Dymondo.

"The Cave."

Fantastic, Dymondo thought. *Another perilous journey.*

"Wait!" Mysteria jumped in. "You don't mean *the* Cave?!"

Baazli did not speak.

Mysteria turned to Dymondo with concerned eyes. "My love, you are not going to the Cave," she protested.

"This is very important, my Queen," Baazli objected.

"Yes, but inside the great, dark Cave, there are creatures that reside in their own world deep underground."

"Yes, my Queen, you are wise indeed. You speak of the Nevala. Abariswidth is their King."

"I am their King!" Dymondo blurted out.

"My King, please, you must show humility. These creatures live in isolation and feed in the forest and jungle. They do not come across any of your citizens nor harm them."

Dymondo relented. "I need time to ponder this," he said deep in thought.

"But Dymondo, there is no time."

"Nevertheless, I need to be alone."

"Wait, husband," Mysteria said, placing her hand on Dymondo's shoulder. "Baazli, are you known to Abariswidth?"

"I am. He knows me."

"So you can make the introduction?"

"I can."

Mysteria took her husband's arm. "Dy, you must listen to Baazli and find a way to meet with Abariswidth, but Baazli…"

"Yes, my Queen?"

"Not the Cave!" she shook her head.

"Will he visit us?" Dymondo asked.

"No, my King…we'll have to go."

Mysteria looked at Dymondo with fear in her eyes and considered the great choice before him. Another dangerous journey with an uncertain outcome.

"So shall we head to the Cave?" Baazli persisted.

"Not yet," Dymondo said, touching Mysteria's face.

Baazli nodded and turned around in frustration.

"I take your leave my King," said Baazli and walked out.

"Why did you let him leave like that?" asked Mysteria after he had left.

"The conversation was over," said Dymondo.

"Call him back."

"But why? You yourself said 'not the Cave.'"

"I did. But by the sounds of it, there is no choice but to go."

Dymondo did not answer her back.

"I am recalling him!" she said and ran to door to call after Baazli. The great bear walked back in with Mysteria holding his large woolly arm.

"Baazli, can you insure an audience with this Abariswidth?" Dymondo asked.

Baazli contained his excitement and bowed. "Certainly, my King!"

"Then we will proceed with the expedition!" Dymondo proclaimed.

CHAPTER 21

TAMARIS

B efore they departed for the Cave, Dymondo agreed to finally accompany Sterferep to the dungeon. The walk down to the dungeon was tough for both men. A strange horrid taste formed in Dymondo's mouth and Sterferep's heart beat fast with worry.

What will happen? Thought Sterferep. *I hope all goes well. O Gods…help us.*

The large dungeon master greeted them and took them to the cell and opened it for them.

The prisoner sat there on a pile of hay in a corner with his head in his knees. It was evident he had been weeping. He looked up to the King and the Lance before him and fresh tears filled his eyes.

"My King!" he said and got up slowly, bowed and knelt. "I thought I'd never see you again. Greetings Lance Sterferep."

"Greeting Tamaris, up with you."

Tamaris got up. He looked thin and weak. He'd been doing push ups in the cell to maintain his shape, but it was not as effective as a Lance's training. He was not as toned as before, but it was clear he had tried his best.

"How do you fare?" asked Dymondo.

"Fare? I suppose well…" answered Tamaris.

171

What a stupid question to ask, Dymondo thought.

"Tamaris…"

"Before you say anything, my King, I seek your forgiveness. Please forgive me for I let you down."

"That you did, Tamaris," replied the King.

"Sentence me to death, my King, but I had no choice. I felt as though I was kicked in the guts when your mother ordered the woman dead and that I had to be the one to carry out the task. But if I had disobeyed her, then I would have disobeyed you, because you yourself said any command she gave superseded yours. I was lost. I felt so alone. I didn't know what to do."

"You could have told the King," said Sterferep.

"She forbade me from that course, dear Sterferep." Tamaris began sobbing.

Dymondo and Sterferep stood and watched this once strong man break down.

"My future is over, that I know. But I will only be able to die in peace once I know you both have forgiven me."

"I have already forgiven you," said Sterferep.

"Gratitude Sterferep. My King…?"

"Oromi is still alive, Tamaris. Yet she is unconscious. Every day that she battles for life, a ray of hope shines through. But still there is no revival. You tried to kill her."

"She tried to kill someone…your chief scholar, Lorca…and you gave her the guest chamber."

"Tamaris!"

"He's right, Dy," Sterferep backed Tamaris.

"I know what I did!" shouted Dymondo, turning to Sterferep with anger in his eyes.

There was silence. After a while, Dymondo placed his hands on his face and then shook his head.

"What do you think, Sterferep? That I don't love this fool like a brother, like I love you and Kor? I love this idiot…and I have kept that close to my heart." Dymondo turned away from both of them and removed his hands from his face.

"Then if you love me, Dy, forgive me."

"Don't Dy me, Tam…" Dymondo looked at him harshly, but at the same time he couldn't contain his smile.

Sterferep and Tamaris too smiled.

Dymondo walked up to him and embraced him tight. Tears began to flow from Tamaris's eyes.

"There, my strong man! Stop those tears," said Dymondo his eyes were numb too as Sterferep thanked the Gods that the King and Tamaris had embraced.

"So you forgive me?"

"I do, Tamaris."

"It could have happened to any of us three, Tamaris," Sterferep added. "Kor could have received the order to remove Oromi. I could have. But you should have spoken to us."

"I didn't know what to do, Sterferep. I went blank."

"Well let it be known. I am the King now. My orders are final!"

"I heard about Queen Ohio. My condolences."

Dymondo nodded in acceptance.

"Right…"

"So, is it the block for me or banishment?" smiled Tamaris with wet eyes.

"Block? Banishment? What on earth are you talking about?" asked Dymondo.

"Hung, Drawn, Quartered?" asked Tamaris.

Dymondo looked at Sterferep. "What on earth is he babbling?"

"Tamaris have you lost your mind?"

"I am just asking what my punishment will be."

"Ah…now I get you." Dymondo decided to jest with him and turned his back to him and winked at Sterferep. Sterferep understood and kept a straight face.

Dymondo turned back around and spoke with a stern expression. "First, Tamaris, we shall boil you in a cauldron, then hang you, draw you and quarter you. Then we will remove your limbs on the block and if you survive that, we will banish you," explained Dymondo.

Tamaris nodded stoically, accepting his punishment.

There was a silence in the cell until Sterferep burst out laughing.

"Great, tremendous integrity, Ster!" laughed Dymondo and both started laughing loudly.

Tamaris looked up at both of them confused.

"Don't be a fool, Tamaris! I don't intend to sentence you!" said Dymondo. "I was hurt—upset and angry with you, but not to the extent that I couldn't forgive you and keep you away from me."

Tears rolled down Tamaris's eyes at this, and Dymondo again hugged him tight.

"You're a friend, Tamaris, and friends are valuable and certainly not punishable."

"How can I thank you? Does that mean I am free to go?"

"What?!"

"Fuck no!" said Sterferep.

"You have a lot of work to do, Lance!"

"You still call me Lance?"

"You are a Lance! Are you not? Then you will remain one," clarified Dymondo.

"And my position?"

"Yes, that too with honour, Tamaris," Sterferep assured him. "King Dymondo said you were away on personal leave. No one knows anything apart from us friends."

"Oh gratitude, gratitude, my King! How can I ever repay you?"

"Just tell me before doing anything like that again...please," smiled Dymondo.

They all laughed.

"So who helped you whilst I was gone?"

"Dan and Dwarpal. They are Lances now!" announced Sterferep.

"Tremendous, if I knew anyone could rise to the task, it would be those two. But..."

"But what?"

"It took *both of them* to replace me?" winked Tamaris. They all laughed.

"Looks like we have our old Tamaris back," smiled Dymondo.

"I but jest. Great boys, those two," said Tamaris.

"Good to have you back. Now, for the task at hand."

"Yes, my King?"

"I am going on a journey."

"Let me come with you, my King."

"Next time, Tamaris. For now, we need you to resume your former role and see to your tasks. Get back into shape. See yourself to a nice bath and a sharp blade. Train hard and eat well. Regain your strength. By the time I have returned I need you ready for we will set off on the most dangerous quest of our lives."

"Where?"

"Haask!

CHAPTER 22

GIFT FROM THE GODS

As Dymondo prepared to depart for the Cave, Mysteria was on edge. She understood Baazli's point that in order to defeat Sanpsarp's venomous army, the Nevala would have to fight under Dymondo's banner, but she was apprehensive. Nobody wandered near the Cave, and no man had ever ventured inside. It was a forbidding place, therefore deserted. To ease her nerves, Mysteria demanded that Sterferep, Kor, Dan and Dwarpal go along with Baazli and Dymondo.

Thus the party set off on yet another journey outside the city gate toward a barren, stony field near the mouth of the jungle. There they found the Cave. From a distance, it looked like a large crater in the ground hidden behind a large rocky hill.

The five warriors reached the Cave on horseback with Baazli galloping alongside. The ground was dry from the heat and the large crater sat before them like a lion with its jaws wide open. Baazli immediately jumped inside and disappeared from view. When the others approached the edge they could see the bear standing on a lower level. Baazli then started down what looked like spiral steps that went deeper underground. He stopped after four steps and turned back.

"The first jump is deep. Be careful!" warned Baazli.

Sterferep jumped next and slipped the landing and grazed himself. "Ouch... Baazli is correct! Careful! The jump is deep!" Sterferep shouted up to them as he stood up.

Dwarpal went next and took a rough landing, falling forwards as he touched the ground, tumbling down three steps, and stopping at Baazli's feet. Baazli caught the Lance and lifted him up. It was Dan next. He fell flat on his face and ate the dust and tiny particle of rock as he smacked the ground. Sterferep helped him up. Next it was Dymondo's turn. He took Kor's hand and asked the Lance to lower him down, making his descent less dramatic. Kor then followed and his landing was not heroic either. Everyone brushed off the dirt from the rough start and started down the spiral steps behind Baazli.

The further down they ventured, the darker it got, until they reached an underground passage with glowing lamps on the either side of the walls. At the end of the passage, there stood two large Nevala warriors. Just as Baazli had described, they were incredible creatures and stood as strong and tall as humans.

"Halt!" shouted one of them and crossed his spear with that of the other Nevala warrior, preventing the guests from entering.

"I am Baazli, the great blue bear! I came a few days ago to visit King Abariswidth."

"Ah yes, the great bear! Do not enter for I know your history Baazla!" shouted one of them.

"I am not Baazla!" screamed Baazli. "He is *red*! I am Baazli! The great *blue* bear!"

"Blue good, red bad," whispered the other.

"No! Its blue bad, red good!" the other Nevala guard argued back.

"Apologies, Baazli, he is new, he does not know," corrected the seasoned guard. "You may enter...but who are these five?"

"This is King Dymondo, of Gammafor and Fourtfor and his friends."

"There is only one King, and that is King Abariswidth!" corrected the seasoned Nevala.

177

"True! Please can you send word, to King Abariswidth that Dymondo of Gammafor and Fourtfor seeks his audience?" asked Baazli politely.

The Nevala did not answer back and just left. The other unseasoned Nevala stood with his legs wide apart in front of Baazli, covering the entire entrance. "The blue is a bad bear!" he whispered.

"No dear Nevala, for you shall see for yourself!" answered Baazli, discontented.

Shortly after, the seasoned guard returned and pushed his colleague out of the path of the entrance.

"Enter!" he said to Baazli and the others. The other five kept quiet and followed Baazli in.

"Rude, aren't they?" whispered Sterferep.

"Ssh!" said Baazli.

They walked further in until an entire underground city came into view. There were countless Nevala. There were children, young, old, male and female. The families made their homes out of small craters and used other craters for small shops for Nevala vendors.

The four, led by Baazli, observed this new world in astonishment. Some Nevala stared at them as they passed, but they said nothing and continued with their lives. As Baazli walked through, some Nevala guards bowed to him. Baazli walked past many habitats and many vendors and headed towards another set of steps that led to another large hole: the Royal Crater.

Baazli took them straight up to Abariswidth's assembly hall, where it was full of strong Nevala warriors. The common Nevala were dressed in large linen cloths, while the warriors wore metal armour and carried spears. On the rock throne sat their King.

A fat Nevala announced Baazli's arrival in a squeaky yet clear voice:

"Bear Baazli enters!" It was evident that he was well spoken.

"Baazli!" shouted Abariswidth.

"King Abariswidth!" screamed Baazli.

"Enter! Who have you brought with you?"

"This is King Dymondo."

"There is only one King, that is King Abariswidth!" shouted Amasong, a strong Nevala warrior, sitting closest to Abariswidth.

"Quiet Amasong. True I am King, but there are many Kingdoms! Dymondo is King of his Kingdom." Amasong went quiet. "Fetch seats for our guests!" Rocks were placed as seats, and the working Nevala placed cloths over the rocks. "Please, take a seat."

As they sat, Dwarpal and Dan looked around in awe at all the Nevala congregated together. Sterferep kept a straight face. Kor too was observant but was trying not to make eye contact with any particular Nevala creature.

"So, King Dymondo Rain! What brings you here?"

"O great King. I seek your friendship."

"Honeyed words, Dymondo! I shall gladly accept your friendship. In any case, we live away from men. We do not trouble you and you do not trouble us. But I appreciate your gesture." His voice was strong and heavy.

"Gratitude, O great Nevala King."

"Is that all King Dymondo? Or is there something else you seek?"

"A great war is approaching, O King of the Nevala—a war so great, no warrior in the realm shall remain impartial. Every true and great warrior must pick a side. It will be the ultimate battle between good and evil. I come here not only to seek your friendship but your allegiance."

"Men engaging in war with other men…that has nothing to do with us, King," remarked Werther, another Nevala sitting very close to Abariswidth but on the other side. He was another strong warrior but spoke in a calmer tone.

"You live underground. Any war above ground does not concern us," added Abariswidth

"What if you found out Sanpsarp was involved? Would you not come to our aid then?" asked Dymondo.

"Sanpsarp! That wretch! He is my sworn enemy!" yelled Abariswidth and curled his paws into a fist.

"It is he whom we seek allegiance against. There are rumours that he has sided with our sworn enemy. Hence if the great war takes place, we shall be facing him and his army of snakes along with the other warriors in this realm. The only warriors who can defeat that poisonous beast and his army are seated before us now: the fearless Nevala!"

Amasong was pleased with the praise and nodded. Werther sat up straight with pride.

"Hmm…!" pondered Abariswidth and placed his paws on his snout. "You do not have a chance against him without us!" he laughed. Sterferep did not like his tone, but the creature was right.

"Yes, that is true," said Dymondo humbly. "However, with our combined armies and friendship, we can burn any army down!"

"We are very modest creatures, Dymondo. We are happy where we are," resisted Werther. "We do not wish to get involved. But, the final decision will be made by the King Nevala."

"We despise Sanpsarp!" Abariswidth said. "So, to finish him off, we can aid you, Dymondo. But putting my warriors and my people in danger and throwing them into an inferno does not seem wise."

"Then I cannot compel you further, my friend," said Dymondo and stood up. "If your heart tells you not to take part in the war, then you must listen. You are free creatures. I am the King of this entire land—this land on which your crater is situated, inside which your underground city flourishes. Yet I have accepted your claim."

Abariswidth stood up as did the other Nevala warriors and grabbed their spears. Sterferep, Kor, Dan and Dwarpal and the bear too rose from their seats. Sterferep placed his hand upon the hilt of his sword.

"This Cave is *ours*, Dymondo Rain!…Do not cross your limits!"

"You will call him *King* Dymondo Rain!" barked Sterferep.

"Go now, for I do not wish to partake in this war. If this snake is coming for you, then you will have to deal with it. I can promise you that we shall not fight in any army alongside that snake. That is all I can do for you. Now Baazli, please be so kind to lead these men out. The meeting is over."

"Abariswidth, you must listen to what I have to say—"

"Enough!" shouted Abariswidth. The Lances drew their swords and the Nevala pointed their spears as their King raised his voice.

The Nevala King walked over to Dymondo amidst the unsheathed swords and sharp spears.

"Listen to me, *King* Dymondo Rain. Leave at once and we shall allow you to go in peace. Otherwise you are no match for me," challenged Abariswidth.

Dymondo scoffed at his comment and lowered his head and put his hand over his mouth.

"Amusing was it, King? Would you kindly like to tell me why you find this humorous?"

Dymondo laughed under his breath trying to disguise it under a fake cough.

"Speak!"

"Apologies, Abariswidth but—"

"*King* Abariswidth!" shouted Amasong.

"Excuse Abariswidth, but…" Dymondo turned to Amasong. "What is your name, if I may ask?"

"I am Amasong the great Nevala that—"

"Ok, whatever…Amasong…shut the fuck up!" Amasong eyes widened with amazement. "When two *Kings* are talking, then courtiers should not interrupt! I know he's King and he knows I'm King, so spare your excrement!" said Dymondo sternly. Amasong was embarrassed and fuming but kept quiet. Sterferep and Kor looked at each other and swelled with pride at their King's strength.

"Apologies, Abariswidth, for *his* interruption and *my* chuckle, but…" Dymondo moved closer to his ear. "With all due respect, you are no match for me. This is not my arrogance speaking.

You can't beat me…not in a duel."

"Ludicrous! How dare you?" screamed Abariswidth.

"What does he say?" asked Werther. "Does he speak ill?" All the Nevala started shouting and came closer.

"Silence!" a voice came from behind loud enough to overpower the loud ruckus.

"Let me come forth, you fluff!" It was a fat, short, old Nevala with white, thinning fur. He barged his way forward into the circle where the Kings and their subordinates stood at arms.

"Let me see this man!" the old Nevala said in his old crackling voice. He came very close to Dymondo, too close for Dymondo's liking. Dymondo moved back as the Nevala's long whiskers touched his nostrils. The old Nevala's eyes widened.

"What do you see old wise Ham?" asked Werther. Old Ham put his paw on his snout and looked carefully at Dymondo and shook his head and pulled a disgusted face.

"Does not seem so, but you never know…" said Ham.

"Ham, say something, or just step aside," said Werther.

The old Nevala looked down and scratched his head and moved back.

"Does not seem so, but you never know…" Ham said again.

The old Nevala eventually went and stood next to Sterferep and broke malodorous silent wind. Kor, who was standing on the other side of Sterferep, noticed the foul smell.

"There is a time and place, man!" whispered Kor into Sterferep's ear.

"What?" replied Sterferep under his breath.

"That is awful!" Kor reprimanded him.

"What is? Oh…! That wasn't me! It was him!" Sterferep whispered back sternly.

Kor held his nose. "Tremendous. Now you blame the poor old Nevala."

Sterferep shook his head and ignored him.

"Ignore the old one, Dymondo. It sounds as though you have challenged me."

"Challenge?" screamed the old Nevala and turned back and rushed back up to Dymondo to look at him again with widened eyes but soon pulled another disgusted face and turned and shook his head.

"Does not seem so, but you never know…" repeated Ham and everyone ignored him.

Abariswidth swung his spear in the air.

"Good with a spear?" Abariswidth threw one at Dymondo and he caught it.

Baazli walked up to Dymondo and whispered in his ear.

"We can leave, King. There was no need to challenge him. We could have been on our way. Why the arrogance?"

Dymondo looked at him strangely and whispered, "Not arrogance, Baazli…confidence."

Baazli read his eyes and smiled. He moved back and patted his shoulder. "May you be victorious."

The Nevala, the bear and the Lances moved back making the centre of the assembly hall an arena for the duellers. The strong Nevala King was an expert spear fighter. Dymondo for his part knew the basics, but he still needed to take advanced lessons from Kor.

Abariswidth leapt in the air towards him with his first thrust and Dymondo waiting for the right moment parried away the attack. The two circled the arena. Abariswidth again came at him, and this time, Dymondo went to one knee as Abariswidth's high lunging thrust pierced nothing but the air. Dymondo returned the attack and his low lunge thrust dug into Abariswidth's knee.

The Nevala yelled out in pain. The other Nevala jeered at Dymondo, whereas the Lances and the bear cheered him on.

"It can stop right here, Abariswidth."

"Never!" came the reply and Abariswidth launched another onslaught. This time he charged towards Dymondo and swung the spear over his head in a semi-circle attempting to cut into Dymondo's chest, which he very nearly did. The attack left a long gash from Dymondo's chest down to his stomach, but it was not deep. This angered Dymondo, but he regained his focus for the next three attacks which he deflected away with great skill.

Kor was impressed by Dymondo's spear fighting technique. The man and the Nevala clashed hard and a series of attacks made by Abariswidth were again blocked, defended and repelled by Dymondo. Abariswidth was getting more frustrated at being unable to disarm Dymondo and beat him. He increased his speed and eventually managed to snap the head off Dymondo's spear and continued lunging at him to cause maximum damage.

Dymondo now just had a staff in his hand to defend with which he used well, parrying more of Abariswidth's skilled thrusts and lunges. In anger, Abariswidth lunged aggressively in an attempt to finish Dymondo off. Dymondo stepped to the side, grabbed the Nevala's spear and elbowed the creature in the face, disarming him. He then turned and with the blunt end of his staff, he smashed hard upon the side of the King's neck causing Abariswidth to go down on his knees. The furious, defeated and humiliated Abariswidth looked up at Dymondo with glaring eyes as King Dymondo stood victorious above him.

"There! I have bested you!" said Dymondo and threw his staff at him and began to turn away. The Lances cheered at Dymondo's victory, but the applause was short lived. Abariswidth seized his fallen spear which had not dropped far and burrowed its spearhead into Dymondo's left shoulder. Dymondo fell to his knees and roared in pain. Abariswidth kept the spear in and pushed it further to keep Dymondo down.

Sterferep, Kor, Dan and Dwarpal drew their swords and were about to charge at the Nevala King, but they were held back by two Nevala each—it took three to hold Sterferep. But Baazli could not be stopped. He kicked Abariswidth away and pulled out the spear. Dymondo yelled in pain as the spearhead was removed. Baazli took a cloth from upon the rock seats to tie it around Dymondo's shoulder to cover the wound and stop blood flow.

"Fool! You fucking fool. You have no honour!" screamed Baazli. "You believe he cannot beat you. He can strike you all down in one swing!"

"Hah! We saw his swing!" jeered Abariswidth.

"King! Show him!" advised Baazli.

Dymondo regained his balance and invoked the Emispear. The sight of the magnificent light from the Emispear shone bright and sent a shiver down everyone's spine—the Lances too. Baazli moved and took a gigantic rock from the side of the assembly chamber which was larger than Dymondo and Abariswidth and placed it in the middle of the arena.

The old Nevala screamed: "It did not seem to be, but now I know—"

"King!" Baazli screamed.

Dymondo swung the weapon and the rock obliterated into thousands of particles.

Abariswidth and everyone moved back as the tiny rock pieces flew into their faces.

"Now Abariswidth it is your turn!" Baazli's eyes were red. "King Dymondo…end his life!"

"No! Forgive him, he did not know!" shouted the old Nevala, Ham.

"Time for that has gone! King Dymondo! Do it!"

Everyone looked fearfully at Dymondo, and so did Abariswidth who moved further back, stepping behind the other Nevala.

Dymondo walked up to him slowly with eyes of fury, holding his deathly spear at the ready, but when he got face to face with the King, he stopped.

"With this weapon I can strike you down with one swing, Abariswidth. During our duel I did not attack you. Only you attacked me. I just defended, in case you did not notice, because I came here to seek help from you…to befriend you."

Abariswidth's eyes lowered in disgrace and dishonour.

"You displayed your arrogance and challenged me to a duel, which I won, with a blunt weapon! But you! You used deception and wounded me and dishonoured yourself. You are a great fighter. You didn't need to drop to this level. Shame on you."

Abariswidth looked at Dymondo, his eyes betraying both anger and humiliation.

"Nevertheless, I am going to have mercy on you and spare your life."

Abariswidth was further mortified.

"I am now leaving Abariswidth, but I hope you have learned something from this, and in the future you will not use deceit when someone has beaten you in a duel."

Dymondo turned away from the dejected creature.

"Wait…end my life," said Abariswidth. "I do not deserve to live after what I have done."

"Damn right! But you are a strong Nevala. You don't need to cheat."

"Forgive me, my King. I am not used to defeat. I have not been beaten by any creature before. I crush poisonous snakes and scorpions, so having been defeated by a man made me lose my senses. I went mad."

Dymondo shook his head.

"He is no ordinary man!" said Ham.

"Quiet Ham!" said Abariswidth.

"He wields the bright lance! Only the Sons of God get to do that!" said Ham and walked off.

"Is that so?" asked Abariswidth.

"Ignore the senile Nevala, Abariswidth," said Dymondo. "Even if a man has bested you, you should respect him and not humiliate him and yourself by doing what you did!"

"I am humbled before you…King Dymondo. Punish me as you wish."

"Away with you, Abariswidth. Baazli! Lances! Let's go from here!"

The Lances shrugged off the creatures and moved to depart the quiet and humiliated assembly chamber. Dymondo turned and spoke.

"I continue to accept your claim to this part of the land. This is a fascinating city you have built. I let you live only for your people. Be grateful to them. And I have already called you a friend. Dymondo will come to your aid if you ever need it, whoever the enemy may be, even if it is the venomous Sanpsarp. I know his acid venom will burn through me and my men and take our lives, but I will still come and embrace death for my friends. Continue to rule here and I assure you on behalf of all men, your territory shall be respected. And you will continue to respect ours. I now take your leave. As your friend, if you wish for some of my sculptors to come down here and strengthen your walls and passages, do not hesitate to ask. There are no formalities among friends," Dymondo said and began to walk out.

"Wait!" exclaimed Abariswidth. "You will send sculptors to strength our rocks?"

"Why not?"

"Why would you? I have not given you my support or help. Why would you give me yours?"

"Because when I walked by the beautiful families of your Kingdom, I felt in my heart that I wanted to do this for them. I moved through your gracious city to reach your assembly hall and I saw many loving parents and their baby Nevala. Stronger walls and surroundings will truly help them, along with softer clothes, and perhaps some food. I have decided to support you, whether you give me your support or not."

Abariswidth lowered his head in shame and began to weep. "Dymondo, I am disgusted by my behaviour towards you." He walked up to the King. "So gracious of you to say this. It is true that we live on your land. We are your citizens, yet you regard and respect me as a sovereign. This shows you are truly great."

"The land is yours, King Abariswidth. You built this magnificent splendour! I cannot even dream of staking a claim to it. If you'll allow me, I can place some of my Lances to safeguard the entrance of the crater so no enemy enters to trouble you?"

"Bravo, Dymondo. You keep on giving, yet I have given you nothing!"

"That is not true, King. You can still honour me your friendship for I long for it. Friendship is a gift from the Gods."

Abariswidth embraced Dymondo immediately after he said those words. His whiskers annoyed Dymondo's ear, but Dymondo did not react to it though the embrace did hurt the wound on his shoulder.

"Ouch!"

"Forgive me for this, my friend. Amasong bring two sticks of wood and light a fire!"

"It is quite alright, Abariswidth, I don't need fire to treat this."

"It's not for the wound. It is our tradition. Please bear with me."

The tough Nevala got two sticks and rubbed them together which sparked into flames. He placed the two burning sticks together on the ground in front of Abariswidth, while Dymondo stood on the other side of the fire. Abariswidth then grabbed Dymondo's hand over the small flame.

"I am honoured to be your friend, Dymondo. Let the God of Fire, Ignio, bear witness to our friendship. I promise you, King Dymondo Rain, I will lead my Nevala army into any battle against any enemy under your banner at any time. It shall be an honour to fight under the banner of such a strong King. May it be day or night, I shall answer my friend's call and come to his aid! I Nevala Abariswidth Atiliax take this solemn vow!"

"And I, Dymondo Rain of Landsfor, take a solemn vow. I will ride into any battle for my dear friend, King Abariswidth Atiliax of the Cave, and promise to help him, his Kingdom, and his people in every way I can! Your enemies are my enemies and your friends are my friends." Dymondo embraced Abariswidth as Baazli, Sterferep, Dan and Dwarpal and Kor looked on and all the Nevala creatures cheered.

"Aargh!" screamed Amasong and everyone looked in his direction. He was one of the Nevala holding Sterferep. "No wonder it took three of us to hold this man back! Stand back! Stand back!" shouted Amasong.

"Calm, Amasong! Why this fuss?" asked Abariswidth. All the Nevala moved away from Sterferep.

"Stand back!" Amasong kept shouting.

"Is everything alright? Sterferep?" asked Dymondo.

Sterferep shrugged his shoulders.

"Did you fart?" whispered Kor in Sterferep's ear.

"Fuck no!" whispered back Sterferep.

Dymondo, Baazli and Abariswidth walked over to Amasong

and Sterferep.

Abariswidth shook Amasong violently to calm him down.

"What is the matter with you, Amasong?" asked Abariswidth.

"King, look!" shouted Amasong pointing at Sterferep's shoulder.

"What are we looking at, dear Nevala?" asked Dymondo gently.

"His shoulder, it's on his shoulder! I'm not touching it!" Amasong was getting hysterical.

"Sterferep lift your tassels," said Dymondo.

Sterferep did so and revealed the Cecrops mark.

"Oh dear!" spoke Abariswidth and moved back. "I command all the Nevala to move back!"

"Is there a problem, dear friend?"

"That mark, King Dymondo! Who is this man?"

"With all due respect, King Abariswidth, it is slightly rude to ask about him when he stands before you. Sterferep Unknown is a Lance in my army and above all one of my best friends. All these men and this bear are my friends."

"Forgive me, King…" with hesitation Abariswidth spoke. "And…apologies Sterferep. But where did you get this mark?"

"I don't know, King of the Nevala."

"Surely you must! You bear the mark of Cecrops, half man/half serpent!"

"I am adopted my King! I was found on the banks of the river Krool. A poor couple brought me up. Hence I am called Sterferep Unknown. I had this mark when they found me. That's all I know."

Abariswidth placed his paw upon his snout and thought.

"What shall we do now?" asked Werther.

"I don't know anything about this mark. If you do, then tell me!" There was urgency and pleading in Sterferep's voice, which was very rare.

"Everyone, calm! Let me ponder…call upon Ham!"

The old wise Ham was called upon and he gasped at the mark and started coughing until he passed out in Werther's arm.

Amasong splashed water upon his face to revive him.

Ham composed himself and went close to the mark and touched it. As he did, all the Nevala gasped in shock. He then looked at Sterferep carefully.

"No…this is odd! Generally it is a bad omen, but I cannot see anything wrong in this man's eyes."

"But he bears the—!"

"Yes! I know. But his eyes tell me he is good."

Kor sniffed at the words of the wise Nevala.

"Amusing, is it now?"

"Kor!" shouted Dymondo.

"Apologies."

"Tell me, strong man, what do you know about this mark?" Sterferep repeated himself.

"Hmm…No King. You don't have to fear him."

"Are you sure?"

"Of course I am!" barked the old Nevala and ended up breaking wind as he shouted. Everyone covered their noses and snouts. "He won't harm us. If anything he will help us," said the old Nevala and walked away leaving his smell behind.

"I don't know what to say," said Abariswidth. "The wise old Ham is always right."

"Sterferep is a good man, Abariswidth," vouched Dymondo.

Abariswidth nodded. "Very well! Go in peace."

"This doesn't affect our promises and vows, does it?" asked Dymondo.

"No. Nevala has promised, but…Sterferep…are you sure you know nothing? Nothing at all? Even the smallest of things will help."

Sterferep looked at Dymondo and Dymondo nodded for him to come clean.

"I don't know why I have it. But I know of three other people, who are our enemies that bear this very same mark."

"Who?"

"Silvenia Rain, Kratos Laaris and Yatus Laaris."

Everyone again murmured.

"Silence! Where do they hail from?"

"Forprimiera and Orakray."

"Orakray! That rings a bell…Orakray…"

"Do you know anything, King Abariswidth? Tell me if you do."

"Not sure whether I should, Sterferep. After all, you were slow to tell me——."

"Please, King, your oath. Tell him what you know," urged Dymondo.

"Very well then. You cannot be killed by just any person. You can only be killed by the person that bears the same mark as you. Likewise, those three cannot be killed by just any person, only by one who carries the same mark."

Everyone went silent after that.

"Worry not! I shall find out more for you, and when I do, I shall visit my friend King Dymondo at his palace and ask him to summon you."

"You are most welcome, my friend," said Dymondo. Abariswidth smiled.

Sterferep was amazed at the revelation.

"So if one of your Nevala drove their spears into my stomach… I wouldn't die?"

"No," replied Abariswidth.

Everyone went silent.

"Would you like to try…?"

Again no one spoke.

"Yes!"

"Sterferep are you mad?"

"I need to know, Dy. King order one of your warriors to stab me!"

Abariswidth took a deep breath and nodded at Amasong. Amasong took his dagger and without warning planted it in Sterferep's chest. Sterferep roared in discomfort and punched Amasong away. Slowly, he extracted the dagger from his chest and fell to the ground on his knees in severe pain. Blood began to flow.

"No!" Everyone shouted.

"Wait!" Abariswidth shouted.

Sterferep's mark began to glow yellow and so did his wound and as everyone looked on, Sterferep's fatal wound was healed.

"Amazing!" said Dymondo.

"You are invincible!" said Kor.

"But I get hurt in training. I am grazed. I get cuts. I bleed!" shouted Sterferep.

"Ever notice how long it takes for you to heal? Ever been ill for long? No, right!?" said Abariswidth.

Sterferep had no answer.

"Your wounds heal quicker than a normal person, but your mark truly comes into effect when you receive a fatal blow. Other than that, it works discretely but fast," said Abariswidth and turned to Dymondo. "Is he your best?"

"By far," answered Dymondo.

"I am not surprised. You four should be proud," said Abariswidth turning to the other four Lances. "To be as good as him must take some power. He has an advantage."

Kor, Tamaris, Dan and Dwarpal smiled and their chest broadened with pride.

"Apologies, dear Nevala," said Sterferep to Amasong, who had been picked up by Werther after Sterferep's blow.

"I suppose it is alright," he said dejectedly holding his snout.

"It is a shock I know. I can understand, Sterferep. But do not let this deter your focus. I shall help you find out more about this. It is a gift, embrace it. We Nevala don't side with the people that bear the mark because the Cecrops is half man/half serpent, and we do not associate ourselves with snakes or serpents."

"Gratitude, Abariswidth, for making an exception for me."

"I am still apprehensive, but I believe Ham and your companions that you are good person, I shall research more for you."

Sterferep nodded, the two Kings embraced once more, and the men and the bear exchanged pleasantries with the Nevala and left.

CHAPTER 23

THE MISSION

Baazli's heart and mind were both at rest after the successful visit to the Cave despite the wound Dymondo picked up. He knew the tougher quest still lay ahead of them: the frightening journey to Haask.

When Dymondo arrived at Gammafor palace, it was dark. Under the canopy of night, he rode through the vacant streets to his palace and was greeted at the palace entrance by Olivious and Puyol, who had obeyed their King's orders and kept his journey a secret. All quietly exchanged pleasantries, but the King's wounds needed attention. Sterferep and Kor took him to the apothecary immediately.

Dymondo's wound was treated with haste. Luckily, it was not as deep as Oromi's. After receiving treatment, Dymondo headed over to the chamber where Oromi lay. Two strong Lances stood outside safe-guarding her chamber whilst the beauty remained unconscious. Though she lay there motionless, Dymondo could detect her slow and soft breathing.

"Any news of her recovery?" asked Dymondo to the thin apothecary.

"No, my King. The wound is sealed and by now the internal wounds have healed too, but she is yet unconscious."

"Let your medicine work its charm on that blue-eyed

woman," said Kor.

"Lance Kor, she breathes. The medicine has run its course. If she is to open her eyes, it must come from her will to live."

Dymondo nodded and left with Sterferep and Kor.

The next day as per his promise, Dymondo sent sculptors to strengthen the Cave, and ten of his strongest Lances took positions to safeguard the territory surrounding the mouth of the crater.

Mysteria was upset to see her man wounded, but pleased he had returned at all and that his quest had been successful. That night, Dymondo slept peacefully. The nightmare no longer troubled him for Dymondo was content at heart that through his own strength and friendships he at last had the ability to defend his realm. Morning came and Mysteria lay on her side, watching him sleep with a gentle smile on his face. Eventually his slumber broke, and she gently greeted him.

"Good morning."

"Morning, my Queen,"

"How do you fare?"

"Well…the sun is bright today…Oh gosh! The court…"

"…Ssh! Just rest! Lie back down and relax yourself. Your wound is still healing."

Dymondo sat up.

"I overslept."

"You did. What did you dream of?"

Dymondo took a deep breath of the fresh air blowing into the room. The gust bore the mixed scent of flowers and fresh soil. Dymondo looked out the window and pondered her question.

"I don't know, my dear. I just…slept."

"That's great to know, my love," she smiled. "Rest for a few days and spend time with me until your wound heals. Then you can rise and go forth to secure the friendship of Haask."

Mention of Haask no longer formed creases of fear upon Dymondo's forehead. He nodded confidently and smiled at her.

After many days' rest, Baazli came to visit Dymondo in his chamber. Mysteria was not there, so it was just the two of them.

"How is your wound, my King?"

"It has healed, Baazli. Gratitude."

"That is great. My King, you should start planning our journey to Haask."

"Yes, I must announce that very soon."

Dymondo went quiet.

"What is it that bothers the King?"

"Do your recall what the shrub said about my mother?"

"I do."

"I'd like to investigate that prior to leaving for Haask."

"If that is your wish, but why can you not set both tasks in motion at the same time? Send someone to Forprimiera to investigate while we journey to Haask."

"Now that I have had time to think of all that has happened, I still cannot believe my brother sent those men who tried to take my life. But there is no denying his war preparations…"

"May the Gods give your brothers sense."

Dymondo did not respond.

Suddenly there was a violent knock at the door.

"Enter!"

"My King, Greetings…" said Sterferep, huffing out of breath. "You must come with me."

"What is it?"

"You must come now!"

"Go, my King, I shall see myself out," said Baazli.

"Gratitude, O great Bear," answered Sterferep.

Dymondo nodded at both of them and left with Sterferep whilst Baazli left for his own chamber.

"Where do you take me?" asked Dymondo on the way.

"To the apothecary!"

Dymondo's eyes widened in shock.

"Is she…?"

"Yes!"

Dymondo and Sterferep hurried down and into Oromi's cell. There she was sitting up upon the bed as the apothecary fed her water from a bowl.

"My lady!" shouted Dymondo.

Oromi's heart fluttered as she saw Dymondo. She could not believe her eyes.

"My King!" she said roughly. Her throat was still sore.

"Apothecary, may I have a word with her?"

"She is weak, my King. She mustn't exert herself. You must not break words with her for long," said the thin man as he went.

"Sterferep, stand outside with the Lances. I wish to speak to her in private."

Sterferep looked at both of them and did not say anything. He just did as he was told and shut the door on his way out.

"So good to see you, Oromi," said Dymondo when they were alone.

"It is so good to see you, too."

"How do you feel?" he asked as he sat beside her and held her hand.

"I have just woken up," she smiled. Her face had faded from the illness. Her lips were dry. But her blue eyes were still as deep as the Aquacaves.

Dymondo slowly went forward and kissed her on her lips. She kissed him back but then withdrew.

"My, my…I don't know what to think."

"Don't think anything. Just let it be for now."

She nodded in contentment and smiled. He placed his hand on her cheek and rubbed it gently.

"I am happy to see you alive."

"I am happy to be alive, my King."

"I guess more rest is required."

"Rest…yes…And then I leave?"

"Leave, yes, but not for your banishment."

Oromi was shocked to hear his words.

"Lady Oromi, I have a task for you."

"A task?"

"Yes. Once you are well and healthy, I would have you do something for me. Will you?"

"What kind of task? My life is still in danger—"

"Not anymore. Queen Ohio has left for the afterlife."

Oromi covered her mouth and her eyes began to fill with

196

water, but then she gathered herself and did not cry.

"Apologies, my King...I mean condolences. What happened?"

"She died in her sleep."

"In her sleep? Impossible."

"Why do you say that?"

"She was a light sleeper and woke up from time to time during the night, but I suppose that has nothing to do with anything. But your mother was a tough woman...and now she's gone...unbelievable."

"Oromi, once you have recovered, I want you to escape from here."

"Escape? Where to...Why?"

"You don't ask how?"

Oromi smiled. She got close to him and brought her lips near his. "I can escape from anywhere. Your guest chamber was penetrable. I could have left whenever I wanted."

Dymondo smiled back.

"I'm sure you could have. That is why I am not going to insult your intelligence."

"Gratitude, but what is it that you ask of me?"

Dymondo got up and walked away from the bed. "Discretion and loyalty. Only you and I will know of the mission and no one else. If you decide to choose someone to help you, then they must not know why they are helping you and nothing shall lead to me."

She struggled to get up but followed him and turned him toward her.

"After Queen Ohio's demise, I am only loyal to you. Your secret and your mission are safe with me."

"Great. Now listen very carefully... I suspect Queen Ohio was murdered in Forprimiera."

Oromi put her hand over her mouth. "Why do you suspect this?"

"I have my reasons. But she died in the royal palace whilst she was on a visit to meet my brothers there. Your task is to investigate this. But no one must know who you are and why you're there."

"That won't be too difficult, my King."

"Why?"

"I can get anyone to talk once I've ensnared them with my beauty."

"Try to do it *without* having to bed someone."

"Why? You're disarming me of one of my greatest weapons."

"Oromi, please…no sex."

Oromi smiled.

"Ok… but why?"

Dymondo smiled back and scratched his head.

"Just because I said so. Use other tactics."

"You just said you didn't want to insult me by telling me how to do my job."

"I am not telling you…just a small condition."

"Why?" she bit her bottom lip and continued to smile.

"I won't answer that."

"Why?" she whispered. "You can tell me in my ear."

Dymondo's face went red.

"Because I wouldn't like it."

"Why?"

"Because…"

"Why?"

"Because I don't want you to bed someone else."

"My King, I have been without cock for a long time now. As a part of my job, if I get the opportunity to fuck a handsome man, then I won't be able to stop myself."

"Still, I'd rather you didn't."

"Tell me the reason and I won't."

"I won't like it."

"Do *you* want me all to yourself, then, eh?" she tempted fate by saying that.

Dymondo remained silently gazing into her eyes watching her pupils dilate.

"You can say that…"

Oromi's blue eyes lit up. Her heart raced and her jaw dropped.

"What did you say?" she asked in a deeper voice, coming close and placing her hand behind his neck, bringing his face close to hers.

"You heard me," he said with confidence.

She kissed him deeply and he too reciprocated.

"I cannot believe it," she said.

"Do not weave a web of dreams for I may not be able to fulfil them. I have taken a Queen."

"And yet you stand here alone with a criminal, kissing her in her chamber?"

"Oromi, look… I don't know where my mind is right now—"

"Who is this new *man*? What happened to the innocent and caring person I knew before I got stabbed? What the fuck happened?"

"I don't know what the *fuck* happened. But Oromi, let us remain focused on your task."

She nodded and ran her fingers through his hair at the back of his head. He too held her face in his hands.

"Will you do it for me? I don't want you getting caught. Make an exit from here when you find the opportunity and get yourself to Forprimiera and find out who killed Queen Ohio."

"I shall do it for you."

"Good girl."

Oromi smiled and touched his cheek gently.

"What would you like as a reward?"

Oromi again enlarged her eyes.

"Anything I like?"

"I cannot marry you, and I will not take you as a mistress."

"Anything else?"

"Anything else."

"I am shocked!" she blurted.

"Give words to your desires, Oromi."

"I want to be here with you, forever. I don't want to be banished. I want you to show me your love from time to time."

Dymondo smiled.

"We shall see."

Oromi smiled.

"Get better soon. May the Gods be with you. When does the Apothecary say you'll recover completely?"

"Seven days."

"I set sail on the seventh day."

"To where?"

"Haask."

"What?!" Oromi's eyes took on a look of worry. "Why? O Dymondo you're making me wet with all this bravery. I cannot believe you are the same person."

"Perhaps not. But I must go."

"The sixth night will be my last night in this chamber as well…After midnight…I shall set the task in motion…" she spoke slowly, suggestively.

Dymondo smirked and raised his eye brows and nodded.

"Rest well these five nights, then."

"And why is that?

"For the sixth night…you'll have little rest," said Dymondo and left.

Oromi could not contain her joy. At her King's parting words, she jumped back onto to her bed, forgetting her weakness as she looked up to the wooden ceiling, dreaming of the night to come.

The next day Dymondo announced at court that he would be travelling to Haask in seven days' time. Queen Mysteria Rain asked his courtiers to send word ahead. Dymondo asked Baazli, Sterferep, Kor, Dan and Dwarpal to accompany him on the journey.

Dymondo did not mention to anyone the task he had set to Oromi or his suspicion that his mother may have been killed, but Sterferep could tell that the King had grown distracted since his visit with Oromi, yet he decided not to question him.

Meanwhile, Lance Tamaris had regained his strength and was now prepared to accompany his King on his mission. He was introduced to Baazli and welcomed into the fold as a Lance once again.

CHAPTER 24

THE SIXTH DAY AND THE SIXTH NIGHT

The sixth day arrived and at court, Dymondo noticed her standing among the courtiers and the noblemen of the land. He looked away for a moment and continued his announcements. He thought he must have been imagining things. He then looked back in that direction. He was certain. It was her. She noticed the joy on his face, and her heart beat faster.

Could that man truly have pushed my brother off that cliff? She thought.

The words of Grygerious rang in her head, and she soon regained her focus.

"That shall be all," finished Dymondo, prompting the courtiers to disperse. Sterferep and Kor started walking up to him, but Dymondo passed them and made his way swiftly up to her.

"I cannot believe it is you!" he said holding her lovingly by her arms.

She smiled back. "It is I!"

"Where on Landsfor have you been?"

Her heart fluttered and began to race, but she kept her

emotions at bay, reciprocating his enthusiasm to defuse any suspicion.

"Symera, it is so good to see you!" Dymondo was ecstatic. He grabbed hold of her gloved hand causing her to flinch slightly. Only a thin cloth kept her nails from making contact with his skin.

She was dressed elegantly in a beautiful, reddish-brown velvet dress which covered her from head to toe and matched her velvet gloves. Atop her head, she wore a lovely cream hat with a netted veil.

"Come! I shall take you to one of my guest chambers where we can talk!"

Sterferep and Kor walked up to join them.

"Sterferep do you remember, Symera?" asked the excited Dymondo.

"I do! Gods! It is been a long time! How do you fare?" asked Sterferep.

"I fare well. Gratitude for asking, Sterferep. Lance now eh?" she responded by looking at his uniform.

"Yes, finally!" Sterferep said.

"And you as well, Kor?" Symera was surprised. "I knew Sterferep would make it, but how did you find the time to train, with your wine and…erm..erm!" Symera jested.

Kor smiled at her comment. "Now that's not fair, Symera. I always worked hard!"

Everyone laughed at that.

"Oh you have missed so much, Symera!" said Dymondo. "We must take her to the guest chamber, Sterferep."

"Indeed! Let us go there now and get you settled in."

"How very kind!" smiled Symera.

Dymondo kept hold of her hand and walked her out with Sterferep and Kor following.

"There is so much to talk about…and ask," said Dymondo on the way.

"We have time for that. Plenty of time," replied Symera.

"Indeed, we do!" proclaimed Dymondo.

"My King, we do not. We have to leave," reminded

Sterferep.

"I almost forgot! I am just so excited to see you, Symera," answered Dymondo.

"You're leaving?" Symera stopped walking and looked concerned.

Dymondo turned back towards her.

"Apologies Symera! I have to leave and I will not be back for a while. Had I had known you were going to come I would have postponed my visit."

"So what am I supposed to do here all alone?"

"You shall be my royal guest and stay with us until I return. I'm afraid I will have to see you to the guest chamber and then leave straight after."

Symera's face dropped and she started to look around helplessly. Sterferep noticed her odd reaction.

"The King will return very soon from his journey, Symera," reassured Sterferep.

She prevented her inner thoughts from further spilling out and veiled them with an innocent smile.

"Of course, Dymondo! You go, and when you come back, we shall talk. There is so much I have to tell you and I'm sure there is so much for me to hear from you!" She again appeared excited. Sterferep was not convinced but he did not say anymore.

"Yes!" said Dymondo. "Come let's get you settled."

The three men and the damsel walked up to the guest chamber.

"This is beautiful! Gratitude, Dymondo."

"He is King now, Symera," said Sterferep.

"Oh leave it, Sterferep," Symera jibed. "We are friends first! Are we not, Dymondo?"

"Indeed! Sterferep, Kor do wait outside for me. I won't be long," said Dymondo.

Sterferep nodded and went out with Kor and looked back at Symera as he went through the door. Symera gathered she may have aroused his suspicion. But she also knew if he suspected danger, he would not had left Dymondo's side. Still, she would have to be more careful around him.

After the two went out, Dymondo grabbed her arms again.

"Where did you go? I searched everywhere for you!"

"I had to go, Dy."

"But why? Was it because we—"

"No! No, not at all! That was the most magical night of my life!"

"Then what?"

"My father died that night!"

Dymondo let go of her.

"Symera, I am so sorry."

"I could not withstand the loss. I did not know what to do. With my brother, mother *and* father gone. I was all alone."

"But you had me."

"Did I?"

"Of course!"

"The Prime Minister's daughter and the Prince of Landsfor! Sounds like a tale grandmothers would tell their grandchildren. Your father would have not had agreed to that alliance."

"I would have fought for you, but you did not give me the chance to do so. You didn't even speak to me or send me a message. You just...

"I know."

"I searched for you everywhere."

Symera's heart again fluttered upon hearing of his devotion.

"You would have fought for me?"

"Of course! I...I..."

"What?"

"I was beginning to fall in love with you."

"Oh, Dy, don't say that." She turned from him.

There was silence in the chamber.

"Right, what is done is done! We cannot change that now. But I am so happy that we have met again!"

"Me too," she said with her back still towards him.

"Well, we shall talk more, when I return."

She turned around to face him.

"When will you be back? Where are you going?"

"I shall return soon."

She smiled and nodded.

"I shall wait, but if you are gone for too long, then I may go back home. You may not find me here."

"Stay as long as you can."

"I will. But I shall come back to court once you have returned," she said as she removed her gloves and threw them onto the bed."

"Very well."

"Farewell then…" she said extending her arms out to him.

He moved swiftly to embrace her. His hold was so tender, caring and loving that again her heart melted. She too held him tight with love and got lost in the intimate embrace. She opened her eyes and realised what a great opportunity this was. She took one hand away from his back and brought her clawed nails slowly toward his neck, but by the time she could do anything, Dymondo had withdrawn from the embrace and she disguised her move cunningly by gently ruffling his hair.

Dymondo smiled and winked at her and she smiled and winked back. Dymondo put his finger on his lip and then placed it on hers over the netted veil of her hat. She smiled and nodded, and Dymondo went in for the kiss.

Another opportunity for Symera to take her revenge, and this time she had decided she was not going to let her emotions get in the way, but as Dymondo's lips came near, she suddenly turned her face to present her cheek to his lips. Dymondo's lips connected with her cheek, and she gently moved him back and smiled.

"That is not fair," said Dymondo.

"You are a married man! Have you no shame?" she smiled and laughed.

They both laughed.

"Just a small kiss?"

"No," she looked away.

"Alright…then I take your leave," Dymondo smiled and began to walk out.

"How about…"

"What?" Dymondo turned swiftly to face her again.

"When you get back…we can go riding into the sunset…and camp on the banks of the river Krool?"

Dymondo was speechless.

"We can spend the night there… and…in the morning, bathe in the river before we head back home…?"

Dymondo was still mum, but eventually he managed to put together a reply.

"I have done that before…with a very special friend of mine."

"Then why not do it again?" she replied.

Dymondo nodded and she smiled in return.

"Wait for my return!" he shouted and marched out without looking back at her.

After he left, Symera was disgusted with herself. She threw herself onto the bed. Her mind and heart was in turmoil.

The sixth night arrived and the Apothecary and Royal Physician had retired to their chambers. Two Lances stood tall outside Oromi's chamber when a figure approached the door dressed in a long black gown with a hood with two guards beside him.

"Who goes there?" asked one of the Lances.

The figure removed the hood.

"My King!"

"Quiet, both of you!"

"What brings you here, my King?" asked the other Lance.

"Something troubles me. I have to break words with Lady Oromi before I set sail."

The two Lances bowed. Dymondo entered and the two guards and two Lances waited outside.

"Remain here. But stand away from the door," commanded Dymondo and the men did as they were told. Dymondo had spent most of the nights up to the sixth day with Mysteria and had slipped out on this night while she was asleep.

Dymondo found Oromi sitting on the bed inside her chamber. She stood up as he walked in. She was dressed in a royal blue outfit. The neckline of the dress went all the way down the middle of her chest to her navel. She was adorned with matching royal-blue-gemmed trinkets and jewellery. There were several clips in her hair, which made her look like a wife of a wealthy dignitary. Since their last meeting, she had regained much of the volume and shine to her hair. It was certain the young woman was miraculously beautiful. The combination of her deep, blue eyes and natural, thick, black hair was a true rarity and suited her lovely face.

"I can see you've seen yourself to a bath?"

"These baths here in your medical facility are not as beautiful as the ones for your guests."

"My apologies."

"None required. They served their purpose," she replied in her sultry voice.

"I can see that."

Dymondo removed his cloak. He, too, was dressed in his best. He looked sharp with his recent close shave and clean hair. The veins of his biceps were visible beneath his sleeves as he had been spending his spare time after court in the training sands, preparing for his dangerous journey. Tied to his waist was a small container.

"Would you like a drink?" he asked.

"I would love one."

"To this evening," Dymondo raised his container, took a large gulp from it and handed it to her.

"To this evening," she replied draining the rest, wiping her chin and setting the container on the table.

Dymondo ignored her presumption and sat down on the bed and crossed his legs, keeping his eyes fixed on her. She stood where she was staring at him with hungry eyes.

"So, my lady, I guess we both know why I am here this evening?"

"Of course."

Dymondo picked up the container from the table and seeing that it was already empty, laughed quietly.

"Woo! Too much too soon," spoke Oromi approached the

bed, then wobbled on her feet, making them both laugh. "It's been a while since wine has passed my lips."

Oromi came closer adjusting her right earring, then turned to face him as she realised he was watching her. Without saying much more, she leapt upon him like a tigress and the two commenced having rigorous and rough sex.

When finished, Oromi and Dymondo lay beside one another on the small bed.

"Gosh! What in Landsfor have you been eating?" she squealed, still breathing heavily and between moans of pleasure.

"Landsfor…eh?"

"You call it that, too, so don't stop me," she laughed.

He let her catch her breath, and before she knew it, he pounced on her again.

"Hang on there, I need…mmm…"

It was too late. He had already started kissing her, and she already melting in his strong arms, let him take her again. They continued until midnight, Oromi gasping and moaning through the evening.

"Right it's time we moved on,"

"Oh! Must we? Can't we leave it till tomorrow?"

"No, it must be done this evening," he said as he began to get up.

"No, no, come back here."

"No Oromi, we must now bid each other farewell."

Oromi threw up her hands and got up and got dressed, as did he.

"Come on, let me take you outside to the gate," said Dymondo.

"You don't need to. I'll manage. You go and be careful in Haask."

"I shall, and you too. Be watchful as you leave and travel to Forprimiera. Do you require anything?"

"Give me your cloak, a rope, a knife and a folded cloth."

"I cannot ask the guards to fetch a rope now, for they shall grow suspicious. But take what you need from this chamber. Take the sheets, and take my dagger," he said handing her his royal dagger.

"Please, do not kill anyone on your way out."

"Of course not."

"Farewell."

"Farewell…" she replied and he went for the door.

"My King?" she asked before he'd opened it.

"Answer me. How do you think of me? A friend, a lover, a mistress, a servant with whom you just had sex with?"

Dymondo lowered his head.

"I see you as friend—a special friend who has earned a special space in my heart. That is all I can say to you right now. I don't know what the future holds."

Oromi smiled and nodded.

"Come back soon," Dymondo said, winking at her.

She winked back and nodded and walked up to him again. They kissed each other goodbye and Dymondo bid farewell to Oromi that evening.

The day of the voyage arrived. As the deck crew prepared the ship to set sail, Dymondo and his five trusted men marched aboard along with his mount and mentor, Baazli. Queen Mysteria, Prime Minister Kriptus, Commander-in-Chief of the Army Hitius Opecious, and Courtiers, Olivious, Urayu, Majesma, Lorca and Puyol, came to the shore to bid them farewell. The ship sailed into the darkness and silence of the early morning. By the time the sun climbed into the blue sky, the ship was far from the coast and out of sight of any land.

Dymondo knew Oromi would have slipped away already in the dead of the night. By the time the Apothecary and the Royal Physician checked on her, she would be gone.

***

Back in the kingdom, Symera suffered a restless night fighting her thoughts. She knew very well she was not going to get another audience with the King before he left, so she didn't make an attempt to seek one. Not wishing to remain in the royal guest chamber any longer, she decided to leave. Far away from the palace, she found a discreet spot to send a message to

Grygerious of the situation and that the mission was on hold. When Grygerious received the message, he was furious.

"Damnation!" Grygerious shouted as he clenched his fist.

"What is the matter, my King? What does the message say?" asked Cresenia.

"It is a message from Symera—"

"Was she caught?" Cresenia interrupted.

"No! Thank the Gods, no!"

"Then what!"

"Dymondo has set sail for Haask!"

"Haask?" Cresenia eyes widened with fear.

"Yes, she arrived too late."

"But all she needed to do was scratch him…no?"

"My lady, if I may?" Karnigol intervened.

Cresenia and Grygerious both looked at him.

"Many aspects may have prevented her from striking," Karnigol continued. "She could not just walk up to him and scratch him. She is required to be discreet. She cannot get caught. If she does, then she'll be tortured until she confesses. If that happens, then Doosranfor will be at war with Gammafor and Fourtfor. We cannot afford that."

"Most certainly not," agreed Grygerious.

"Then what do you think she will do? Will she find a quiet moment and strike?" asked Cresenia.

"As a last resort, but if she does that, then surely she will be the prime suspect. They will search for her and if she is caught, then we face the same problem. But—"

"Oh, dear!" Grygerious slumped in his chair with his hand upon his head.

"Fear not, my King," spoke Karnigol. "She is clever and will find a way to win their trust so she can remain in the kingdom and not have to run, but—"

"But what if she cannot win their hearts and does have to run?" asked Grygerious.

"As I was about to finish…If that happens, then I assure you, My King, no one will be able to catch her once she is incognito."

Grygerious breathed a sigh of relief.

"Leave us, Karnigol!" commanded Grygerious.

Karnigol bowed and left.

"My King, you worry needlessly," said Cresenia, as the old man left.

"Perhaps…" Grygerious was deep in thought and looked the other way. He was still slumped in his chair.

Cresenia smiled, walked over, stood before him and removed her light green dress. She had his attention now, and Grygerious's mind and eyes were fixed on her naked body.

She smiled at him, turned her back and strutted over to the bed, and slowly got under the sheets.

Grygerious's worries fled, and he rose and followed her under the sheets.

***

The voyage for Dymondo was monotonous, as only Sterferep and Kor exchanged words with each other and then dispersed, leaving Dymondo alone on deck. Dymondo kept quiet throughout the voyage, only giving the odd instruction here and there until Baazli gathered the Lances and approached the King.

"My King,"

Dymondo turned to face his bear and his men. Baazli stood in the middle with Lances on either side.

"What concerns you, my King?" asked Baazli.

Dymondo turned around and looked to the sea.

"Haask…Gods knows what will happen."

"All shall be well," said Baazli as he walked up to stand beside Dymondo.

"Baazli is right," said Sterferep, walking up to stand on the other side of Dymondo. "As long as we remain together and help one another, we shall be fine and accomplish our task."

"It is dangerous…" started Dymondo.

"Then so be it! When has danger ever deterred us?" exclaimed Kor, now standing next to Baazli. Baazli put his paw gently on the Lance's shoulder and Kor put his arm behind Baazli's back to return the gesture.

"We ready are to face any risk and any danger for you, my ing," said Tamaris, joining Sterferep.

"He's right. No matter where and no matter what, you shall always find us beside you." added Dwarpal walking up behind Tamaris to stand beside him.

"And we cannot for one moment believe we might fail. We have to believe that we will succeed…and succeed we shall!" proclaimed Dan as he too walked up and stood next to Kor.

Dymondo's spirits raised after hearing the encouraging words of his comrades.

"To Haask then!" roared Dymondo.

"To the King!" Sterferep led.

"To the King!" everyone repeated.

The ship sailed on towards the bright sun cutting through the blue waves as the King, the bear and the Lances looked ahead to their next adventure.

The end.

ABOUT THE AUTHOR

Raj Bansal was born in Southampton Hampshire and currently resides with his wife in Ashford Middlesex. Raj is an IT consultant by profession, but writing is his passion. Thank you for reading his book. If you enjoyed it, then please take a moment to leave a review at your favourite retailer.

Raj Bansal